A DEADLY INVITATION

CHRISTY CARLYLE

Chapter One

April 1879

A mourning dove's call carried on the breeze as Electra Poole approached the mist-shrouded graveyard where her mother and father lay side by side. She'd brought a cluster of violets for her mother, though it was in remembrance of her father that she'd come.

Four years had passed since the death of Detective Inspector Erasmus Poole on a cool April morning in 1875. Her father had been killed on his way home from Scotland Yard at around midnight. The detective assigned to the case had never apprehended the ruffians who'd attacked him, picked his pockets clean, and left him battered and bleeding on the cobblestones less than a mile from their front door.

Detective Inspector Gideon Pierce, who'd been a mudlark and pickpocket himself when her father had taken him in when he was twelve, had never stopped trying to solve her father's murder. He had informants throughout the city, and yet even those who'd perpetrated similar crimes could not be linked to or provide information about the death of her father.

Her feelings about him were complicated. He'd been a respected police officer, a diligent detective, a strong and guiding influence in her life, and yet he was also the man who'd signed a document allowing her mother to be committed to an asylum. Electra wrestled with forgiving him for that decision, and she still woke from nightmares, imagining what her mother had endured inside the Elmhurst Asylum. And nightmares fearing she would end up in such a place herself plagued her too.

But she could not fail to come to the cemetery and acknowledge the day she lost him either. His death, even after all the estrangement between them in those years after her mother was taken away, had struck her hard.

At the sound of movement, Electra turned to see a familiar figure approaching. The pale light of dawn flickered over his bowler hat and broad shoulders. Of course, Gideon would come. He had loved her father devotedly, with no knowledge about the truth of her mother's "illness" or what sort of hospital she'd been sent away to.

For three years after her father's death, she'd cut ties with Gideon—her feelings had been too raw and she'd needed distance. Then, last year, she'd become embroiled in a murder case that he'd been tasked with investigating. In the end, she'd assisted him in finding the killer and gained a sort of notoriety she'd never wanted.

She'd held psychic readings prior to the Becknell murder case, but once the papers ran away with the story, painting it in the most lurid terms, letters had begun arriving at the Russell Square townhouse of her friend, Lady Cordelia Redmayne, who hosted most of Electra's sessions in her elegant and spacious drawing room.

"I don't wish to disturb you," Gideon said from the spot where he'd stopped a few feet away.

"I suspected you'd come." Looking over her shoulder, she noticed he'd removed his hat and clutched it in his hands. "It seems a fitting coincidence that we chose the same ungodly hour."

Gideon's mouth softened into something close to a smile, and he approached to stand shoulder to shoulder with her. He tilted his head down to look at her father's headstone. After a moment, he lifted an object from his overcoat pocket and knelt to place a small, stoppered bottle on the stone's edge.

"Whiskey?" she asked.

"His favorite." Gideon straightened again and glanced over at her. "How have you been?"

Electra grimaced and turned to look his way. "Forgive me for not coming to call."

"That was not intended as anything other than a genuine inquiry."

"In all honesty, it has been a strange few months. Journalists still contact me, even months later."

"It will die down." He tilted his head as he appraised her. "And are you continuing your...work?"

Electra's jaw tightened at the hesitation in his tone. Though her inexplicable abilities had proven useful during the Becknell investigation, Gideon still doubted. He was a man of logic and reason, and she herself could not explain why she saw and sensed the things she did.

"Many have contacted me, but I've refused most requests."

"Why?"

Electra drew in a breath and thought of all the desperation, the fear, the anxious yearning she sensed as she held each envelope, read each letter. She took the precaution of donning gloves before reading her post now, as they tended to dull her abilities.

"Most want one thing." She looked over at him, meeting his gaze. "They want a death prediction."

His brows furrowed and then understanding smoothed them again. "Because of what happened in the Becknell case?"

Electra nodded. She'd foreseen the death of Lady Helen Becknell, though the vision had come unexpectedly. She'd never told the noblewoman what she'd seen, and Lady Becknell had been murdered later that night.

Now, it seemed many who'd read of her in the newspapers had seized on the idea that she could predict the day of their death, or that of someone close to them.

"It isn't how I prefer to use my abilities. I don't even know for certain if I could. What happened with Lady Becknell was unexpected."

"I wouldn't wish to know the day I was going to die," he said softly, as if mulling the prospect.

A little shiver ran down Electra's spine at the very thought of a world without Gideon Pierce in it. She wasn't sure she could bear it.

"Part of what makes life precious is that we do not know how much of it we have left." He said the words solemnly while fixing his gaze on the side-by-side tombstones of her parents.

"I agree."

"So have you sought some other employment?"

Electra tried not to be riled by the slight lilt of hopefulness in his tone.

"Cordelia introduced me to a countess who I type correspondence for. And I've been helping Cordelia plan events she'll host during the upcoming Season." The work was tedious, except for the challenge of teaching herself to use a typewriter efficiently. After her father's death, she had committed herself to using the psychic abilities she had denied for so long. But after the Becknell case, she was no longer certain it was the right path.

"And you?" she asked. "You must be occupied with other cases now."

"Very much so, but I will always regret being unable to deliver justice for him." He gestured at her father's grave.

Electra reached out with a gloved hand and brushed Gideon's sleeve. "You mustn't let it eat away at you. He wouldn't want that. Whatever he might have been, a vengeful man he was not."

He turned to her again, head tilted as if hoping she might look back at him. "Your anger toward him. Does it have to do with your mother?" he asked, his voice gentler than his usual tone.

"Yes." Electra bit her tongue, refusing to let herself give in to the anger that simmered deep in her chest. "Let us talk about it another day." Electra knew she should tell Gideon the truth, and she would. He deserved to know, even if it shattered some of his illusions about her father, who'd been a mentor and father figure to him too. But now wasn't the moment.

When they fell silent, she prepared to take her leave. He seemed to sense it and turned to face her. Electra turned too.

"Will you come to dinner next Sunday?" he asked, a bit of anxiousness in his gaze. He was a man who rarely revealed when he was troubled to anyone, so it was notable. "Mrs. Perkins continually reminds me that I should invite you."

After their work together on the Becknell case, Electra had considered allowing their reconciliation to grow into the sort of rapport that had existed between them in the past. But something held her back.

Still, it had been months since they'd seen each other, and she had missed him. She could admit that much to herself.

"Dinner on Sunday sounds lovely."

"Good." He rocked back on his heels and smiled.

"I should be on my way. Cordelia will wonder where I've gone."

"Are you staying with the Redmaynes then?"

"For the time being." She'd given up her boarding house room due to lack of funds. That had nicked at her pride. In the past weeks, an aimlessness seemed to envelop her, and she remained undecided about how to proceed. Should she continue to use her abilities, or should she pursue some other course?

She'd always thrived on having a purpose and was tenacious to a fault. To be unmoored made her uneasy.

"I'll see you on Sunday," she told Gideon. They exchanged a nod and Electra made her way out of the cemetery to find a cab to take her back to Russell Square.

CORDELIA EMERGED from the drawing room to greet Electra as soon as she stepped into the townhouse's main hall.

"You were up quite early," she said, worry lacing her tone. "Is something amiss?"

Since the Becknell case and the attention it had brought, Cordelia had become protective. More so than usual.

"Nothing is amiss," Electra assured her. "I visited Father's grave."

"Oh, Electra. Of course, I remember now. I should have accompanied you."

"It's all right. I wanted to go on my own. Though in the end, I wasn't alone."

At Cordelia's questioning look, Electra steeled herself. "Inspector Pierce came along while I was there."

"Did he indeed?" Cordelia arched a brow and couldn't quite hold back her smile. "And how is your inspector?"

Despite Electra's repeated corrections, Cordelia insisted on referring to Gideon Pierce as hers.

"He seems well and invited me to dine with him and Mrs. Perkins on Sunday."

"How lovely."

"Yes, it was…kind of him." Electra ignored Cordelia's not so subtle glee. Her friend imagined that there was something more between them than a bond built in childhood, but Electra was not prepared to discuss her feelings about Gideon Pierce with anyone. She wasn't even prepared to fully examine them herself. She only knew that they ran deep, and he was on her mind more than she liked to admit.

"You sound almost reluctant." Cordelia's manner turned serious. "I do worry about you of late."

"Please don't." Electra knew she had to shake her restless uncertainty. She had no desire to return to a time when she denied her abilities, but neither did she know how to proceed with embracing them.

"Maybe this will cheer you up." Cordelia offered her an envelope.

Though Electra had done her best not to reveal her worries for all to see, Cordelia knew her better than anyone other than Gideon. Still, as she reached to take the envelope with ungloved hands, she hesitated. She wasn't hopeful that whatever it contained would lift her spirits. In all probability, it was another request for a death prediction that she would not be keen to fulfill.

Her address had been typed on the envelope, which was intriguing since typewriters were considered newfangled by most. Yet when she opened the letter, she was struck with an odd sense of familiar knowing. Then she saw Lady Alice Kirkham's signature at the bottom. They'd been classmates at the finishing school Electra's father had sent her to. Now, they exchanged letters about twice a year.

Somehow, the eldest daughter of an earl and the only daughter of a London police inspector had found they had a great deal in common, and Electra had found a true kinship with Alice, who often claimed she felt different from the other girls too. She'd been shy but keenly intelligent and always watchful, studying others and then drawing them. Electra couldn't recall a time when Alice didn't have a sketchbook nearby. But when it was just the two of them on a long walk or sitting side by side in the dining hall, she spoke freely about her opinions, fears, and anxieties.

Though Alice had finer clothes and wore gem-encrusted jewelry and spoke with perfect elocution, Electra had soon realized that her pampered life came with more expectations too. Electra's father had been proud to save enough to send her away to a prestigious boarding school, but he'd never insisted she find a husband or become a dutiful wife. Indeed, he'd encouraged her to consider an occupation that she loved as much as he loved being a police officer. She'd often teased him that she'd happily follow in his footsteps if ever ladies were allowed to do so.

Alice's letter was full of affection, though Electra had sensed worry when she opened it.

> *Dearest Electra,*
>
> *I think of you frequently. Please forgive my long delay in replying to your last letter. Lately, I've been reminiscing about Fairgate Finishing School. I remember our days together there fondly, and I miss that camaraderie that seemed to grow so easily between us—more easily than with other classmates.*
>
> *I am also writing because my Aunt Gertrude, who I know you became quite fond of and she of you, is with us at Carthorpe due to my father's ill health. She speaks of you often and encouraged me to pen this letter. In truth, I fear that her own constitution is not what it used to be.*

We both agree it would be an enormous pleasure to see you again and catch up on all that has passed in our lives since we saw one another. Forgive the abrupt nature of this request, but could you find the time to do us the very great favor of visiting Carthorpe Hall forthwith?

I've been presumptuous and have enclosed a train ticket for Friday, which will, if the royal post may be counted upon, be the day after you receive this letter. If you cannot come then, please write and suggest a more convenient time.

Yours warmly,

Alice

When Electra looked up from the letter, she found Cordelia's gaze fixed on her.

"She's asked me to come for a visit. Her aunt is with her. Do you recall Lady Dalrymple?"

"Of course. How could I forget?" Cordelia said brightly. "She adopted us as honorary nieces."

Electra had liked Alice's aunt the first time she'd attended a luncheon at her London townhouse. The eccentric Lady Dalrymple had taken a liking to Electra too. Even after the Kirkhams returned to their countryside estate, she'd often invited Electra to tea or to accompany her on shopping trips. She'd once confessed to Electra that she felt a maternal affection for her because she'd lost her own mother as a young girl and knew how hard it was to be without such an influence in one's life.

They'd lost touch after the death of Electra's father when Electra spent time in Ireland and pulled away from Gideon and nearly everyone who'd been part of her life before her father's death.

"Will you go?" Cordelia asked softly.

She'd missed Alice and Lady Dalrymple, and with her

uncertainty about how to proceed with using her powers or seeking some other form of employment, time away from London sounded quite appealing.

"I'm considering it." Electra's chest felt looser, almost as if something inside her had been wound tight, and the prospect of leaving the city for a short while caused it to release its hold. "I think I will."

"Good." Cordelia smiled. "I suspect it's precisely what you need. I'd considered suggesting a small holiday for the two of us, but Kit's grandmother is unwell, and he's asked me to accompany him to Scotland for a fortnight."

Then it truly was best that she went to visit Alice in Oxford. It wouldn't feel right to remain at the Redmayne townhouse without Cordelia.

"When do you depart?" Cordelia asked with an eager tone.

"She sent a train ticket for tomorrow."

"Good heavens." Cordelia's brows arched. "Well, then you haven't much time. Would you like assistance preparing your travel trunk?"

"I'll manage."

Electra smiled. There were servants in the household who'd help her if she required it, but she appreciated that Cordelia would never consider aiding a friend to be below her station.

Her traveling trunk would be far lighter than Cordelia's would have been, and her wardrobe was far less fashionable. Indeed, the prospect of spending time at Alice's father's estate made her realize she didn't truly have the proper selection of gowns for socializing with nobility for more than a couple of days.

"I can loan you anything you might need."

Electra chuckled. "I was just thinking of my gowns. Are you certain you don't also have the ability to read the thoughts of others?"

Cordelia smiled mischievously. "Perhaps you are rubbing off on me a bit."

They parted ways, and Electra began climbing the stairs to her room when Cordelia called out, "Don't forget to send a note to Inspector Pierce to let him know you won't make your Sunday dinner visit with him."

Electra let out a sigh. She would send him a message, and as much as Oxford felt like a pleasant escape from London, she couldn't help but feel a bit disappointed that she'd miss out on a visit with Gideon and Mrs. Perkins.

Then and there, she vowed to make a point of visiting as soon as she returned to London. Maybe by then, she would feel less out of sorts. After a few days in Oxford, perhaps some clarity about her future course would become evident to her.

Chapter Two

The note had been hand-delivered by a messenger boy to Gideon the previous evening, and he hadn't felt at ease since he'd read the few lines written in Electra's neat, tight script. She'd let him know that she would not be coming to dinner on Sunday because she'd been invited to visit a friend in Oxford.

Gideon had half-expected her to decline the invitation when he'd proffered it the previous day. He'd been surprised when she'd agreed so readily. After resuming their acquaintance the previous autumn during the Becknell case, he'd hoped they might return to the rapport that had come so easily between them years ago.

Secretly, a part of him had hoped that rapport would grow into something more.

But she'd withdrawn again over the winter. She had to come to visit once over Christmastide to give him a gift—a volume of Shakespeare's sonnets, as she remembered how fond he was of the bard. He'd given her a leather-bound journal, remembering that she'd kept one daily as a girl. A committed diarist always appreciated a fresh journal, and she'd thanked him profusely.

Then the distance between them had widened again. He'd become busy with a flurry of new cases, and he'd assumed she'd found herself in even more demand after the notoriety the Becknell case had brought. The papers had mentioned her far too much for Gideon's taste, and it had revived the protective instinct he'd often felt for her in their youth. She'd been a truer friend to him than he'd ever known. That sort of caring wasn't something he'd been used to, but Erasmus Poole and his only daughter had been the family Gideon never believed he would have after being orphaned.

Still, there had been secrets in the Poole household. When he'd attempted to broach the topic of Electra's mother, both of them had refused to reveal anything other than that she'd been ill and hospitalized. At times, the secrecy made him recognize his separateness. Yet he'd also understood that the secrets weren't only hidden from Gideon; Erasmus and Electra Poole were burying truths that had scarred both of them.

Now, as Gideon sat in his office at Vine Street station, rereading Electra's short letter, something tickled in the back of his mind. The name of her friend, Lady Alice Kirkham, was familiar because he recalled times Electra had visited her.

Noting the time her train to Oxfordshire would depart from Paddington station, he looked at the clock, then looked back at her letter. He could not shake the oddest sense of foreboding.

He'd never put much stock in soothsaying before discovering that Electra claimed to have powers beyond the senses he knew and understood. After working with her last year, he now believed she *did* possess abilities he couldn't understand. She had seen things in individual's minds, gained knowledge from objects she touched. None of it fit well into his perception of the world, but he trusted her. She would not feign such a thing.

And he trusted his own instincts too, that feeling in his gut about certain cases or suspects. That was also a sort of knowing he could not quite explain.

That feeling—that tightness in his middle that told him something wasn't quite right—was present now at the prospect of Electra leaving London.

He'd told himself he would not allow his feelings for her to hinder their friendship, that he would hope only for the resumption of amity between them. But she'd distanced herself again, and he wasn't certain why.

Glancing up, he noted the time once more, then looked at the case files strewn across his desk and groaned. He had plenty to occupy his time, and so he laid Electra's note aside and got to work.

RESTING against the bench of the elegant carriage that had been sent to collect her from Oxford station, Electra took a deep breath. The air was filled with green scents—new leaves emerging on tree limbs after winter's chill, flowers blooming, fresh-cut grass, all the verdant indicators of spring. London had always been and would ever feel like home, but there was no denying the appeal of fresh country air.

By the time the carriage began winding along a narrow, graveled path that she guessed was the approach to Carthorpe Hall, dusk had turned to early evening. Electra was eager to get out, stretch her legs, and see her old friend again.

Yet as the old country house came into view, unexpected trepidation raised gooseflesh on her arms. She'd never visited Carthorpe, but she knew that parts of the house were constructed centuries ago. Against the moonlit sky, the Hall loomed tall and oddly misshapen. One half looked like a remnant of an Anglo-Saxon stronghold with a half-ruined tower and crenelated battlements. The other half and front of the house were all Palladian elegance, with columns and an impressive pediment.

Most intriguing of all, the Hall was ablaze with light, making it seem as if every room was occupied. All of the ground floor windows and a few of the upper story windows were aglow, and she could see shadows of figures moving about on the ground floor.

Alice's letter had made it sound as if the house was lonely, too big and rambling and that she craved company to combat its emptiness. But it wasn't empty at all. Indeed, there seemed to be a passel of guests at the moment.

As a footman handed her down from the carriage and collected her traveling case, she saw several shadowy figures beyond the open drapes. Then a flickering light in the grounds of the estate caught her eye. Servants in livery strode through the garden with lanterns held high, lighting their faces.

A man appeared, framed against the light of the open front door, and he began a quick stride toward her. He had a lanky build and wore an elegant black evening suit with a white waistcoat and tie. As he drew closer, Electra realized he was young, perhaps a few years younger than her seven and twenty. His thick wavy light brown hair looked mussed, as if he'd run his fingers through it. Breath gusting out as if he'd sprinted out to meet her, he offered a nod of greeting.

"Miss Poole," he said in a strained baritone, "I regret the lack of a proper introduction. I am James Lockhart."

Electra recognized the surname from one of Alice's letters, but the name she'd mentioned was Lord *Henry* Lockhart.

"My brother asked me to ensure that you were greeted and shown to your room."

Behind Mr. Lockhart, voices filtered out into the night. She heard the raised voice of a woman, a gentleman's bark in retort, and then what sounded like a lady crying.

"There's been an unexpected turn of events this evening," he said, crooking his arm and lifting it as if urging her to rest her hand on him.

Electra merely looked at his arm, then up into his face, half hidden by shadows. "What events, Mr. Lockhart?"

"Allow me to escort you inside, and I'll explain."

When he realized she was not going to take his arm, Mr. Lockhart began a slow walk toward the front door. Electra followed.

The moment she stepped onto the marble-floored entryway, a wave of fear and anxiety washed over her. It clouded the air like smoke, and to her left, two young women in black and white servants' uniforms rushed into a room that looked to be a drawing room.

Electra turned, feeling a tug as if something were pulling her toward the room.

"This way, Miss Poole. I'll show you up to your guest chamber," Mr. Lockhart said, a hand out as if to usher her toward the stairs. Under the gaslights, his face had the softness of youth and yet his blue eyes flickered with irritation that she would not cooperate as he expected her to.

"Where is Lady Alice?" Electra felt a compulsion to see her before taking another step farther inside Carthorpe Hall. "I was invited by her to visit. I'd like to speak with her before I go up."

"She's in here," a gentleman's voice called from the drawing room threshold.

Electra turned to find a tall, russet-haired man with a neatly trimmed mustache and beard watching them. His blue eyes were large and arresting, and he held them focused on Mr. Lockhart. The two stared at each other a moment, as if some silent message was being relayed between the two.

"My brother, Henry," Mr. Lockhart said from behind her as if by way of introduction.

That was the name Electra recognized. Lord Henry Lockhart, Viscount Lockhart. Alice's fiancé. In a letter she'd sent the previous winter, Alice had mentioned their engagement in a single sparsely worded line. It had struck Electra as odd. Most young ladies seemed eager to gush about their intended, but Alice had always been the sort to guard her finer feelings. Even when they were at school and the closest of confidantes, Electra had sensed her friend was not entirely forthcoming. But she never urged Alice to confide her secrets. How could she? She'd kept her own, never revealing her abilities or the truth of what had happened to her mother to anyone.

"Miss Poole, I'm afraid you've arrived in the midst of most unexpected circumstances. Yet I believe your arrival will prove very useful," Lord Lockhart said. He had a confident, commanding voice. "Would you be willing to sit with Alice for a bit? This has distressed her immensely."

"Of course."

Lord Lockhart led her into the drawing room, and Electra found it occupied by half a dozen guests. Ladies and gentlemen were scattered around the room, either seated or gathered in small clusters, all of them looking fretful. A few looked her way, eyeing her curiously.

On a chair on the far side of the room, near a window, she spotted Alice. The same delicate features and expressive face. The same chestnut-brown hair, a few wisps always spilling out of her coiffure.

The moment she noticed Electra, Alice stood and the shawl around her narrow shoulders slipped down. She wore a wobbly smile on her face.

Electra started toward her, Alice came forward, and they met in the middle of the room. Green eyes glittering, brow pinched, Alice immediately took up Electra's gloved hands. "My dear, this is not at all how I hoped to welcome you on your first night at Carthorpe."

A tear dropped down her cheek, and Electra felt a tremor run through her friend. Her hands shook as Electra clasped them.

"Darling, why don't you and Miss Poole find a spot by the fire," Lord Lockhart encouraged, cupping Alice's elbow and guiding her.

Alice released Electra's hands and let herself be escorted to a pair of chairs arranged at the edge of facing settees. When she sat, she let out a sigh and immediately lifted a handkerchief to dab at her cheek.

"I must go and join the search party. I'll return as quickly as I can." Lord Lockhart bent and took Alice's hand, placing a brief kiss against her knuckles.

"Please take care, Henry."

"Of course, my love."

Once he'd gone, Electra took the chair across from her friend and removed her gloves. They often worked to dim her abilities, keeping her from being unexpectedly overwhelmed when touching a person or an object. But she couldn't quite make out what Alice was feeling, and she was curious. Though it was obvious her friend was deeply unsettled, she sensed it was more than whatever had occurred that night. She looked pale and a bit gaunt. The rosy cheeks and the spark she was used to seeing in her friend's eyes seemed to have dimmed.

Electra reached out and brushed Alice's arm, but nothing came—no sensations or images to give her more insight.

"Can you tell me what's happened?" Electra asked quietly, then glanced around at the other guests, some of whom were looking her way.

"It's dreadful." Alice's voice broke and she swept a lock of hair behind her ear. "Aunt Gertrude has gone missing."

Electra felt her own heart stutter in her chest and a cold chill swept down her back. She laid a hand on Alice's arm again and sensed immense fear, thick and palpable, though no images came.

"When did she go missing?" Electra kept her voice low.

"Less than an hour ago."

"Then she can't have gone far." Electra had the urge to bolt up and rush outside to assist with the search.

"This house party was a dreadful idea. We thought it might lift Papa's spirits, but he's taken poorly again and hasn't been down since the guests began arriving." Alice finally lifted her gaze to Electra's. "My goodness, you've not been introduced to anyone, have you?"

"I met Mr. Lockhart and Lord Lockhart. There will be time for me to meet the others."

"I should have mentioned in my letter that we'd have other guests."

Electra would have preferred to be forewarned, but all she wanted now was to find Lady Dalrymple.

"When was your aunt last seen?"

"Earlier this evening. It was such a lovely night, and the moon was so bright, so we all decided to walk the hedge maze. Everyone took to their own nooks or paths. When the rest of us returned, many went back up to their rooms to refresh before dinner. It was some time before Ophelia informed us that she hadn't returned."

"Ophelia?" Electra sensed the young lady in question approaching almost the moment she said her name.

"Hello, Electra." Her voice had the same musical quality Electra recalled from years ago. "It's been far too long."

Ophelia Winters had been the most beautiful girl at their finishing school. Her strawberry-blonde hair and bright blue eyes seemed to enthrall everyone, and she had a winning manner too. Friendly and charming. Electra had sometimes wondered if all that sereneness was feigned, but then they'd become friends, and she'd realized that she was genuinely warm and amiable. Yet they'd never grown as close as Electra had to Alice.

Electra stood and Ophelia leaned in to buss a kiss against her cheek as had been her habit when they were at school together. When she straightened again, Ophelia glanced across the room.

"Alex is here too, though he's out searching with the other gentlemen."

Another familiar name. Alex Winters. Ophelia's elder brother. Hearing his name after so many years caused an unwanted ripple of awareness to run through Electra.

"How long have they been searching?" she asked as Ophelia took up a spot on the settee near them.

"About thirty minutes," Alice said in a low shuddery tone. "I cannot imagine where she's gone."

"I believe all will be well," Ophelia said, displaying that hopeful nature that Electra recalled from when they were schoolmates. At times, it seemed somewhat forced, as if Ophelia smiled to hide whatever she might truly be feeling.

"I recall from stories Lady Dalrymple told me," Electra began, "that she likes to explore on her own. She told me she prefers to be fearless when she goes on holiday, and she said she quite scandalizes the tour group who'd lose sight of her in a marketplace or a museum when she went off on her own."

Ophelia smiled, but Alice looked more fretful.

"But where would she wander to in the Oxfordshire countryside in the middle of the night?" Alice said, her tone almost at a panicked pitch. "And after what she said last evening…"

"You mustn't think on that," Ophelia said, cutting off whatever Alice meant to say. "Lady Dalrymple seems quite fascinated with spiritualism and the macabre," Ophelia said in an amused tone. "She reads too much Wilkie Collins, if you ask me."

At the mention of spiritualism, Alice turned toward Electra, brows arched expectantly. Had she read about the murder of Lady Becknell? Did she know Electra had been called a spiritualist by the London papers for the last several months?

When Alice said nothing, Electra couldn't resist inquiring. "What did Lady Dalrymple say last evening?"

"She believes Carthorpe is haunted," Alice said, directing her words at Electra. "Henry and Alex tried to dissuade her, but there's a long-standing legend about the spirit of a young man haunting the grounds. I've seen odd things at Carthorpe all my life."

Ophelia inhaled sharply but said nothing. When Electra looked her way, she gave the slightest shake of her head, as if she didn't believe any of it.

"Well, I give no credence to any of it," she said confirming Electra's assumption. "I refuse to believe in what I cannot see with my own two eyes," Ophelia said, then frowned as she looked at Electra. "Do you truly believe in such nonsense, Electra? I read about you in the London papers and was taken aback. I always thought you were the cleverest of us all."

Ophelia, it seemed, had shed some of her meek demeanor since their time together at school, but Electra still found herself shocked by the tinge of bitterness in her old friend's tone.

Before she could form a suitable reply, footsteps sounded in the hallway, and Lady Honoria, Alice's younger sister, rushed into the room, her honey-blonde hair disheveled and her cheeks red from the cold.

"We've found her!" she said breathlessly.

Alice shot to her feet and rushed over to Honoria, who immediately took her hands and said something quietly to her that Electra could not hear.

Not two minutes later, the silver-haired lady who Electra felt a swell of affection for staggered into the room, guided by Alex Winters, who held one of her arms while Lord Lockhart held the other. Pale-skinned and shivering, she still seemed to be fighting to walk on her own. When she turned her face, Electra saw abrasions and a trickle of blood on her cheek.

"We should take you to your room," Mr. Winters told her.

"Nonsense." But Lady Dalrymple waved a hand covered with rings and flicked her wrist tinkling with stacked bracelets, brushing off the notion. "I must tell all of you what I saw. Now help me to sit."

"You've sustained injuries," Lord Lockhart said gruffly. "They must be tended to."

"Send for a doctor," her ladyship said in the sharp, perfectly enunciated tone Electra recalled fondly. She flicked her hand again. "Do what you will, but I must speak of it, and I shall not be silenced."

Both gentlemen continued holding onto her until she lowered herself to the settee where Ophelia had been sitting. Ophelia scooted over to make room for the noblewoman.

"We need bandaging, water, and antiseptic to clean her wound." These words came from Lord Lockhart. He barked them at one of the housemaids who'd come into the room soon after Lady Dalrymple. "And send a footman to fetch Dr. Brownlow." The girl skittered off.

Alex Winters crossed the room and sprawled on the settee opposite Lady Dalrymple.

Lord Lockhart strode over to Alice and laid a hand on her shoulder, as if to reassure her. Electra noticed Alice's subtle flinch away from his hand, as if the viscount's touch did not seem to comfort her. Lockhart glanced down at her, eyes narrowed, lip curled, but then it was gone so fast that Electra could almost convince herself she hadn't seen it.

James Lockhart entered the room last and went to stand near the mantel, holding his hands out to the fire as if to warm them.

"I saw what I thought at first was an apparition. A shadowy figure crossing the grounds. He moved so quickly, but I followed the specter," Lady Dalrymple said. "It was a young man. I followed him into the hedge maze, but then he vanished. I wouldn't be daunted. I called to him. And then he was there again. I heard the sound of footsteps, felt a shift in the air. I am loath to admit it, but I stumbled, fell to the ground, and must have fainted."

Lady Dalrymple's agitation seemed to create a hum of tension in the room. Ophelia reached out to stroke her arm, as if to offer comfort. At that moment, the noblewoman lifted her gaze and seemed to spot Electra for the first time.

"My dear," she said on a gasp. "My dear Miss Electra Poole. You've come." She lifted a hand, and Electra stood and drew close, taking the noblewoman's hands. She was cold and Electra chafed her fingers between her own.

"Whatever you saw," Ophelia said in a warm, soothing tone, "we're glad you're back safe with us, my lady."

"Of course, I am," Lady Dalrymple snapped, then turned a soft smile Electra's way. "Perhaps I should go up to my room. I'd like to get all of this down in my journal. Honoria dear, would you be so good as to write it out for me? My hands aren't as steady as they once were."

"Yes, Aunt, of course."

Both Alex and Lockhart helped to get Lady Dalrymple to her feet again, though she still held fast to Electra's hand.

"We shall speak to each other soon, my dear. You and Alice and I must take tea together," she said, then released Electra's hand. Honoria immediately took her aunt's arm and led her slowly from the room.

Alex Winters turned a look Electra's way. "Miss Poole, you arrived to a bit of drama." His voice held too much amusement for the seriousness of the moment. "How many years has it been?"

"A long while." It had been nine years, but she was not at all surprised that he didn't recall that as well as she did.

Electra found it oddly unsettling to have his dark eyes on her again after so many years. For one summer of her life, she'd thought of him far too often, but he'd rarely crossed her mind since.

He didn't seem to have changed. He was a complete contrast to his sister, with nearly black hair, dark eyes, a crooked smile, and a sense of humor that seemed always on display. That humor was sometimes entertaining, but more often biting.

"I read about you in the papers. You predicted a lady's death, did you not?"

Though the room had been quiet since Lady Dalrymple's exit, it fell completely silent at Winters' question, and all eyes seemed to swing her way. Something in the center of Electra's chest felt heavy. Perhaps coming to Oxford hadn't been an escape from her dubious fame after all.

"Yes, I did, Mr. Winters," Electra finally said into the quiet.

"Then you may prove very useful to Lady Dalrymple." He still wore an irritating half grin on his face. "She's determined to have a séance conducted at Carthorpe. According to Alice, Lady Dalrymple insists the restless spirit of the young man's ghost must be contacted."

Electra shook her head before Mr. Winters finished speaking. "I'm afraid I do not do that."

"I see. How very disappointing." Mr. Winters shrugged as if he did not care at all. "Well, then I suspect she will call upon someone who will."

Chapter Three

The next morning, Electra woke to a scratching sound that roused her from sleep.

She noticed a slip of paper on the floor just inside the threshold of her closed bedchamber door. She slipped out of bed and made her way over to pick it up.

A rush of fear spiked through her when she touched the folded slip of paper, making the hair on the back of her neck stand on end. Closing her eyes, she summoned whatever else might come.

She saw an overgrown folly, as one might find on an old, abandoned estate. And she walked toward it purposely, eager. Someone was waiting for whoever's memory she was seeing.

Then it faded and she came back to herself in her room at Carthorpe, her hand trembling slightly as she held the note in her hand. She unfolded the paper and found a short message from Alice written inside.

Would you come to visit me in my chamber as soon as you receive this? Alice

Electra washed and dressed quickly, pulling her hair up into a knot at her nape. Then she made her way down the hall, not entirely certain which door might be the one to Alice's bedroom.

A dark-haired housemaid rounded the top of the servants' staircase and started down the hall, her arms stretched wide as she carried a tea tray.

"Would you be so kind as to direct me to Lady Alice's room?"

"First at the top of the stairs, miss."

At the farthest end from her own room. She made her way down and heard raised voices echoing through the walls as she drew nearer. By the time she reached the threshold of Alice's room, a loud clatter echoed in the hall, as if something had fallen against the room's wall, and then a scream rang out.

Electra twisted the door knob and swung the door open.

Inside, she saw Lord Lockhart with one hand gripping Alice's wrist and the other raised as if to strike her.

"Stop!" the shout startled both of them. Lockhart loosened his grip. Then he turned to face Electra so swiftly that Alice stumbled back, lost her footing, and tumbled to the floor.

"This is madness," Lockhart shouted, his glare now turned Alice's way.

Alice wouldn't look at him. She'd landed on her backside and pushed herself up to a sitting position, hands braced on the floor.

"Please leave us, Henry," she said in a broken whisper.

"I'm not certain I should leave you alone with Miss Poole," he said, his voice shaking with emotion. "You're not well, Alice. You're mad—"

"I must speak to Alice, Lord Lockhart." Electra made no attempt to keep the disdain from her tone. "Right now, if you please."

He stared at her, almost dumbfounded, as if he'd just

recalled that she'd entered the room. Electra stepped closer to Alice.

"Please allow me to speak with her," she told him.

Lockhart's intense blue eyes bored into Electra's, and she sensed more shock than anger from him. Not only in his expression, but the feeling itself moved out toward her. She could identify confusion among his emotions more vivid than any other. Indeed, the man looked thoroughly rattled.

"Watch yourself," he told Electra.

Then he offered Alice one long inscrutable look and strode from the room. Electra closed the door behind him, twisting the key in the lock to secure them inside.

By the time she'd turned around to assist Alice, her friend had already gotten to her feet and was righting her clothing and hair. A straight-backed chair lay on its side against the wall, and Electra lifted it, settling its legs on the carpet.

"Did he strike you?" Electra gestured toward Alice's arm, scanning for any sign of injury, but Alice flinched away. Almost as if she did not trust anyone to touch her at that moment.

"No, he did not. I am unharmed. A bit shaken, perhaps."

"Of course you would be." Electra gestured to a pair of chairs near the fireplace. "Let's sit. Shall I ring for tea?"

"I already have some. Will you pour me a cup?" Alice gestured toward a tray set out on a low table, half obscured by one of the wingback chairs.

After Electra poured tea, they each took a few sips as they turned their attention to the fire, watching the low flames flickering in the hearth. Electra glanced over at Alice's wrist, but Alice immediately pulled the cuff of her dress down.

"I found the note that had been slipped under my door," Electra began quietly. "You wished to see me?"

"Oh," Alice said, almost as if she'd forgotten ever writing the note. "Yes, I wanted to speak to you about this evening's event, but..." She trailed off and then fell silent. "First," she finally began again, "I must apologize for last night. What a dreadful way to welcome you to Carthorpe. Talk of ghosts and Aunt Gertrude's little mishap."

"Why would you apologize? Whatever happened to your aunt—"

"I do believe her, Electra. That she saw a phantasm of some sort." Alice turned a questioning look her way. "You must too since you... Well, you're a spiritualist yourself now, are you not? Or do you prefer to be called a medium?"

Electra far preferred to speak about what she'd just seen pass between her friend and Lockhart, but it was clear Alice wasn't ready to discuss the matter.

"I don't feel any affinity for those descriptions," she told her friend. "I do not consider myself a medium. I don't quite know how I should define myself. The abilities I possess are still a bit of a mystery to me."

Alice assessed her a moment. "But how can that be? Are they not a part of you?"

"Yes, but I've denied them for most of my life. I never told you. I never told anyone, especially not my father. Acknowledging them doesn't mean I fully understand how they work. I'm learning."

Electra took a sip of her tea and when she set her cup down, she got a clearer look at the mark on Alice's wrist, half hidden by the draped shawl. The reddened skin didn't surprise her, but what looked like an older, faded bruise did. Had Lockhart manhandled her in the past too?

"But you do know things, or see things, don't you?" Alice asked.

"Sometimes, yes, I do."

"How do you know what you see is true? And what sorts of things do you see?"

"When I touch people, I can sometimes sense their thoughts, or see their memories, or feel their feelings. It might happen when I touch an object too, especially if someone has held it recently. Occasionally, emotions will have a shape or a color that I can see." Electra thought back to that night last November when Helen Becknell had embraced her. "And quite rarely, I will have a vision of a future event."

"That's remarkable, Electra. Truly." She sounded awestruck, and it made Electra uncomfortable. She'd made the decision to embrace her gifts after her father's death, but she was discovering that it set her apart from others too. It made her an oddity.

"Will you tell me about what I observed just now when I walked in?" Electra asked, gentling her tone. "Is that the true reason you wanted me to visit your room? Do you fear him, Alice?"

For several ticks of the mantel clock, Alice observed her and said nothing. Electra suspected her friend was weighing how much to divulge.

"I don't know what to do." Tears welled in Alice's amber eyes. "And you were the person I thought to call upon for advice." She sniffed and lifted a handkerchief she clutched in one hand. "Now that I know you are gifted as you are, perhaps you have unique insights."

"I'll help in any way I am able to, but you must tell me what's troubling you."

Electra sensed fear as she had with Alice the previous evening, but now the reason seemed clear. Lord Lockhart was a violent man.

"Had he harmed you before today?"

"Today was a...misunderstanding," she said quickly. "But..."

Alice lifted a hand and covered her mouth, seemingly determined to hold some terrible secret inside herself. "I fear him," she finally whispered, then lowered her hand.

"So he is violent?" Electra wore no gloves and considered reaching out to determine what she might from touching Alice. Yet something held her back. Perhaps the notion that it was best if this was a confession Alice spoke aloud.

Alice licked her lips and opened her mouth, then hesitated before saying, "Henry has a temper. Don't all men? My father does. But Henry's temper is unpredictable. I seem to displease him when I least expect to."

Every time Alice spoke his name, Electra felt an echo of fear pulse in the air.

"He's harmed you before?"

"Henry is very exacting. And when I don't behave as he wishes, or when matters don't go to his liking... He lashes out." She lifted her shoulders. "And I tend to be closest when he does."

"Alice, you must consider ending the engagement."

"Oh, I don't think—"

"Once you're wed, his control over your life and choices will not be your own. Ending an engagement is far easier than severing a marriage."

Alice shook her head sharply. "It is out of the question. Father adores Henry, and it's a fortuitous match. I can't recall ever seeing him so pleased as the day I told him that Henry and I were to marry."

"You cannot make choices simply to please your father." Electra felt the hypocrisy of her words. She herself had hidden parts of herself for years to satisfy her father, or perhaps to avoid his judgment. "Especially if your own well-being is at stake."

She lifted her head and gave Electra a half-smile. "You, my

friend, have never met my father. If he's well enough today, perhaps you shall have an opportunity to."

As if she wished to speak no more of Lord Lockhart, Alice lifted her teacup and took a few sips.

Electra could not let the matter rest. "How many times has he laid his hands on you, Alice?"

She shook her head. "Not many. Only when he's very displeased. Especially if he's had too much whiskey. At those times, he occasionally clutches my wrist too hard or..."

"Or?"

Alice shook her head. "I feel I am imposing on you with these dreadful confidences."

"I walked in upon on him manhandling you. You are not imposing on me at all. You are confiding in me, and I appreciate that you trust me enough to do so." Electra reached out, gently laying a hand on Alice's.

To her surprise, Alice smiled but slid her hand out from beneath Electra's hold. "There was an incident, a while back, that he deeply regrets. He has apologized for it numerous times, and I have forgiven him. So why speak of it?"

"What incident?"

"He pushed me," Alice said with surprising softness in her tone, almost a sad regret. "It was my fault. I was beseeching him, clinging to him, and he pushed me away. I stumbled and fell." She reached up and brushed at a fall of curls that she wore framing her face. "My head struck the table's edge. You can still see the scar perhaps."

"You fell today too." Electra couldn't detect any mark on Alice's skin, but presumably the incident had taken place long enough ago that the wound had faded.

"I must emphasize that he did not mean for me to injure myself."

"Yet he was the cause of you doing so." Electra realized

she'd pushed too far when Alice shifted in her chair to turn away.

"He apologized, but I struggle to forget. And between father's failing health and Aunt Gertrude's insistence on speaking of specters at Carthorpe, my nerves are a bit jangled." She stared into the fire's flames. "Henry suggested I go away for a bit to settle my mind."

"No." The word burst out of Electra, so loud and forcefully that it shocked her.

Alice looked at her in stunned silence.

"I won't let you be sent away."

Alice frowned, her expression softening. "I think he only meant to the seaside, my friend. Not to a hospital."

Alice knew that Electra's mother had been ill and hospitalized, though she wasn't aware that the asylum she'd been sent to was meant to treat maladies of the mind, or that its treatments were cruel rather than curative.

"Of course," Electra said, feeling suddenly embarrassed. "How may I help? You've invited me here, you've confided in me, and I wish to help."

Alice stood and walked over to the long window that looked out onto the garden and hedge maze at the west side of the house.

"You say you can read thoughts when you touch someone," she said with her back to Electra.

"Sometimes I can."

Alice turned to her, framed in the golden glow of early morning light. "Would you do so with Henry? Could you lay a hand on his arm and...read him?"

Electra's immediate reaction was hesitation. After what Alice told her, she didn't imagine Lord Lockhart would be amenable to a sitting with her. Unless Alice was asking her to do it surreptitiously, which she had done with individuals during the Becknell investigation. She was not averse to doing so if necessary.

"What is it you think I might discover if I do?"

"I will sound paranoid if I admit it."

"You can trust me, Alice."

"I want to know if he truly has ill will toward me. If he loves me. At times, I've wondered if it's just my dowry he wants. Papa has insisted on quite a sum."

Electra rose from her chair and walked over to where Alice stood by the window. Beyond the open curtains, she could see the symmetrical patterns of the garden's beds and the dark, twisting lanes of the hedge maze stretching out at its edge, where early morning fog seemed trapped, hovering just above the ground.

"If I agree, will you promise me one thing?" Electra asked.

"What is that?"

"If I determine that Lord Lockhart has ill intentions toward you, or if I foresee some future vision to indicate he might harm you, will you break the engagement? Regardless of what your father may think."

"That is quite a promise to ask of me, Electra."

"What is the point of me asking this of me if not to keep you safe?" Perhaps it was naive of her, but that had been part of Electra's motivation to begin offering sittings to others in the first place. She clung to the notion that the gifts her mother was condemned for might be used to help others. And if they could, then that would somehow help to rectify her mother's inability to use her gifts without the dreadful consequence of being locked away in an asylum.

"Very well," Alice said, reaching out and laying a hand on Electra's sleeve. "I promise."

"Then I'll do it."

"Thank you, my friend." Alice's blue eyes were brighter

when she looked at Electra and a smile softened her features. "I knew I could count on you." Her whole demeanor seemed lighter, yet she still remained at the window, staring out. "Aunt Gertrude has arranged a séance for this evening, and that's when I'll ensure you're seated near Henry. The lady she's hired to lead the spectacle will no doubt ask us to join hands."

"Mr. Winters said something about a séance, but I had no idea your aunt could arrange one so quickly."

"It's a lady she knows in Oxford. Apparently, she's quite proficient and renowned. She doesn't do table rappings or even transform in speech or visage, but she can speak to the dead." Alice looked over her shoulder. "Can you?"

"No," she told Alice.

It didn't surprise Electra to be asked such a question, since many assumed her skills extended to mediumship. She had tried once, attempting to reach out beyond the veil that separates the living and the dead. That moment had frightened her enough that she'd never tried again. Not because of what she'd seen, for the shapes were just beginning to take form in her vision before she pulled herself back from the brink. No, it had been what she'd felt, a loss of control, a surrender, as if she was being enveloped.

Alice stared at her, head titled. "But you've *seen* ghosts, haven't you?"

"No, in truth I have not, but I...do not doubt their existence." Electra was on the verge of telling Alice the rest, but it seemed too raw, too revealing.

Her father, when he'd had far too much to drink, would sometimes talk to her mother as if she was standing in the room. And once, when Electra had stormed in to take the bottle away from her father before he drained it to the dregs, she'd sensed something. A shift in the air, her mother's familiar scent, though she'd seen nothing. And later, she'd told herself that her emotions had gotten away from her, as they had with her father.

"Lady Dalrymple has insisted that we bring in a medium," Alice said, then arched a brow. "Unless you're willing to change your mind and conduct a séance yourself."

"As I told you, I'm not a medium. Does your father approve of hosting a séance at Carthorpe?" She recalled from Alice's letters that her father could be quite stern.

Alice's face brightened. "Father adores his sister. He won't gainsay her."

Suddenly, Alice tensed and fixed her gaze on something outside. Electra approached and looked down to see Lord Lockhart and his brother James striding into the hedge maze.

"He wanders there when he's in a foul mood, and James usually chases after him," she said quietly. "They're very close, but I don't think James would ever tell me anything Henry didn't want him to. That is why I need your help." Lifting her head, she looked over at Electra. "Tonight, hopefully you can determine his true intentions."

"It still seems precipitous to hold a séance tonight. Has your aunt even had sufficient time to recover?"

"Oh, she only took a little tumble. Scratched her face on one of the hedges. As you know her well, you must know she's fiercely determined when she makes up her mind. Perhaps you'll be able to determine whether the lady she's chosen to lead the séance is a charlatan."

"I don't know about that." Electra realized many assumed anyone with abilities beyond those most could comprehend were viewed as charlatans or performers who provided entertainment.

"I do hope she can contact the restless spirit Aunt Gertrude saw. And that when you lay a hand on Henry's, you can discover something to allay my worries."

Electra tried for a reassuring smile but suspected it came out as more of a grimace. She felt no certainty about anything but wanting to help her friend. And if Henry Lockhart meant Alice harm, and she could somehow sense or foresee it, she would warn her. She would never again remain quiet about what she saw in a vision.

DINNER WAS SERVED LATE that night at Carthorpe because the guests were expected to remain up until the hour of midnight. Mrs. Markland, the medium Lady Dalrymple had employed deemed it the optimal hour for the séance that was to be held in Carthorpe's drawing room.

After dinner, Electra went upstairs briefly, then headed downstairs again, anxious to see how Lady Dalrymple was faring after the previous night's events. It was about an hour before the séance would commence, and the butler, Mr. Jenks, informed Electra that everyone was to gather in the parlor. Mrs. Markland had commandeered the drawing room and would allow no others to enter until the séance commenced.

Electra found the parlor empty, but the room contained a bookshelf and a rack filled with recent newspapers and magazines. She selected a copy of the *Illustrated London News* and took a spot on the settee. Some minutes later, Lady Honoria entered the room and sat next to her.

"Are you well after last evening?" Electra asked her, recalling how animated she'd been when she rushed into the drawing room to announce that they'd found Lady Dalrymple.

"It was all distressing, but Aunt Gertrude has always been high-spirited." She smiled warmly. "I suppose that's an odd way to put, considering what she has planned for this evening."

"She's quite interested in spiritualism, I take it." She hadn't been when Electra had known her, though that was over three years ago.

"Of late, it is her preoccupation. She's even drawn Father into it, though I think he simply likes that she visits with him and talks for hours."

The lady in question entered the room in a swirl of lavender silk. She had a cane in hand, but didn't seem to rely on it much as she made her way to the chair next to Electra's.

"So pleased you're here, my dear," she said to Electra once she sat and arranged a shawl across her shoulders. Alice trailed behind her aunt and offered Electra a smile, then chose a chair arranged near her sister.

James Lockhart arrived soon after and reclined on a settee across from Lady Honoria. Electra couldn't help but notice that the looks the two exchanged seemed more than merely polite.

When Alex Winters strode into the room, he beelined for the drinks cart and poured himself a snifter of liquor. Then he lingered near the mantel and took a sip as he surveyed the room, swiping a hand through the fall of black hair on his forehead. To Electra's shock, his gaze locked on her as soon as she glanced his way. That crooked smile of his inched up, and he immediately approached, settling on the edge of the settee.

"Miss Poole."

"Mr. Winters."

He didn't unnerve her the way he had almost a decade ago, though he seemed to think he did.

"Have you always had your"—he wiggled his fingers in the air—"magical powers?"

"I'm not a magician, Mr. Winters."

He leaned a bit closer. "I was teasing you, Electra. You were more fun when we knew each other years ago."

Electra scooted away from him. "As you say, that was many years ago."

"Can we not be friends again?"

"Were we ever friends?" One summer, Electra had visited the Winters' home during summer break from Fairgate Finishing School. For one week, she'd romped the grounds around their country house with Alice, and Alex had smiled at her in a way no young man ever had. Except for Gideon, but even then, her feelings for him had been too complicated to ponder.

She'd been eighteen that summer, and for a few days, she'd been entirely smitten.

"Perhaps not." He smirked. "But there's no time like the present."

"I'll return to London in a day or so, and I doubt we shall ever see each other again," she told him.

"Ah, well, a pity."

Looking back, she realized she'd simply liked the attention of a handsome young man, but she'd also discovered a cruelty in Alex Winters that repelled her. His teasing was biting. And once he'd gained her attention, he quickly became uninterested in possessing it.

At the parlor's threshold, Carthorpe's butler cleared his throat.

"Miss Electra Poole?" Mr. Jenks said.

Every gaze swung toward her.

"Would you come with me, miss?"

Electra frowned but stood and crossed the room.

"Please allow me to escort you, Miss Poole?" With that, he turned and led her to Carthorpe's front door. For a moment, she thought he meant to escort her out, but he opened the door and then gestured toward the house's grounds.

"His lordship asked that I direct you to the garden. He's waiting there to speak with you."

"Lord Carthorpe?" Electra couldn't imagine why Alice's

father, who she'd yet to meet and understood to be quite ill, would insist they speak outdoors.

"No, miss, Lord Lockhart." He arched a silvery brow. "Shall I escort you?"

The request stunned her, so much so that her curiosity overcame her wariness, and she followed the servant to the threshold. Electra looked out onto grounds, lit by the light of an almost full moon.

"I believe I can find my way. Thank you, Mr. Jenks."

Chapter Four

Lord Lockhart stood at the edge of the carriage circle, near the green swaths of neatly trimmed grass that led into the garden and the hedge maze. Light from the ground floor windows spilled out, casting a warm glow upon his features.

Electra couldn't determine his mood, either from her abilities or his expression. He held himself in stony stillness, as if keeping all his emotions under tight restraint.

"You wished to speak with me, my lord?" Electra sensed anger as she closed the distance between them. The emotion wasn't visible in his expression, but she felt it emanating from him like the heat of a banked fire.

"I wished to apologize, Miss Poole." His tone didn't match what she sensed from him. His voice was almost reticent and he spoke softly. "What you came upon this morning..."

Electra had to bite her tongue when he paused.

"It was not at all how I wish to conduct myself. And yet such clashes have become more frequent." He looked up, his brow furrowed, eyes stricken. "I worry for my Alice, Miss Poole."

"As do I, Lord Lockhart, and I admit that I'm quite dismayed." Electra drew in a breath, knowing that her next words might cause offense, though she was determined to get them out nonetheless. "I do not believe a gentleman should put his hands on a lady in the manner I observed this morning."

He snapped his gaze to hers, notching up his chin up. "You are gravely mistaken, Miss Poole, and yet you cast judgment quite freely."

"I know what I saw, my lord."

"She struck me," he said simply. "*That* moment you did not see, and I am grateful for it. I do not wish for anyone to see Alice in such a state, when she is not herself. And I suspect she doesn't either. She had been...raving for some time, and when she lifted her arm to strike again, I held her off."

Electra assessed Lockhart, trying to weigh the truthfulness of what he claimed, whether his emotions matched the assertion. Nothing came to her. If she touched him, she might be able to see a memory of this morning's events through his eyes, but she couldn't think of a polite reason to do so. At least not until they were seated around the table this evening.

"What was the cause of the altercation between you?"

Electra took a step closer, wanting to get a better look at his features. Feelings came to her then, though all she sensed was sadness. No longer anger, nor even annoyance at her forthrightness. Only sadness.

"When she told me she'd invited you to Carthorpe, I had hoped your visit would help her."

"I want to help her, Lord Lockhart, and I will, however I can. But I also wish to know that she's safe, my lord."

Once again, he seemed taken aback. "I desire the same. I love her, Miss Poole. But if she is unwell, then I must consider how best to care for her. Being here at this house with its history and Lady Dalrymple's carrying on... Well, I've begged her to accompany me to London. There are doctors there who could treat—"

"Alice is not mad." Talk of doctors made Electra's heart thrash in her chest.

Her father told a doctor her mother was not of sound mind. Days later, she was taken from their home by that so-called doctor and never returned. For years, and sometimes even now, Electra feared the same fate would befall her too. No matter how many people sought her out or seemed to value her abilities, the fear remained, and the nightmares still came on occasion.

"She does not seem unwell to me, my lord. Perhaps a bit fretful, but with her father's illness, is that not to be expected? If a man I intended to marry left bruises on my wrists—"

Lockhart lunged toward her in the darkness, his greater height allowing him to loom over her. Electra took two back steps and wobbled when her boot heel hit a large bit of gravel.

Lockhart gripped her arm lightly. "Watch yourself."

As soon as he touched her, emotions flowed over Electra in a rush. Lockhart's frustration, his anger, and flickers of an image in his mind. An argument, not with Alice but with his brother, James.

Electra pulled out of his hold. "You cannot send Alice away."

"What are you implying, Miss Poole?" Lockhart remained close, anger tightening his jaw. "You think I wish Alice harm? Even after I confided to you what happened this morning?" He inched closer.

Electra instinctively took a step back. He was a tall man, broad shouldered, and Alice was even more slight in frame than Electra. She could imagine the fear her friend must feel when the viscount towered over her.

"Do you plan to send Alice away?"

"Did she tell you that?"

Electra wouldn't divulge any of what Alice had shared. "If you send her to a…hospital, or an asylum, I assure you they will do her far more harm than good."

Footsteps sounded behind her, and Electra turned to see Alex Winters approaching.

"Are you two going to remain out in the cold all evening or do you plan to join the mystical event?" Winters called.

"Go inside, Miss Poole," Lord Lockhart said, waving her off.

Electra immediately turned on her heel and strode quickly toward the front door of Carthorpe. She felt instant relief, a loosening in her chest, as she walked away from Lord Lockhart. Inside Carthorpe, the gaslight sconces in the main hall had been dimmed, and the butler directed her to the drawing room.

The room had been entirely transformed. All the gaslights had been dimmed and the room was strewn with candles in candlesticks and candelabrums that had not been in place hours before. Black cloth had been draped over some of the furnishings, which had been pushed back to the room's edges. A wide round table sat in the center of the room, also draped in black, and a scent wafted in the air. Something with a spicy undertone.

Electra wondered if the butler had mistakenly sent her to the room too early, as it was empty but for a tall woman who stood tapping her chin and pondering the arrangement of candles on the table. She noticed Electra and turned her way.

"You must be Miss Poole," the lady said. She wore a striking gown of sapphire, and the darkness of the dress contrasted with her pale skin and red hair.

She had to be the medium Lady Dalrymple had secured for this evening's séance.

A strange sensation filled Electra, and for a moment, it was as if the rest of the room faded. She felt an odd pull toward the woman, as if part of her was bending toward the medium.

"I am Mrs. Cora Markland," she said in a firm, strong voice. "Lady Dalrymple told me about you and your notoriety in the London papers."

"Did she?" Electra dipped her head. "Not the sort of notoriety I wish for, but the public was quite fascinated with the case."

"Yes, but also with you and your abilities." She smiled and assessed Electra, seemingly searching for something. "We have much in common, I think. Did you always know you possessed your gifts?"

It felt odd to speak openly to a stranger about aspects of her life she'd denied for so long, but it was a silly bit of reticence now. "I only noticed them when I was about ten years old, but I explained it all away to myself. My mother..."

"It's not uncommon for others in our families to be gifted too."

"No one in my mother's life considered it a gift. Especially not my father."

"I understand." Mrs. Markland nodded, and Electra felt a sense of empathy and understanding from the woman, as if it were a tangible object that she was pushing toward her.

"I think you should come and sit beside me, Miss Poole." She gestured to a spot to the left of a chair centered in front of a bowl of water, paper, and an ink pen.

"Oh, that works perfectly," Alice interjected as she entered the drawing room. "Electra must sit there beside you, Mrs. Markland." Alice stopped behind one chair and gestured to another one on her right. "And Henry will sit here when he arrives." She gestured to a spot situated on the right side of Electra's. "And James can go on the other side next to Honoria and Mr. Winters."

"I would like to sit on Mrs. Markland's right," Lady Dalrymple announced as she entered the room and then proceeded to do precisely that. "That is how I usually do it at the various séances I've attended."

That would put Lord Lockhart between Alice on his left, Electra on his right.

Once Lady Dalrymple took her chair, Alice and Electra did the same.

"We've a little more than quarter of an hour before the session begins," Mrs. Markland said. She'd not taken a seat and now eyed the doorway. "I'd like to see if Mr. Jenks has a few more candles. If you'll excuse me, ladies."

She swept from the room, and Electra turned her attention to Lady Dalrymple. "We haven't had a chance to talk, my lady. I trust you're well after last evening." Electra noticed that the abrasion on her cheek had scabbed over, though there was a bit of discoloration. Still, she looked bright-eyed, as if eager for the evening's event.

"Thank you, my dear. I am quite well and most intrigued about the séance. Have you led many yourself?" She beamed that smile Electra had become used to when she'd visited her. Always open. Forever curious.

"I lead sittings, my lady, not séances."

"No? Never?" Lady Dalrymple looked confused yet intrigued. "We'll take tea soon. You must tell me more."

Alice took her seat, one chair from Electra's. She looked much better than she had that morning. Her cheeks were bright, her hair was swept up into an artful style, and jewels glinted in her hair and at her throat.

"You're feeling better?" Electra asked quietly, knowing other guests might join them at any moment.

"I'm much better, yes." Her smile lit her eyes, and she looked young again, so like the girl Electra had known years before. "Thank you for asking, and thank you for being here." She gestured toward the empty chair between them, where Lord Lockhart would soon sit. "And for what you've agreed to do," she whispered.

Electra considered whether to mention her brief conversation with Lord Lockhart. "If I sense anything, I will tell you."

"And maybe Mrs. Markland will reveal something too," Alice said hopefully. "Aunt Gertrude insists she's quite good."

Electra had no desire to dim Alice's improved spirits. She *had* felt an odd frisson of awareness when she'd first met Mrs. Markland, but the theatricality of how the room had been arranged made her wonder whether they would see a true revelation of the medium's powers or a show rehearsed and staged like a theatrical event.

Several minutes later, Ophelia came into the room, her cheeks pink and eyes darting around at each of them. "Is there a particular chair I should sit in?"

"How about that one, my dear." Alice gestured to a chair across the table from hers.

A while later, Alex Winters burst into the room and locked his gaze on his sister, eyes wide. He appeared slightly disheveled. His necktie was askew and one of his waistcoat buttons was undone. "I couldn't find you," he said to Ophelia, a bit breathlessly.

"Well, you have now," she told him with a pert smile.

He gave his sister a look through narrowed eyes and then took the chair next to her. With a nod to Mrs. Markland, he laid his clasped hands upon the table top. Electra noted his hands were shaking slightly and his chest rose and fell visibly as if he was catching his breath.

"I wonder where the rest of the guests are," Alice murmured, glancing at the mantel clock.

"I'm here," James Lockhart announced as he entered the

drawing room. His hands were fixed at the neck of his tie, adjusting the fabric as if to make sure he looked presentable. "Am I late?"

"Not at all," Mrs. Markland told him with a smile.

Electra noticed that his cheeks were full of color and his hair damp. She glanced across the hall at the parlor window, wondering if he might have been outdoors and rain had come on unexpectedly. But she could see no drops on the windowpanes.

The Winters engaged in quiet conversation while Alice looked increasingly fretful as the hands on the clock moved toward midnight.

Lady Honoria came in just as the clock struck the midnight hour, chafing her hands together and choosing a spot on the opposite side of her sister.

"Henry should have been here by now," Alice said quietly to Electra. "Perhaps he means to avoid it all together." She turned her attention to a footman who was passing in the hall. "Hobbes, would you find Lord Lockhart and remind him that the séance is set to begin?"

"We can wait for him," Mrs. Markland offered in a polite tone.

"No, I don't think we should," Lady Dalrymple insisted. "Perhaps he means to dissuade us. He told me he disapproved of this evening's event. But in that case, we must continue without him. Do you not agree, Alice?"

"We're all eager to begin, Aunt, but I think we should wait until Hobbes returns," Alice told her in a most congenial denial.

They waited and Electra watched as the clock's hands moved past the midnight hour.

After four minutes past the hour, the young footman, Hobbes, approached the drawing room threshold. "I could not locate him, my lady, but Carter said he may have gone out to stables. He's heading there now."

Alice gave a tremulous smile. "One of his stallions is ailing of late, and he's been worried for the beast. Let us continue on. Perhaps we shouldn't wait for him after all. Please close the door, Hobbes."

A solemn, weighted silence fell over the room when they'd all been closed inside together.

Mrs. Markland slid her gaze over each person seated around the table, then lifted a small bronze bell, ringing it gently. At the tinny sound, everyone focused intently on the medium.

"Welcome, all," Mrs. Markland began in a low, resonant voice. "I am honored to have been invited to lead this séance. If you've entered our gathering with doubt in your heart, I ask that you to embrace a spirit of curiosity. Question as you will, but do not judge what manifestations emerge this evening until you witness them for yourself."

The tension in the air became palpable, and as Electra looked around at the faces of those assembled, she noted that several guests, Lady Dalrymple and Honoria, looked eager to begin. Others, like Alex Winters and James Lockhart, wore fearsome frowns, seemingly just as anxious for the whole thing to be over.

The medium remained entirely focused on her purpose as she stared into the bowl of water before her, then waved her hands slowly over the bowl, as if wafting a fragrance toward her. Suddenly, she lifted her gaze and fixed on some far-off point beyond the table.

"Would you please join hands with the individuals seated on either side of you?" she murmured.

Alice turned a glance Electra's way. The spot where Lockhart would have sat was empty beside her, but they could stretch out their arms to hold each other's hands easily.

Electra clasped Alice's hand and then that of Mrs. Markland, who sat to her right.

"We are quite safe within this circle," Mrs. Markland said in a firm, steady tone. "So I ask that you all close your eyes, at least during the invocation."

Electra lowered her eyes, then side-eyed Alice, curious if she would comply.

She had, though her brow was furrowed.

Electra closed her eyes and felt an odd mix of energy from the ladies on either side of her. Through her connection to Mrs. Markland, she sensed power. Raw, almost elemental power. It felt as if her focus was being pulled toward the medium, though no thoughts or images came through.

But from Alice, something more emerged. Electra's chest burned and her muscles tensed at the unbridled anger she sensed in Alice. A tremor ran through Alice's body, and Electra felt it through their linked hands, as if emotion was overwhelming her friend.

Images came. Electra saw a man stretched out in bed, his face pale and gaunt. Alice's father, she assumed. Alice looked down at him and felt enormous rage. He'd disappointed her in some way, or perhaps hurt her feelings, but Electra couldn't determine any details. Then sadness came, the feeling of Alice being powerless in her disappointment.

"If you come to this circle with questions, hold them in your mind now," Mrs. Markland said.

Her voice scattered the images in Electra's mind.

The medium's tone had dropped lower, to an almost reverent whisper. "I invite those who are beyond the veil to come forward if you wish to speak to us this night. But we welcome only those whose intentions are for our good. If you come with menace, you will not be admitted to this circle."

Mrs. Markland fell silent, and Electra focused again on Alice.

Once again, images took shape in her mind. Alice's memory

of a gentleman in her bedchamber. To Electra's shock, it wasn't Lord Lockhart. It was Alex Winters, smirking in his maddening way. Her perception of him through Alice's eyes came with a rush of fury, heat filling Electra's chest.

The two were arguing, but Electra heard no words. Alex seemed to shout, and she suspected he was saying something biting, as he was so talented at doing. A taunting sort of gleam lit his eyes. In her experience, when defending himself, he struck back with harsh words.

Then the pictures in Electra's mind shifted. Winters faded as another memory took shape. Lord Lockhart knelt in a bedchamber embracing someone, his face pressed to their cheek. Electra saw through Alice's eyes, and the two she observed didn't seem to be aware of her presence. When Lockhart arched back, Electra held her breath, wondering who'd she see. It was Honoria, cheeks pink, eyes glistening. The viscount lifted a hand to her cheek.

"Mary," Mrs. Markland said, her voice whispery. "A Mary has come forward and wishes to speak to someone in the circle."

Alice squeezed Electra's hand, and the image of Honoria and Lord Lockhart faded.

"Who here knows a Mary?" Mrs. Markland's voice rose.

"I knew a Mary." Alex Winters uttered the words tightly.

Mary was a common name. Electra had known a Mary at the boarding school she'd attended with Alice and Ophelia. Electra wondered if Alex might be referring to the same young woman. Though if he was, why hadn't Ophelia replied?

"And we will honor Mary's presence," Mrs. Markland said. "Yes, she tells me you are the one she's come to speak to. Mr. Winters, is it? She is on the other side now and watches over you."

Electra heard the rustle of fabric, and once again, Alice tightened her grip on Electra's hand. She lifted her head and opened her eyes to get a glimpse of Alice, but her friend's eyes remained closed, her head bent low. Electra kept her eyes open. Lady Dalrymple's were too, as were all of the gentlemen's.

"The decision you're making, Mr. Winters. Mary says it is the wrong choice." Mrs. Markland kept her head bent and her voice emerged as a monotone, as if she were reading the contents of a telegram. "She says you should turn back from that path. They will have deadly consequences."

"We were not close," Alex said bitterly. "She would have no knowledge of my choices."

He looked boldly at the others around the table, his gaze eventually falling on Electra.

"But she does, Mr. Winters," Mrs. Markland retorted. "She came this evening to offer a word of warning. You may take it or leave it. We may accept it or deny that which is offered, but that is the message which has come through."

"Well, that is rather unhelpful," Alex quipped, shooting a glare toward the medium. Electra detected a change in his tone. The message had affected him more than he was willing to admit.

"May we not seek to speak to the young man who haunts the grounds?" Lady Dalrymple asked in a breathy tone.

"I have summoned him," Mrs. Markland reassured, "but he has not come forth."

The room fell silent but for the flicker of candlelight and the snap of the fire in the drawing room hearth.

Quiet reigned so long, Electra wondered if Mrs. Markland's séance would come to a close early. Then the medium shifted in her chair and inhaled sharply.

"Greetings," Mrs. Markland whispered, her voice pitched higher. "Come. You are welcome to join our gathering and share your message, which I will convey."

The medium made an odd sound, a sort of half-strangled gasp and said, "Another spirit has come forward."

Someone at the table emitted a sound of dismay. It sounded like one of the ladies, but Electra couldn't tell if it was Ophelia or Honoria as she searched their faces. The two sat side by side, their heads bent, eyes still closed.

"I sense maternal love." Mrs. Markland spoke softly now, her voice resonating with warmth. "Julia. She says that is her name is."

Alice's fingers tightened around Electra's hand almost painfully.

"That is our mother's name," Alice whispered.

"She's here with us, Lady Alice, Lady Honoria. She loves both of you. Her beloved daughters. She wants the best for you, but she fears for you as well. For you especially."

"For me?" Honoria asked, voice breaking as if she was on the verge of tears.

"No," Mrs. Markland told her softly. "This message is intended for Lady Alice."

Electra squeezed Alice's hand, trying to offer reassurance and comfort. Alice only tensed in response. Mrs. Markland breathed heavily and her hand had gone oddly cool in Electra's.

"What else does she say?" Honoria asked.

"She's fading," Mrs. Markland replied, "but her concern for Lady Alice is vivid and unmistakable. She believes you are in danger, Lady Alice." The medium drew in a sharp breath. "Lady Carthorpe?" Unlike her earlier strident tone, Mrs. Markland spoke softly, almost beseeching. "Are you still with us, my lady?"

Honoria opened her eyes and began weeping. James Lockhart and Alex Winters both turned their attention toward her, and Lockhart seemed to offer her something below the table's edge. Electra guessed it might be a handkerchief, but Honoria did not immediately dry her tears.

Only the medium, Alice, and Lady Dalrymple kept their eyes closed and their heads bowed as Honoria sobbed. Electra found it odd that her sister's distress did not seem to disturb Alice enough for her to open her eyes.

"Will you not come to us?" Mrs. Markland queried. "We seek to ease your wandering."

Electra thought the medium must be speaking of the ghost Lady Dalrymple was eager to contact. Mrs. Markland let out an odd little moan into the tense silence of the room.

Suddenly, the drawing room door burst open. Alex Winters whipped around so quickly, his body caught the tablecloth and dislodged it, causing candles to gutter, spilling wax onto the dark tablecloth.

Hobbes, the young footman, stood on the threshold, his eyes enormous, mouth agape, chest heaving as if he'd been running. The servant fixed his gaze on Alice.

"Lord Lockhart's been found, my lady," he gasped out.

Alice sprang to her feet, chair scraping the floor. "Where is he?"

The young man hesitated, shifting his gaze to Mr. Lockhart and then back to Alice. "In the garden, my lady. He's..."

"Tell us," James Lockhart snapped.

"Out with it, Hobbes," Alice added breathlessly.

"He's bleeding, my lady. I...I think he's dead."

Chapter Five

In the next minutes, all the solemnity of the séance was swept away by chaos.

Lady Dalrymple cried out and slumped in her chair as if she'd swooned. Mrs. Markland immediately reached for her, placing a hand on her shoulder, then bending to speak to her quietly. Ophelia leaned in too, a hand on her ladyship's arm.

The men burst up from their chairs, almost toppling them, then they followed the footman out into the night. Alex Winters led the way; James Lockhart followed behind.

Honoria burst into tears again, and Ophelia embraced her, letting Honoria collapse into her arms. A moment later, two housemaids rushed into the room. One approached Alice.

"What should we do, miss? They're bringing his lordship through."

"Doctor Brownlow," Honoria cried. "We must send for him."

"Yes." Alice had been standing frozen, staring into the distance, but she turned to look at the young housemaid. "Do call him immediately. He said he would come at any hour to tend to father. Go, go!"

The girl rushed from the room so quickly, she slipped for a moment on the front hall's marble floor. Meanwhile, the second housemaid stood waiting, looking frightened and eager to be dismissed.

Alice regained her calm and said to her, "Lord Lockhart must be brought to his room. Dr. Brownlow can attend to him there."

"And the authorities must be called," Electra added.

The second maid nodded, then scurried off.

Electra moved a bit closer to Alice, yearning to offer comfort. The footman said Lockhart was possibly dead, not ill, but she understood how the mind fought against such a devastating truth.

She laid a hand on Alice's arm, but as she had in her bedroom earlier, Alice flinched away.

"I should go up and wait for them to bring him—"

Before Alice could finish her sentence, a startled scream echoed from the hallway. Everyone in the drawing room moved toward the threshold. Alice and Honoria clasped hands as they reached the doorway together. But Alice almost immediately faltered back, and Electra, standing behind her, reached out to steady her.

Beyond her shoulder, Electra saw what had upset her so. Three men, including the young footman, Mr. Lockhart, and Mr. Winters carried Lord Lockhart's body through the hall. One of the viscount's arms hung limp at his side, and the white waistcoat he wore was soaked with blood. Someone had placed their suit coat over Lockhart's face, but the stains were still visible around his neck and shoulders.

Unless he'd suffered a fall that had caused grave injuries, it looked as if Lockhart had come to violence. A shiver chased down Electra's spine at the realization that someone at Carthorpe Hall might be responsible for the viscount's injuries.

"Is he...alive?" Honoria whispered.

James Lockhart lifted his gaze to Honoria's and shook his head, his expression grim, eyes glassy.

The men moved as quickly as they could, and the butler immediately shifted toward the drawing room threshold, as if to block the ladies' view as the men carried Lord Lockhart's body up the stairs.

"I don't understand," Alice whispered. "What's happened?"

She turned to Electra, looking dazed, as if not quite fully aware of all that had just transpired.

"I must go to him," she said suddenly, all but lurching into the hallway.

"No, don't," Honoria pleaded, gripping her sister's hand. "Let the men see to him until the authorities are called."

"We don't need authorities," Alice countered. "We need Dr. Brownlow."

"Oh, Alice." Honoria pressed a fist to her mouth and lifted tear-filled eyes to Electra. "Will you help her?"

"Alice, come with me, won't you?" Electra asked, laying a hand gently on her friend's arm.

This time Alice didn't flinch away. She merely nodded and allowed Electra to lead her to the parlor, where they'd all assembled earlier that evening.

When Alice slumped down on the settee, Electra went to the bell pull. Shortly after Electra took a seat next to Alice, the blonde housemaid entered the room. The girl's hair was askew and her face was tear-streaked. She seemed to be fighting to collect herself.

"May we have a tea service brought to the parlor?" Electra asked the young woman, who bobbed a curtsy and hied off again.

"I don't want tea," Alice said weakly. "I should be with Henry."

Electra took Alice's hands in hers. They were worryingly cool, so she chafed them between her own. "Let's wait until the doctor arrives, and the authorities."

"But what if he needs me?" Alice asked, eyes wide and brimming with tears.

Electra didn't take Alice's confusion as any sort of mental decline, as Lord Lockhart had implied earlier. When she'd learned of the death of her mother, she'd wrestled with the truth of it for days.

"I'm so very sorry, Alice, but he is no longer with us." Electra spoke the words slowly, hoping they might sink in past the shock.

Tears that had gotten caught in the lashes of Alice's eyes welled and spilled down her cheeks. "Is he? Are you certain?" she whispered.

"Mr. Lockhart seemed to confirm it when Honoria asked him."

Alice nodded. "Yes, I saw that, but it's hard to bear."

"It is. Of course it is."

"And what happened to him, Electra? What could have happened to him?"

"Dr. Brownlow will determine that in short order." Electra had seen the bloodstains. Lord Lockhart had not died peacefully, but she would not speculate. A grieving mind conjured the worst possibilities all on its own.

"Our last words to each other this morning were not kind ones," Alice said, "but I trusted that we'd make amends. We always do." She looked up, her eyes red-rimmed. "Now we never shall."

"I'm sorry, Alice." The words seemed insufficient because Electra knew the pain of unspoken words between oneself and a lost loved one. There was much she would have said to her father, and her mother, if she'd known she'd run out of time.

Alice dipped her head a moment, then snapped her chin up. "Mrs. Markland," she said, her voice quavering. "Do you think she could contact Henry?"

"Oh, I don't think it's the time for such a thing. I know it feels impossible, but now is the time to wait. I know patience is difficult at such a moment, but we'll learn more soon. I'm certain of it."

The maid returned, bearing a wide silver tray containing cups, a pot of tea, and plates filled with biscuits. Electra prepared a cup for Alice and then for herself. That sat quietly for a while as Alice took a few dainty sips of tea.

A knock echoed from the hall, and Alice looked toward the drawing room threshold anxiously. Minutes later, Mr. Jenks passed by, leading a balding, brown-haired gentleman, wearing spectacles and carrying a satchel.

"Dr. Brownlow," Alice called, standing and nearly spilling her tea as she set the cup down.

"My lady," the older man said in a grave tone, "I understand Lord Lockhart has come to some trouble."

"Yes, you must see to him. Do what you can for him," she said, her voice cracking.

"Of course, my lady." Dr. Brownlow nodded, then turned to proceed toward the stairs.

Almost as soon as Alice had taken up a spot beside Electra on the settee again, a commotion drew their attention to the hallway once more.

Carthorpe's butler rushed past, and a youthful-looking, blond-haired police constable followed in his wake. The constable turned a look into the open parlor door. Alice stood as if she might speak to him, but then James Lockhart appeared, having come from the opposite end of the hallway.

"Hello, sir. I am Constable Withers. Your man here says there's been an incident at the hall."

Lockhart said something quietly to the constable that Electra couldn't hear, and then the two men disappeared from view.

Electra had the urge to follow them, to learn what the doctor might determine about Lockhart's death and how the constable would proceed with investigating the matter, but she had to stay with Alice.

They sat down again. Alice took only a single sip of her tea. She closed her eyes and then slid them open, as if catching herself before falling into slumber.

"You must be exhausted," Electra told her. "Why don't I accompany you up to your room so that you can rest?"

Restful sleep would likely be hard to achieve after the night's events, but Electra suspected it would help her friend immensely if she could face all of this in the light of morning.

"Would you check in on Honoria too? She may have already returned to her room."

"Of course."

Electra was anxious to protect Alice from seeing too much when they went upstairs, but once they'd climbed the stairs, she realized all of the bedchamber doors were closed. Only the faint sound of voices carried from one on the left, farther down the hall. Alice glanced over, and Electra guessed that must be Lord Lockhart's room.

At the threshold of Alice's bedroom, she turned to Electra. "I'll be all right, my dear. I'm going to sleep, but if anything more happens, promise you'll come and wake me."

"I promise I will."

Alice offered her a half-smile, then stepped into her room and closed the door behind her.

Electra turned to head down the hall to check on Honoria just as the constable emerged from Lord Lockhart's room.

"Pardon me, miss. May I ask your name?"

"Electra Poole."

The young man glanced down at a notepad in his hand. "And may I ask your relationship to others in the household? Are you visiting or do you reside at Carthorpe Hall?"

"I'm visiting from London. Lady Alice invited me."

"I intend to speak to each guest and resident. Would you be willing to speak to me now, Miss Poole?"

The hour was past one in the morning, and yet Electra suspected she wouldn't be able to sleep even if she returned to her guest chamber.

"Of course."

He gestured toward the staircase. "Shall we head down to the dining room? I've asked the staff to provide a space for my inquiries. I mean to speak to everyone I can before Sergeant Ormsbee arrives."

"Will he be in charge of investigating the...crime?" she asked as they proceeded downstairs.

"Yes, miss. He's been sent for and shall arrive at first light."

"Was Lord Lockhart murdered?"

On the dining room threshold, the young man gave her a stern look. "Why would you presume such a thing, Miss Poole?"

"I did not presume, Constable, but I saw the blood when he was carried in. It did not seem a peaceful death."

Constable Withers regarded her quietly.

Once they'd both stepped into the dining room, he nodded. "Yes, he was indeed murdered."

Confirmation of what she'd suspected tied a knot of worry in Electra's middle. It meant the killer was likely with them at that very moment inside Carthorpe Hall.

"Shall we sit?" Withers gestured toward a silver urn and a collection of teacups. "The staff has provided tea if you like."

Electra declined to partake and instead settled into a straight-backed chair on one side of the table. Constable Withers sat opposite her.

He opened a notepad much like the one Gideon carried with him. "Thank you for speaking to me at this late hour, Miss Poole. Tell me when you arrived at Carthorpe."

"I arrived last evening."

"And you mentioned that you came at Lady Alice Kirkham's request?"

"I did, yes."

The young man tipped his head and assessed her. "A friendly visit or did she invite you for a particular occasion?"

"A friendly visit." Electra wondered now if gleaning something from Lockhart had been Alice's reason for inviting her, and it had never had anything to do with Lady Dalrymple at all.

"When did you first meet Lord Henry Lockhart, Miss Poole?"

"Last evening. I met everyone staying at Carthorpe last evening."

"Had you never met the viscount before?"

"No, never."

"And did you speak to him at length last evening?"

"No, I did not."

"Yet you spoke to him this evening?" The constable looked up from his notepad, all the focus of his dark gaze homed in on Electra.

"I did, though briefly."

"And what was the substance of that discussion, Miss Poole?"

Electra stared at the young man, knowing that whatever she said next might lead him to discover the contentious relationship between Alice and Lockhart.

"He said that he believed my visit would help Alice."

"Why did Lady Alice require assistance?"

"I believe it has been a stressful time for her. Between her upcoming nuptials and the earl's convalescence."

"Did any of her stress relate to Lord Lockhart?"

"I cannot say." Electra knew the answer was most likely yes, but she didn't even know if Alice would admit that much.

"I was provided information regarding an argument between Lord Lockhart and Lady Alice this morning. Were you aware that they'd rowed?"

"Yes." Electra couldn't help but wonder how he'd learned of the incident after being in the hall such a short while. Could he have already spoken to staff?

The constable's brows arched at that. "Do you know the cause or content of that argument?"

"No, Constable."

Constable Withers' dark brows drew down again and then together as he glanced at his notepad, flipping back to a previous page before looking at her again.

"Another guest of Lord Carthorpe's, a Mr. Alexander Winters, says that you were observed having an altercation with Lord Lockhart shortly before he was attacked."

"Attacked?" It seemed strange and unsettling to think that she'd spoken to the man hours ago and left him in the garden. Had someone been waiting to strike at that moment?

"What exactly happened to Lord Lockhart?" Electra asked, though she doubted the policeman would divulge much.

The constable leaned a little closer, his chest almost touching the table's edge. "I was hoping you might be able to shed light on that, Miss Poole. According to the few individuals I've had the opportunity to speak to, you were the last person seen with Lord Lockhart."

"That is untrue." Electra tapped a finger on the tabletop. "Alex Winters, who it seems you've spoken to, did indeed observe me speaking to Lord Lockhart. But he also remained outside while I returned to the house. Mr. Winters was likely the last person to see Lord Lockhart."

The young man's eyes registered surprise, though Electra couldn't sense anything from him through her abilities. He seemed to be one of those people who were impervious to her gifts.

"Can you estimate the time when you re-entered the hall and observed Mr. Winters with Lord Lockhart?"

"It would have been about twenty minutes or a quarter hour until midnight. And I do not know if Mr. Winters spoke to the viscount. I can only say that they were both outside when I stepped back inside Carthorpe Hall."

The constable bent his head a moment to make a notation, and Electra couldn't help but think of how Alex Winters had looked when he'd entered the drawing room prior to the séance. He'd been disheveled, and James Lockhart had looked unsettled too. But Winters claimed he'd been looking for his sister, though he never explained why.

"Constable, may I have a word?" Dr. Brownlow stood on the dining room threshold.

The constable looked up with a brow arched, gave the doctor a nod, then turned his attention back to Electra. "Do you plan to remain at Carthorpe Hall, Miss Poole, or return to London?"

"That is partly dependent on Lady Alice, but my intention had been to remain for several days."

"Excellent. I will be asking all guests and residents to remain until I or Sergeant Ormsbee have spoken to them. Shall we continue this conversation tomorrow morning?"

Electra glanced up at the doctor, who shifted on his heels, seemingly eager to speak to Constable Withers.

"Yes, of course. I will see you tomorrow, Constable." Electra stood and made her way to the door, where Brownlow stepped back, allowing her to exit the room.

The doctor immediately stepped inside and pulled the door almost closed behind him.

Electra turned to head up to her room, but curiosity held her in place. She hesitated, bending her head toward the doorway.

"The object would have been smoother than a rock, but solid enough to cause serious damage."

"And the attack came from behind?"

"That is my opinion, and I will tell the coroner as much." After a pause, the doctor added, "I've sent word, and he should arrive in the morning."

"And the strength needed to commit such an act? Could a lady have managed it?"

For a moment, the two men fell silent.

"It would depend on several factors. The height of the lady. Lockhart's awareness of what was happening. He was a tall man. It might require that he be seated when the incident occurred."

"There are benches in the maze, I'm given to understand," Withers said.

"But is there any blood on those benches? There would be blood, Constable."

"Blood on the culprit who attacked the viscount too?"

"I would say so. Perhaps not a great deal, but I think escaping without a single stain would be unlikely."

"Several of the staff are searching the grounds for the murder weapon, and I'll go out now to see what I can discover. Though daylight will aid us immensely."

"I will return tomorrow to assist the coroner. Will you return in the morning too, Constable?"

"I won't be departing. The constabulary is sending Sergeant

Ormsbee to oversee the case, and I intend to remain until he arrives tomorrow. It would be foolhardy to leave the hall unattended." The two men feel silent, then Withers added, "One fact is unmistakable. Whoever killed Lord Lockhart is under this very roof."

Chapter Six

Gideon arrived at Vine Street station later than usual the next day. His current case had him up much of the evening and into the wee hours of the morning, but it had been worth it. A suspect had been taken into custody. Though he'd not confessed, Gideon felt certain they'd gathered sufficient evidence for justice to be meted out. With a mug of steaming tea beside him, he began composing the reports of all that had transpired during the course of the case in anticipation of a meeting with his chief inspector.

An hour into his work, Constable Clegg rapped on his open office door.

"Seen the newspapers today, gov?"

"No. No doubt they're making a meal of the Halsted case?" The one he was currently writing his report on involved the murder of a nobleman by his wife's paramour. Due to the victim's title and social prestige, it had been the fodder of avid reporters for weeks. Indeed, the details had been so salacious that it had finally overtaken coverage of the Becknell case.

"They are, but that's not what I was referring to." Clegg stepped forward and laid a folded newssheet on Gideon's desk.

He scanned the tiny print and three words stood out. *Murder in Oxford.*

Gideon pulled the paper closer and read the two paragraphs.

A ghastly tragedy befell the well-respected Lord Henry Lockhart during a midnight séance conducted at Carthorpe Hall, the home of his betrothed, Lady Alice Kirkham—

"I recall you saying that Miss Poole had gone to visit a friend in Oxford," Clegg said, "and when I saw mention of a séance. 'Course it could be a coincidence—"

"It's not." Gideon's hand shook slightly as he held the newspaper and read of the unsolved murder of a nobleman at the same estate Electra had traveled to days ago. Lady Alice Kirkham was the friend she said she'd gone to visit.

Despite the mention of a séance, Gideon felt a surge of relief that there was no reference to Electra in the short article describing the case. Yet he suspected she was still in Oxford. He could only conclude that, somehow, in the course of two days away, she'd found herself embroiled in another murder case.

He stood, placing the folded newspaper on his desk. "Thank you, Clegg, for bringing this to my attention."

Clegg nodded. "Of course, gov."

Gideon tried to focus again and finish his reports. His meeting with Chief Constable Douglas would commence soon. Nearly an hour later, he'd finished the reports the chief wished to review and collected them into a neat pile as he stood at his desk. Then he scooped them up and headed down the hall. Anxiety caused him to stretch his gait into a quick clip.

His meeting with the chief wasn't for another half an hour, but seeing the article about the murder at the same estate

Electra had departed for two days ago changed all of his intentions about the day.

After knocking at his superior's door and hearing "come in" barked from the other side, Gideon stepped into the chief's office.

Douglas's thin gray brows inched up. "You're early, Pierce."

"An urgent matter has arisen, sir."

The chief laid his pen aside and settled back into his chair, a furrow pinching his brow. "Tell me there's been no muck up with the Halsted case."

"None at all." Gideon laid the reports he'd written on Chief Douglas's desk. "This regards another matter."

"Go on."

"There's been a murder in Oxford."

The inspector pursed his lips. "And that is the purview of local authorities. How does that present any urgency for you?"

"Could I be sent to assist the local authorities?"

"You know that's not how it works, Pierce. The Metropolitan Police and in particular the Criminal Investigation Division cannot nose in where they're not wanted." He gestured to the piles of documents arranged over the surface of his desk. "Do we not have plenty of crime in the parishes and districts of London to keep you occupied?"

"It is, in part, a personal matter, sir. Whether I assist in the case or not, I would like to request a weeks' leave, Chief Inspector."

Douglas's face creased further, his frown deepening. "This is unexpected, Pierce."

"It is, sir. But I must travel to Oxford to...assist a friend."

The older man lowered his shoulders and clasped his hands atop his desk, pondering the matter. Finally, he looked up and said, "Very well. If the Halsted case were still unresolved, I could not spare you. But as we've made an arrest, I cannot deny that you have gone above and beyond in the past weeks to obtain a much-needed resolution."

"Then I may depart today?"

"Must you travel immediately?"

"Yes, sir, I think I must."

"I would prefer that you see out the day and give me a chance to review these reports."

Gideon clenched his jaw, forcing himself to tamp down his frustration. The worry he felt at the prospect of Electra's name being dragged through the press once again had welled up and would not be dispelled. All of his instincts told him that he needed to go to Oxford immediately. She'd likely bristle at the notion that she needed his help, but the urge to give it remained, nonetheless.

"I have spent the morning producing the reports you see there, and I would prefer to depart now. On the earliest train."

Douglas assessed him silently. "Very well." He waved a hand as if in dismissal. "Be on your way, Pierce. I can see you have no intention of tarrying."

"Thank you, sir." Gideon gave the chief a nod, pivoted on his heel, and all but sprinted down the hall of the station. All the while, he calculated how long it would take to return home, pack a few necessities, and get to Paddington station to catch the next train to Oxford.

Electra had met many police officers in her life.

In her earliest memories of childhood, she recalled her father in his uniform of the Metropolitan Police force. Later, when he became a detective, he wore his own suits to work, but that image of him in his "peeler" uniform—dark-blue swallow-tail suit with a top hat—always stuck in her mind. The few men he called friends, and who were invited to their home, had also been Metropolitan Police officers.

Then, of course, there was Gideon, who'd wanted to follow in her father's footsteps almost from the moment he'd been brought into their household.

None of the policemen she'd known were quite like Sergeant Archibald Ormsbee of the Oxford Constabulary. The sergeant looked to be about her age, perhaps even a couple of years younger and had dark eyes, burnished blond hair, and a neatly trimmed beard and mustache. Yet what stood out was his demeanor. He held himself with the sort of prideful arrogance she'd only ever encountered in powerful noblemen. He'd stepped into Carthorpe Hall as though it was his ancestral holding and was now his to command. He'd managed to ruffle feathers in short order, including his own, if his reddened cheeks and intermittent sighs were any indication.

Constable Withers remained, looking rather more haggard than he had the previous evening. Based on the conversation she'd overheard, Electra suspected he'd had very little sleep.

Ormsbee arrived around ten and began barking out orders to the young constable and every member of the Carthorpe staff that he encountered. He'd been no gentler with the assembled guests.

After Withers gathered everyone in the household into the parlor, Ormsbee decreed that no one should retire to their room until he had a chance to speak with each of them. Only Lady Dalrymple had been excluded, since she'd been so overwrought by the previous night's events. Dr. Brownlow had given her a sedative to help her sleep off the effects of the shock she'd sustained.

Though Electra had spoken to Withers the previous night, she'd been directed back into the parlor to wait for her turn to answer Sergeant Ormsbee's questions. They were all forbidden from entering the drawing room. The sergeant insisted it must remain as it had been the previous night for the time being.

One by one, each guest or resident of Carthorpe left the parlor and then returned. Now, it seemed the only one left to speak to the sergeant was Electra.

Alex Winters stood on the far side of the parlor with his sister, Ophelia. James Lockhart sat with his arms folded, staring out one of the long drawing room windows. Alice had initially sat beside Honoria, speaking softly to her. But Honoria eventually stood and went to stare out another of the windows, her shoulders shaking, as if she wished to weep without anyone seeing her distress. Electra had no sister, but it struck her that Honoria and Alice did not gravitate toward each other at such a moment.

No one truly conversed. Everyone, except for Alex Winters, seemed to have turned inward. Alice had been almost silent throughout the morning, lost in the comfort of drawing in her sketchbook. Electra had remained sitting beside her, but Alice didn't seem in the mood for speaking, and Electra decided not to coax her into doing so.

Alex Winters was the most unsettled of all of them. He could not seem to remain still for more than a quarter of an hour. He paced. He availed himself of the drinks cart, and then he slumped down next to his sister, crossed his arms, and seemed to brood.

"As you know," Ormsbee began, without greeting or preamble, as he strode into the room, "we have taken statements from almost all of you and have begun our initial investigation into Lord Lockhart's grisly demise."

All attention was riveted on the tall, narrow-framed sergeant, and with a slow, deliberate precision, he let his gaze alight on the face of one guest and then the next. Electra imagined it was how she looked when she put all of her focus on an individual and tried to read their emotions or perhaps gain a glimpse into their memories or thoughts.

She had no illusions that Ormsbee had psychical abilities, but he was not subtle about the implication that he suspected every single one of them and would patiently lie in wait until some sign of guilt was revealed.

"When do we get to return to our rooms, Sergeant, or do you intend to keep us herded here like livestock all day?" Alex Winters asked. He'd gotten to his feet and had his hands planted on his hips.

Ormsbee swung his gaze toward Winters and glared. "I was getting to that, Mr. Winters. I do appreciate your *patience*. Our only goal is to see justice done for Lord Lockhart. I'm certain that is your goal too."

"Of course we understand, Sergeant," Honoria said from her spot near the window. "Have you discovered anything that you are able to share with us?"

"Not as yet, my lady."

"I'm acquainted with a superintendent at Scotland Yard," James Lockhart said, his voice rough. "Perhaps he could send assistance if it's required."

Electra watched a series of emotions play out of over the sergeant's face, none of them in the least bit pleased.

"We will discover the culprit, Mr. Lockhart. I hope you'll put your faith in our abilities, but we'll succeed regardless." Ormsbee held James Lockhart's gaze until the nobleman's brother shifted his attention to where Lady Honoria stood.

"May we go up to our rooms now, Sergeant Ormsbee?" Ophelia Winters asked far more sweetly than her brother had. "We were all up late last evening, and I, for one, am exhausted."

"Of course, Miss Winters. All of you may come and go as you please—"

"As if we need your permission," Alex Winters grumbled

under his breath, though loud enough for everyone in the room to hear.

"But I would ask," Ormsbee continued as if he had not been interrupted, "that none of you depart from Carthorpe Hall until the coroner completes his work."

"You can ask, Sergeant Ormsbee, but my sister and I will be returning to London in the morning." Alex Winters' tone had lowered to an icy growl.

Ormsbee merely arched one thin brow. He did not seem a man who was easily baited, though his proud bearing seemed to bait Alex Winters quite readily.

"I'd like to go up to my room," Alice said softly.

"I can go up with you," Ophelia offered.

"I'd like Electra to."

Electra stood and Alice did too, grimacing as if the act of unfolding herself from the sofa where she'd been sitting, sketching for hours, pained her.

"I would like to speak to Miss Poole," Sergeant Ormsbee said. "So perhaps Miss Winters should accompany you, Lady Alice."

Alice gave Electra a look that was half curiosity and half concern, then nodded in the sergeant's direction while allowing Ophelia to take her arm and escort her from the room.

"This way, if you would, Miss Poole," Sergeant Ormsbee said, staring at her expectantly.

"Would you like me to accompany you, Miss Poole?" Alex Winters' question shocked her.

"No, I'll manage on my own, Mr. Winters."

Sergeant Ormsbee looked between them, then pivoted on his heel to exit the drawing room. Electra followed the police officer. Constable Withers' questions had been rather thorough, but she was willing to repeat it all again. She did trust that Ormsbee was determined to find the murderer among them, but all morning she'd had the persistent thought that she wished it was in the hands of someone like Gideon, who'd handled so many other tangled murder cases.

Ormsbee led her to Carthorpe's dining room, gestured to an empty chair, then waited until she was seated to sit down across from her.

"One of my constables has delivered an interesting bit of research to me, Miss Poole." He collected a folder lying on the table and flipped it open.

Inside, Electra saw long, handwritten documents and clippings that had been cut from newspapers. Ormsbee drew out one particular article and slid it toward her across the polished mahogany table.

It was an article that recounted her involvement in the Becknell murder case.

"You've been involved in a noble's murder previously, haven't you, Miss Poole?" Ormsbee asked archly.

"I had nothing to do with the murder itself, Sergeant." Electra flicked her gaze down to the newspaper cutting. "As it says there, I foresaw what would happen."

Ormsbee leaned forward a bit, bracing his hands on the dining room table. "Did you foresee Lord Lockhart's death too?"

"No, not at all." Electra thought of how Alice had wanted her to determine what she could from touching Lockhart's hand. Would she have had a vision of his death too?

"I see from Constable Withers' notes that a servant informed him of an argument between Lockhart and Lady Alice yesterday morning. You told Withers that you were aware of that argument."

"I walked into Alice's room in the middle of it."

He dipped his head in acknowledgement. "Why?"

"She'd left a note, asking me to visit her room. When I went down, I heard noises that disturbed me, so I entered without knocking."

"And what did you see?"

Electra's mouth went dry. She felt that she was somehow betraying her friend by confiding the truth, but she didn't see as she had much choice. "Lord Lockhart gripped her arm and had his other hand raised."

Ormsbee's brows twitched upward. "Did he strike her?"

"No, but I thought he might, so I shouted for him to stop."

"And did he?"

"Yes, immediately, but Alice fell as a result."

From the way his brows twitched and his eyes took on the cast of a fox sighting prey, she suspected this was all new information to him. Perhaps Alice had not mentioned the argument, or had downplayed it when asked.

"Was she injured?"

"She said she was not."

"Did she ever confide in you about whether this was new behavior on his part or regular?"

Electra broke eye contact with the sergeant, and he made a little sound of acknowledgement. He seemed to realize he'd hit upon a line of inquiry that would provide him with new information. Electra hadn't divulged everything to Withers because her impulse had been to protect Alice, but something about Ormsbee made it harder to prevaricate.

"She acknowledged that they'd had conflicts before."

"So, presumably Lady Alice was quite angry with Lord Lockhart on the evening of his murder."

Electra saw a gleam in the sergeant's eyes that she'd seen in Gideon's and her father's when they believed they were on the right path toward finding answers to a case.

"Alice entered the drawing room for the séance very shortly

after I did, Sergeant. Alex Winters was still outside with Lord Lockhart. I had only left Lockhart minutes before." Fear made her fingers curl inward. "Even if there had been conflict between them, Alice would never do such a thing."

Ormsbee sat back in his chair and crossed his arms. Electra didn't know if he was waiting for her to say more after considering her claim about Alice.

"Pardon, sir." Mr. Jenks, the Carthorpe butler, entered the dining room.

"What is it?" Ormsbee looked up with a grimace, not bothering to hide his annoyance at the interruption.

"Forgive me, Constable, but there's a visitor for Miss Poole."

"I asked that no visitors be admitted, Mr. Jenks."

"Yes, sir. We did not admit him, sir, but he insists on speaking to Miss Poole and is waiting for her near the fountain." When Ormsbee said nothing, Mr. Jenks added, "He says it is most urgent, Sergeant."

A muscle ticked at the edge of Ormsbee's jaw, but he nodded. "You may go and speak to your visitor, Miss Poole. But please don't leave the grounds of Carthorpe Hall. I may have other questions to put to you."

Electra found the man too abrasive to offer any words of thanks, but she stood, offered him a nod, and followed the butler out of the dining room.

"The fountain is outside of the conservatory on the west side of the hall." Mr. Jenks pointed in the opposite direction Electra had taken the night before to approach the edge of the gardens where Lord Lockhart stood. "Shall I accompany you, miss?"

"No, Mr. Jenks. I can find my way."

Without waiting for a coat or gloves, Electra stepped out the front door, turned left, and headed toward the far edge of the hall. This was the half of Carthorpe Hall that looked older, as if it had been built when country estates were more defensive than decorative. What she'd not seen when she'd arrived the previous evening was an elegant, arched wrought-iron and glass-walled conservatory jutting out from the edge of the hall.

As she rounded the corner, she spotted a figure near a multi-tiered fountain, and her breath caught in her chest. Until that moment, she hadn't realized how all that had transpired in the last hours had unsettled her. How tight her chest felt, how her head ached and worry had settled in her middle like a stone. She realized it now because she felt a swell of something like relief.

Oddly, it wasn't a surprise to see Gideon. It was as if some intuitive part of her knew the moment the butler said a visitor had called for her who she'd find standing in the neatly clipped grass at the edge of Carthorpe Hall.

Something unraveled in her chest and then warmed. She was so pleased to see him, she couldn't suppress the smile that came to her lips when he turned and spotted her.

He moved first, striding toward her so quickly the tails of his long coat swept out behind him.

Electra matched his quick stride and when they were face to face, he hesitated only a moment, searching her face, then wrapped her in a brief embrace.

At first she stiffened, but only for a moment. Then it was over, and he'd pulled back.

"I read about the murder at Carthorpe in the newspapers."

"Did you? I'm surprised it was noted in London papers so quickly."

Gideon shrugged. "The death of a nobleman will always draw the notice of the press."

"But why did you come?"

He gave her an exasperated look. "Must you ask? I saw Lady Alice's name and the name of the manor house, and I knew you'd left London in part because you'd been embroiled in another murder case."

"You were worried about me?" Electra didn't know why she was forcing him to spell out his motives when she knew him well enough to understand.

"Yes," he said, then darted his gaze around the grounds of Carthorpe Hall. "I didn't like the notion of you being here where you knew no one—"

"Except Lady Alice, who invited me."

"I thought you might... I thought if there was any way I could help you, I would."

Her mouth curved. She couldn't help it. Then she shivered when the breeze kicked up. The air was dense, as if it might soon rain, and the cold cut through her clothing.

"Is there a place where we could speak privately? Preferably indoors, since you've no coat."

"The Oxford Constabulary sergeant has insisted no visitors are to be admitted."

Gideon approached the conservatory and tested the glass door framed in wrought iron. It opened. "Shall we?"

Electra entered first and was struck by how warm, almost sultry, the air was inside the arched glass walls. Though there was greenery nearly everywhere she looked, there was still a clear view of the door that led from the conservatory into the hall. As far as she could tell, the conservatory was unoccupied, so they could speak discreetly.

"Lord Lockhart was murdered in the hedge maze last evening," she told Gideon. "It's on the other side of the house."

"The newspapers described him as well-respected."

"Perhaps he was. He was Alice's fiancé, and I must admit

that I'm afraid for her." Electra lifted a hand to her throat and traced the outline of her mother's necklace beneath the fabric.

Gideon's jaw tensed. "Do you have knowledge of who killed the viscount?"

"No, but I think Sergeant Ormsbee suspects Alice."

"And you?" Gideon crossed his arms and assessed her. "I take it you do not."

"Of course not. Alice is a gentle person. An artist. And she was with me in the drawing room when the murder was likely committed."

"Do you suspect any of the others?"

"No, I can't say that I do. I met a few of the guests, including Lord Lockhart, only a day ago. But I know Alice and her sister, and another fellow student from our boarding school is here visiting too. I can't imagine why any of them would do such a thing." Electra had been turning the matter over in her head since last evening. "I overheard a conversation between the doctor who's been tending the earl and Constable Withers. Lockhart was struck on the head." Electra swallowed, recalling the viscount's stained clothing. "I think he lost a good deal of blood."

Gideon nodded. "It is not uncommon with head wounds." He twisted his mouth, an indication that he was pondering.

Impulsively, Electra asked, "Could you not offer Sergeant Ormsbee your assistance?"

"The constabulary would have to make a formal request." From his tone, he seemed dubious such a request would be forthcoming, but she suspected Gideon had far more experience than Ormsbee.

"Would you speak to him?"

"I suppose I could." Gideon inclined his head and then looked up at her, his brow tense. "The thought of assisting had crossed my mind before I left London."

"Then come now," she said in a tone of challenge that had long ago been quite common between them. "I know you can be quite convincing when you wish to be."

He huffed out a little chuckle, but he did not refuse the challenge she'd put to him.

Chapter Seven

Convincing the Earl of Carthorpe's young housemaid to allow him admittance to the family's home was easier than Gideon expected. She demurred at first, but once he explained that he was a detective with the Metropolitan Police, the tall, apple-cheeked girl relented. He suspected she'd been under the impression he'd been invited by the Oxford Constabulary, though as soon as she directed him to Sergeant Archibald Ormsbee, the young, blond local policeman made it abundantly clear that his unexpected presence was not at all welcome.

"This is most irregular," the younger man said, bristling as they stood face to face in the dining room that seemed to have been commandeered to question the staff. He looked a bit like a boy attempting to exude prowess.

"It is. I admit that, Sergeant. In fact, I am..." For a moment, he considered how best to describe his relationship with Electra. They were friends, at the very least, even if he felt more. "A friend of Miss Electra Poole. I came out of concern for her."

"Lord Lockhart is our victim, Inspector. Does Miss Poole

have something to fear? Has she been threatened? Is she harboring some guilty knowledge?"

Gideon scoffed as the sergeant rattled off his questions, then squared his shoulders when he realized the brusque young man was serious. "If you've questioned Electra, then you have the truth of what she knows."

"How well do you know Miss Poole, Inspector Pierce?"

"Well enough to be certain of her honesty."

Ormsbee eyed him a moment, scraping his gaze down to Gideon's boots and then up to his brow. "What is your history, Pierce?"

"I've been with the Metropolitan Police since I was twenty-one and entered the detective branch five years ago."

Ormsbee offered him an irritatingly condescending look. "And your family history?"

Gideon rocked on his heels and kept his hands clasped behind his back, willing himself not to rise to what seemed to be the young officer's determination to unnerve him. Or perhaps he was oversensitive about his family history, being that he didn't know much about his blood relatives and had never formally been adopted by the man who'd been a true father to him.

"My mentor was also a detective inspector. Is that relevant to you in some regard?" Gideon prided himself on control—his clothes, his accent, his manners were all carefully crafted to present himself as respectable and polished enough to be admitted into any level of society. It was a necessity in order to do his job. But it was damnably hard to hide his irritation at Ormsbee's priggishness.

"I ask only because the earl and his family have a long, respectable association with the county. My father, a baronet, knew his, so it puts the family at ease that I am familiar with their status, even if I must invade their privacy and ask indelicate questions. I'm not sure that would be the case with a Scotland Yard man."

Gideon drew in a slow breath and exhaled with a noncommittal smile. "My most recent case involved the Earl of Halsted. I solved his murder a few days ago. And last year, the Lady Becknell case."

Ormsbee's brow arched. "I recall reading of that case. Garnered a great deal of attention in the press, did it not? There was a psychic involved." Ormsbee's dark eyes sharpened. "And here she is again. That psychic was Miss Poole, was it not? Is that how you met?"

"No, our friendship started in childhood."

"I see." Ormsbee seemed nonplussed by that revelation. "Well, I offer you congratulations on the resolution of two such noteworthy cases, Inspector."

Gideon searched the younger man's dark eyes, the slight grin on his wide mouth, and wondered if he was being baited. "Thank you."

"So, you came to Oxford because your friend, who was embroiled in your recent case, is embroiled in this one too. How did you meet *in childhood?*"

"The mentor I mentioned was Miss Poole's father."

Ormsbee reached up a hand and stroked his beard thoughtfully. "Do you think your chief would allow you leave from your duties to assist?"

"I have been given a week of personal leave, but if you were to telegraph a formal request to Chief Douglas, I believe he would approve." Gideon recalled how eager his chief had been for him to solve the Becknell and Halsted cases with discretion, since they involved respected noble families. He'd proved that he could, and that alone would make him an asset to Ormsbee's investigation.

"Very well," Ormsbee said with an almost relieved sigh. "I'll have a servant send a telegram from the station within the hour." The young man looked at the dining room table, then up at Gideon. "It's already become complicated. There are nearly a dozen staff members and a few of the guests wish to depart, but I've yet to have time to collect sufficient evidence."

He lifted a piece of paper from the dining room table. "This is a list of the servants. I've spoken to all of the guests and residents at Carthorpe, but have only managed to speak to two of the staff members." He drew in a deep breath, then said, "If you're certain your chief will agree, I could use your help immediately, Inspector. Might you question the rest of the Carthorpe staff?"

When Gideon took the sheet of paper, Ormsbee seemed relieved to pass on the task.

Still, Gideon was surprised Ormsbee would allow him to assist before formal permission was granted, but because this case involved Electra, he was satisfied to give aid however he might.

"If you fill me in on the details you've gathered thus far, it will help me when questioning the staff."

Ormsbee gestured toward a chair. "Shall we sit?"

Once they had, the sergeant clasped his hands. "Last evening at approximately one half to one quarter hour before midnight, Lord Henry Lockhart was struck from behind with a large object that caused loss of blood and death in short order. I thought perhaps a large rock, but the doctor suggested the edges were likely smooth. Regardless, after searching the hedge maze where the body was found, and having the family's servants assist with a search of the grounds, no murder weapon has been recovered." He lifted a bundle from his suit coat pocket. It looked like a handkerchief twisted around some object. "We found this near where Lockhart's body was located, but it does not match any on the suit he was wearing or the clothing he brought to Carthorpe."

It was a shiny bronze button with a scrollwork design atop it. The large size put Gideon in mind of a button that might be found on a man's overcoat or suit coat.

"Was it a single blow?"

Ormsbee rolled his shoulders. "The doctor believes so. The local coroner has been delayed but should arrive forthwith."

"Of this list of current staff, you say you've spoken to three?" Gideon pulled out the notepad he carried with him by habit.

"Yes. The butler, Mr. Jenks, and the housekeeper, Mrs. Holcomb, and the first footman who found Lord Lockhart in the hedge maze, Mr. Samuel Hobbes."

"And you learned nothing from the guests and residents you questioned?" Gideon asked, pencil poised to add to his notes.

"I didn't say that." Ormsbee arched a brow and looked every bit as haughty as any nobleman Gideon had ever met. "There was an...event scheduled last evening that nearly all of them were meant to attend, including Lord Lockhart. His absence is what caused them to search for him."

"A dinner party?"

"A séance." Ormsbee spoke the word with a grimace.

Gideon recognized the disdain as not so very different from what he'd felt when he'd discovered that Electra offered psychical sittings among the upper crust of London society.

"Guests and residents of the hall were either inside the drawing room," Ormsbee continued, "or on their way there. All have claimed it as their alibi, but many were not yet in the room between the last moment when Lord Lockhart was seen alive and when he was found by a servant who was sent to search for him. At that point James Lockhart, the viscount's brother, and Alexander Winters, a current house guest, went out to assist the servant to carry the viscount's body into the house. The family doctor, Brownlow, arrived soon after and conducted an initial examination."

"The two housemaids, Lydia and Annie, also assisted with the search within the house and may have seen something they don't realize is significant."

Gideon placed a tick by their names too.

"I intend to speak to Lady Alice once again," Ormsbee told him. "She was Lockhart's intended and failed to inform me of an event that occurred between them." Ormsbee stood as if to signal the end of their conversation.

"I'll introduce myself to the butler and seek out the two housemaids you mentioned."

Ormsbee offered no thanks, merely a nod. "Very good."

Gideon left the dining room feeling as if he'd been relegated to the sort of grunt work he'd been assigned as a new constable, yet he understood that household staff often proved the most helpful witnesses, providing information a noble family might not wish to divulge.

As soon as he stepped into the hallway, he spotted Electra lingering near a potted palm, as if she'd been waiting for him.

Rather than emerge from her spot near the palm, she waved him toward her.

"What did he say?" Her anxious tone was so unlike her usual equanimity that he searched her face a moment, noting the shadows beneath her blue-green eyes.

"He's going to send a telegram to Chief Douglas and formally request my assistance." Gideon lifted the piece of paper he'd folded in half. "Though he's asked me to begin assisting immediately by questioning the staff."

"I'm relieved." Electra let out an exhale as if she'd been holding her breath. "Alice will be too. In fact, would you consider delaying your questioning of the staff and speak to her first?"

Before Gideon could answer, footsteps sounded behind him.

"What's this?" Sergeant Ormsbee asked. "I will be questioning Lady Alice directly, Miss Poole. And Inspector Pierce is on his way to speak to the staff. Shall we let him get on with it?"

Gideon clenched his teeth and turned to face Ormsbee.

"Actually, Sergeant, I would like to speak with the man from Scotland Yard, and I'd like Miss Poole to be present when I do." The voice came from the top of the stairwell. All of them turned their gazes toward a thin, brown-haired young woman who Gideon guessed was Lady Alice Kirkham.

She looked haunted. Her eyes had the hollow look Gideon had seen many times in those wrestling with shock and grief. Her skin was shockingly pale against the black gown she wore.

Behind him, Ormsbee made a sound of displeasure, but Gideon suspected he'd relent. Any reasonable request that got a witness to speak freely was to be encouraged.

"This is most irregular, my lady," Ormsbee said. "Inspector Pierce and Miss Poole are...acquainted."

"I'm aware of that, Sergeant. It is why I feel more comfortable speaking to Inspector Pierce."

Gideon had misjudged the man and suspected he might refuse her ladyship's request after all. For a moment, the two merely observed each other. Lady Alice offered no challenge in her gaze. She exuded the certainty of one who knew she would ultimately obtain whatever she desired.

"Very well," Ormsbee finally said. "Let us convene after you've spoken to her ladyship, Pierce. If I have further questions after you've spoken to the inspector, my lady, I will put them to you personally."

"Of course, Sergeant."

Gideon followed Electra upstairs, and Lady Alice gave her a half-smile before turning to lead them to her chamber.

"Please close the door, Inspector. I know Sergeant Ormsbee will be provided the details of our conversation, but I'd prefer that others in the house are not."

Gideon did as he was bid, then joined the two ladies, who'd settled into side-by-side chairs not far from the fireplace. Gideon took a chair across from them.

Lady Alice lifted a teacup and took a sip, then squared her shoulders as if the brew had fortified her.

Gideon glanced at Electra, who gave him the merest of nods.

"When was the last time you saw Lord Lockhart, my lady?"

"Yesterday afternoon. We took luncheon in the conservatory together." Lady Alice gave Electra a tight smile, and there seemed to be a look of understanding between them.

"What was Lord Lockhart's frame of mind while you shared lunch?"

"He seemed a bit uneasy about a conversation he'd had with Alexander Winters." Lady Alice lifted her teacup again and took a dainty sip. "They'd argued, and Henry did not like such outbursts."

"Why did they argue?"

Lady Alice dipped her head, and ran a hand along the fabric of her dress. "Mr. Winters would not like me speaking of it, no doubt. But I know that all must come to light if it will help you find whoever did this to Henry."

Gideon waited. Alice continued to hesitate, fussing with her gown a bit longer. He recognized it as a delaying tactic, yet the young lady had also just lost her fiancé, and he suspected she was still shaken by all that had occurred.

"Mr. Winters had confronted me earlier in the day, angry at Henry, who'd been exerting enormous pressure on him. Apparently, Henry had loaned him a significant sum of money on more than one occasion. Mr. Winters failed to repay when he said he would, and Henry had lost patience with his deceit."

"What deceit do you refer to, Lady Alice?"

"Oh, I'm not certain, Inspector. Only that Henry said that Mr. Winters is a liar, that I should not trust him, and that he would never trust him again."

Gideon jotted down the characterization in his notepad. Then he looked into Lady Alice's eyes. He sensed a guardedness in her, emphasized by her glances at Electra, as if seeking reassurance.

"Do you know of anyone else at Carthorpe who might have borne ill will toward Lord Lockhart? Any other conflicts you're aware of?"

Lady Alice looked away, staring out the window past Gideon's shoulder. "I don't wish anything I say to be construed as an accusation, Inspector Pierce."

"I'm merely collecting information, Lady Alice, and unless you overtly make an accusation, I would not take it as such."

Electra turned a look Lady Alice's way and said, "It's all right. You can tell him."

Lady Alice swallowed visibly, as if gulping for air. "Ophelia," she said quietly, then looked up at him, her expression strained. "She's been a friend for years, Inspector." With a glance at Electra, she added, "We all met at school."

"What is Ophelia's surname?"

"Winters," Electra told him. "Alice and I attended finishing school with Ophelia, and she's the sister of Alex Winters, who's also currently staying at Carthorpe."

Something about the way Electra said Winters' given name drew Gideon's notice. Her ease with using a diminutive of his name told him she may have been familiar with the man as more than merely a friend's brother.

"Go on, Lady Alice. You wished to tell me something about Miss Winters and Lord Lockhart."

"I think she had a sort of infatuation with him. Well, in truth, Henry told me as much. He said he found it unsettling, especially when it persisted after our engagement."

"And yet you invited the Winters siblings here to Carthorpe for a house party."

Lady Alice's expression sharpened, her eyes narrowing. "Despite everything, they *are* friends, Inspector. Henry urged me to invite them. He was the sort who wished to make amends and did not like allowing bad feelings to linger."

Gideon bent his head and made a few notes on the pad balanced on his thigh. He'd provoked the noblewoman and knew he should press the advantage, whether Electra sat at her side or not.

"Would you tell me where you were last evening at approximately half past eleven in the evening?"

"I was in my room preparing to come down for the séance. You may speak to my lady's maid. She assisted me."

Gideon thought back to the names on the list Ormsbee had given him. "And her name?"

"Madeline." She glanced down at his notepad, where he'd written the maid's name. "Constable Withers may have already spoken to her, but I don't think the sergeant has. I've asked all the staff to make themselves available and answer all questions honestly, so you may speak to her too if you wish."

"Thank you, my lady." Gideon understood that nobles often made it seem like a kind of favorable dispensation when they allowed him or others to do their jobs within a noble household.

"You must tell the rest," Electra said in an almost whisper.

Gideon snapped his gaze up to hers, but she was looking at Lady Alice, who was once again staring out the window behind him.

He saw a little tremor chase through her. "Henry and I had a row yesterday morning. Electra observed some of it." Unlike everything else she'd said in a calm, steady tone, these words burst out of her in a rush. "I believe she's already spoken to the constable and sergeant about it."

"But you may have further insights to share," Electra said softly.

"What was the cause of the argument, my lady?"

Lady Alice turned a look Electra's way. "Henry wished for me to seek a rest cure and we disagreed on that point. When we argued, Henry sometimes became very emphatic."

Electra let out what sounded very much like a scoff. "I saw his lordship gripping Alice's arms forcibly."

Gideon swung a look Electra's way and then back to Lady Alice, who gave him a small, seemingly reluctant nod.

"I must ask, Lady Alice, did Lord Lockhart ever strike you?"

"No! Not at all." The noble lady sat up straighter, squaring her shoulders. "Henry loved me, and I loved him. I would never have accepted his proposal otherwise. We simply disagreed at times, but we always made amends." She glanced at Electra. "He apologized for the incident Electra observed."

"He apologized to me as well," Electra told him. "In the garden, at about twenty past eleven. The butler, Mr. Jenks, told me that Lord Lockhart wished to speak to me and I went outside to do so."

"And he apologized to you?"

"Yes, he told me he was sorry for the incident I witnessed and that he was glad I'd come to visit. He said he'd hoped I might be a comfort to Alice. I assumed he meant because of Lord Carthorpe's illness."

"It has been a long and quite remorseless illness," Lady Alice put in. "Dr. Brownlow does not think Papa shall ever leave his bed again." She lifted a handkerchief clutched in her hand and dabbed at her eyes just as a tear slid across her cheek. "Henry helped in any manner he could. Even brought a special doctor to Carthorpe from Harley Street in London, but the prognosis was the same."

"I'm very sorry, my lady."

The tears continued, and Gideon suspected their conversation was at an end, at least for the time being.

"Thank you being so forthright, Lady Alice."

She nodded but said nothing, just sniffed as she swiped away more tears.

"I'm going to speak to Inspector Pierce a moment, but I'll return if you like," Electra said to her friend in a soft tone.

"I think I'll try for a bit of sleep," Lady Alice replied, her voice rough. "I got very little last evening."

"Of course." Electra patted her arm and then stood.

Gideon got to his feet as well. They walked to the door together, and Electra closed it behind them as they stepped into the upstairs hallway.

"I take it Ormsbee's knowledge regarding the confrontation between Lady Alice and Lockhart is what fueled his suspicion."

Rather than answer him, Electra strode down the hall and opened the door to a room on the left. "Let's talk in here," she whispered.

Gideon followed her into the guest chamber.

"Close the door," Electra told him. "I don't trust anyone in this house at the moment."

Gideon pulled the door shut and looked around the elegantly furnished, pastel-papered room.

Electra went to the fireplace and held her hands out to warm them. "I can't get warm in this house. Is it cold to you?"

Gideon spotted a shawl hanging over the back of a wingback, picked it up, and approached Electra. He offered it to her, and she took it immediately, wrapping it around her shoulders.

It disturbed him to see her so shaken. Though he knew her emotions ran deep, she didn't reveal them to others freely.

"Will you tell me why you're upset?" he asked. The moment the words were out, they seemed rather foolish. A man she'd met yesterday was now dead. Her friend had lost her fiancé.

"I fear for Alice."

Gideon waited. There was more. He could feel it like a heaviness in the air between them, and he knew she would tell him when she was ready.

"That argument that I saw the end of..." She turned to him, her arms crossed, eyes cast down to the carpet. "Alice mentioned that Lockhart wanted her to take a rest cure. But he mentioned hospitalization to me. I believe he thought her afflicted in her mind, but she's not."

"She didn't seem so." Indeed, if anything Gideon thought that Lady Alice Kirkham had more mettle than she portrayed. He'd seen little flashes of it.

Electra lifted her hand and laid it across her throat. "Gideon, my mother. I know you always wondered."

Every muscle in his body tensed, and his breath tangled in his chest as he waited for her to continue. This was a topic Electra never broached. A forbidden subject with her father too.

"She was sent to a...private asylum that she never returned from. My father believed her mind was irreparably ill. Broken." A bleakness came into her vivid blue-green eyes the likes of which he'd never seen. "But she was like me. She saw things. Felt things, and no one believed her. I've always feared I'd share her fate if I told anyone about what I felt and saw."

"Electra." He took a step closer, yearning to comfort her and take away that bleakness. "You're not broken, and she should never have been relegated to such a place."

Anger rose in him toward her father. Erasmus had been a

man who struggled to see beyond the rational, the logical. Gideon sometimes struggled with such constraints of thought too, though of late, because of Electra, his experience and understanding were widening.

"Perhaps you understand my feelings toward him." Tears welled in her eyes. "I know he cared for her, but he refused to believe her."

"I wish he had." Gideon recalled how broken Erasmus looked on the few occasions he referred to Electra's mother. Most of all, he recalled the wall of silence around her.

"My father never wished to speak of it. Perhaps it was guilt or regret. But, in my worst moments, I believe he was simply embarrassed that anyone should know. It hurts to know he was ashamed of her, that he would be ashamed of me."

"I can't ever imagine being ashamed of you."

Her eyes fluttered closed and a tear slipped down her cheek that Gideon dared to swipe gently away with the pad of his thumb.

"Now you understand why neither of us told you," she said, opening her eyes, her breathing shaky.

"I suppose I do, but I wish I had known." The pain of losing her mother to a place like that, of Erasmus, her father and Gideon's mentor and guardian, losing his wife to such an illness must have weighed heavily on both of them. "Though I never met your mother, I knew what she meant to both of you, and I would have shared that grief willingly."

Tears welled in her eyes, but she offered him a soft smile. "I know you would have."

For a moment, as he looked into her eyes, Gideon wanted to offer comfort now. Here, so close to her, the urge to wrap Electra in his arms rose up as it seemed to keep doing since they'd reconnected last year. He realized that the feelings he'd told himself he'd set aside were still very much alive inside his heart.

"Can I tell you something quite shocking?" she whispered.

"You can tell me anything."

"I know Alice had nothing to do with Lockhart's murder, but Gideon, part of me feels relief that he's gone." She bit the edge of her lip and her eyes widened as if her own words shocked her. "If Alice had married him as she'd intended, he could have sent her wherever he wished, and she would have had no choice in the matter."

It wasn't what he'd hoped or expected she might say. He'd misread the moment entirely and felt foolish. Yet her hands were trembling beneath her dark gloves. Instinctively, he reached out, and she responded immediately, clasping her fingers around his. At seeing her so shaken, the protective impulses that always arose where Electra was concerned took hold of him.

"I don't know Ormsbee well, but I know you will find the killer." It wasn't a question. She spoke the words as if they were a certainty. As if her faith in him was unshakable.

"I will." From the little he'd learned, one fact was clear: whoever murdered Lockhart was still at Carthorpe Hall.

"Ormsbee doesn't want anyone to leave the hall, yet that means we're confined her with a murderer," she said, echoing his thoughts. "We must determine who actually killed Lockhart before anyone else comes to harm."

"No doubt eager to be away from Carthorpe as soon as they're able," Gideon mused. "Few killers would wish to remain at the scene of a crime."

Electra crossed her arms and glanced up at him, her expression unreadable.

"You don't agree?" he asked.

"I just have a feeling the danger is not at an end."

"Have you...seen something?"

She shook her head. "No, it's not a vision or anything I've perceived with my abilities. Just an odd sense of foreboding."

Gideon wanted to comfort her, to take away her fear, but he knew the best way to do that was to ensure her safety while he was at Carthorpe and discover who'd murdered Lord Henry Lockhart.

Chapter Eight

Electra decided to accompany Gideon below stairs, as she suspected the Carthorpe staff would treat him with reasonable suspicion. The whole household was fraught with tension. She sensed it from every maid and footman they passed in the hall, and she saw its outward manifestation in the etched frowns worn by Mr. Jenks, the Carthorpe butler, and Mrs. Holcomb, the housekeeper, as she approached with Gideon at her side.

"Mr. Jenks, Mrs. Holcomb, this is Detective Inspector Gideon Pierce from the Metropolitan Police."

"I thought the Oxford Constabulary was seeing to this tragedy," Mrs. Holcomb said, giving Gideon a once-over look.

"Scotland Yard has been asked to assist," Gideon said smoothly. "And to prove useful to Sergeant Ormsbee, I've been asked to speak to the various members of his lordship's staff. Is there a place where I might do so that would provide some quiet and privacy?"

"We share an office," Mr. Jenks said. "You're welcome to use it, Inspector."

"That will do. Thank you." Gideon gave the older man a nod. "I'd like to speak to Madeline first, Lady Alice's lady's maid."

Mr. Jenks led Electra and Gideon to the office he shared with Mrs. Holcomb. It was narrow and spartan, with a shelf of ledgers behind a battered desk. A still-steaming mug and a pile of paperwork were centered on the desk, facing a captain's chair, and two straight-back chairs were arranged in front of the desk.

The butler watched them warily, as if unsure whether he should leave or remain. A few minutes later, he turned toward the sound of approaching footsteps.

A slim, dark-haired young woman with a narrow chin and wide eyes entered the room. The lady's maid looked as if she'd been caught doing something improper and feared being called in for a reprimand. She darted clear blue eyes between them, then tucked a wisp of dark hair behind her ear. Her cheeks had begun to pinken from the moment she crossed the office's threshold, and then she began shivering so fiercely Electra heard the girl's teeth rattle.

"Madeline?" Gideon inquired.

The girl flinched but nodded. "Yes, sir." She lifted a shaking hand to sweep another loose strand of hair behind her ear.

"May I ask your surname?" Gideon softened his tone, noting the young woman's fear and unease.

"Frain, sir." Her voice emerged breathy.

Electra thought she looked as if she might faint if she didn't sit down.

"Please have a seat, Miss Frain," Electra said, gesturing to one of the chairs. "Could I get you a cup of tea?" She felt the girl's fears and anxieties as if they clouded the air in the small office.

Mr. Jenks still lingered in the doorway, and the young maid looked back at him.

"No, miss." The young woman's pale eyes searched Mr. Jenks's face, then Electra's. "Am I being dismissed?"

"Not at all, Miss Frain," Gideon said. "My name is Inspector Pierce, and I've been tasked with asking you some questions."

"I'll leave you to it, Inspector," Mr. Jenks said and then pulled the door of the office mostly closed as he departed.

Gideon approached Electra. "She's skittish as a hare," he whispered. "Would you remain while I speak to her?"

"Of course." The irony did not escape Electra that while he'd worked the Becknell case, he'd chastised her for her involvement several times. But she understood that the girl might feel marginally less frightened if another woman were with her as Gideon asked questions.

"I'm going to stay, if you don't mind," Electra told Miss Frain in a low voice as she settled into the chair beside her. They'd not been formally introduced, but she'd seen the girl leaving Alice's room the previous day.

"Thank you, miss." Miss Frain's voice remained shaky, but she had a look of resolve in her eyes now. The anxiety she'd sensed from her had ebbed a bit.

"Miss Frain," Gideon began, still keeping his voice softer than his usual firm, clear tone. "I trust you are aware of what befell Lord Lockhart last evening."

"Yes, sir."

"When was the last time you saw his lordship last evening?"

"I never saw him in the evening, sir. Only yesterday morning, while I was in Lady Alice's chamber seeing to dressing her hair."

"Please describe his demeanor when you saw him, Miss Frain," Gideon prompted.

"Oh." The lady's maid looked down at her clasped hands, then glanced at Electra.

"It's all right. Inspector Pierce has already spoken to Lady Alice," Electra told her, assuming she'd seen part of the same altercation between Lockhart and Alice that she had.

Gideon gave her a furrowed brow look.

"His lordship seemed agitated," Miss Frain said. Her voice was clearer now and her trembling had eased. "He sent me from the room before I was finished with her ladyship's coiffure."

"Do you recall what he said to you and to Lady Alice?" Gideon asked, then poised his pencil over the notepad he'd laid at the edge of the desk.

Miss Frain licked her lips, glancing down at her hands. "He told me to get out and he…" The maid looked toward Electra. "I don't want to be indiscreet."

"No one will consider you so, and Inspector Pierce is the soul of discretion." Electra felt Gideon's gaze on her as she reassured the girl.

"He burst into the room unexpectedly," Miss Frain said quietly. "He said, 'Alice, are you mad?' and then he saw me and ordered me to leave."

Gideon dipped his head to note her words, then looked up again. "Thank you, Miss Frain. Would you tell me when you last saw Lady Alice last evening?"

"It was late, sir. Sometime near midnight. She was attending the séance and asked me to help her with some combs she wished to wear in her hair."

Gideon tipped his head as he looked at the young woman but said nothing. Electra knew it was his way of hoping a person might reveal more if he allowed his silence to linger.

"She'd changed her mind, you see, and wanted the emerald hair combs to match her gown."

Gideon noted that down, nodding to acknowledge the additional details.

"And then she went down to the séance?"

"Yes, sir, I believe so, sir."

"Did you assist anyone else in the household last evening?"

"No." The girl shook her head and frowned. "I assisted Lady Honoria a bit earlier in the evening. She dressed for dinner early, despite the meal being delayed due to the... evening's entertainment. When I asked if she wanted further assistance before the midnight event, she declined. After the dreadful incident..." Miss Frain shook her head and bit her lip. "After what happened to his lordship, I assisted both ladies to prepare for bed, but it was the early hours of the morning by then."

"Did you venture out into the garden or hedge maze at all last evening?"

Miss Frain shook her head emphatically. "No, sir. Once I had finished with her ladyship's hair, I went straight up to my room. It was quite late. She said she would send for me after the séance to assist her, so I waited there until she did."

"Thank you." He said, then laid his pencil aside.

Miss Frain shifted in her chair for the first time, preparing no doubt to make a hasty exit once her questioning was done.

"One more question, Miss Frain," Gideon said offhandedly. "Did you ever witness any other conflicts between anyone in the household or guests at Carthorpe with Lord Lockhart?"

The young woman stiffened and Electra watched her swallow deeply before responding with a nod. "Yes, sir. Only on one occasion. I was coming through the entry hall and heard Lord Lockhart and Mr. Winters shouting from Lord Carthorpe's study, sir."

"When was this?"

"Two days ago. Around midday."

"Did you hear anything that was said between them?"

"Very little, sir. I did hear someone say 'never again' quite loudly and then a door slammed. Perhaps they shut the study door. Mrs. Holcomb saw me lingering and told me return to my duties."

Electra had watched Miss Frain off and on throughout Gideon's questioning and noticed that this particular answer made her blush brightly. Perhaps from the embarrassment of having been caught lingering in the hallway.

"Thank you for answering my questions, Miss Frain," Gideon said. He flipped his book closed.

Beside her, the young maid sat up straighter in her chair. "May I go now, sir?"

"Yes, of course."

She stood and scurried out of the room, as if terrified Gideon might think of another question to ask.

He stood and slipped his notepad and pencil into his suit coat pocket. "What did you make of Miss Madeline Frain?"

Electra couldn't help but smile. "Are you asking for my assistance with this investigation?"

Gideon scoffed. "No, I'm asking what you made of Miss Frain. Did you find her credible?" He shrugged. "You were sitting close to her. I'd like to know your observations."

"She seemed terrified at first and a little reticent, but everything she said sounded reasonable. The incident with Lockhart and Alice is the same one that I saw, and Lockhart asking if Alice was mad seems in accordance with him wishing to send her away for a rest cure. And Alex Winters—"

"Alex?" Gideon arched one dark brow. "I take it you were acquainted with him prior to coming to Carthorpe Hall?"

Gideon had a habit of reading her reactions, even changes in her tone of voice, all too well. She might have ascribed it to his talent as a detective, if not for the fact that he'd had the same ability since they were children.

"You don't remember me mentioning Ophelia Winters?"

He frowned, pensive. "Now that I think about it, yes. The summer you went away to Essex."

"Yes, I visited the Winters, and Alex was on summer holiday from university." Electra willed her cheeks not to warm. She wasn't affected by Alex Winters' charms, or lack thereof, anymore, but it felt odd to give any sign that she had once been to Gideon.

"And what's your opinion of Mr. Winters?" He watched her closely.

"I do not know Alex Winters well, Gideon. I last saw him that summer. And I thought he was amiable at first, but then I found him rather churlish by the time my visit ended."

Gideon studied her a bit longer. "I've spoken to two members of this household since arriving and both of them report that he's volatile. Did you see that in him?"

"I suppose. He's changeable, and he can be quite rude. Sharp-tongued. But I never saw him strike anyone or have a shouting altercation as Miss Frain described, yet that doesn't mean it's untrue."

"Agreed. I think he should be the next guest questioned if Ormsbee hasn't already done so. I also think his wardrobe should be searched."

"His wardrobe?"

"A piece of evidence was found in the hedge maze." He hesitated and said, "A button. I'm going to go and report to Ormsbee now." Gideon tugged at the cuffs of his suit coat. "Thank you for sitting in. I'll speak to you later?"

"Of course you will."

They both turned toward the office door, and Gideon gestured for her to precede him out. In the main kitchen area, a cluster of servants—two housemaids and two footmen—stood whispering near the servants' stairs.

"She nearly fainted dead away," one of the maids whispered.

"Who fainted?" Electra asked.

The cluster stepped apart, all of them looking sheepish.

"Oh she didn't truly faint, miss," one of the other maids said. "We just thought she might, the way she shrieked and wobbled a bit against her cane."

"Lady Dalrymple," one of the footmen added. "They've come to take Lord Lockhart away. She saw the gentlemen carrying him in the upstairs hall and had a bit of a fright."

Electra wondered if Alice knew they'd taken him and whether she'd had to endure seeing Lockhart's lifeless body as they did so. She glanced back at Gideon. "I should go check on Alice and Lady Dalrymple."

His expression had turned grim, and he dipped his head. "Let's reconvene later."

GIDEON CLIMBED the servant stairs and didn't have to look far to find Sergeant Ormsbee. He stood convening in the front entry hall with a middle-aged black-haired man with a neatly trimmed beard, who Gideon guessed might be either the coroner or the doctor attending on Lord Carthorpe.

"Pierce," Ormsbee said, waving him over. "This is the coroner, Mr. Alton. He concurs with Brownlow's findings and will convene an inquest at the local meeting house tomorrow."

"I understand you're a Scotland Yard man," Alton said in a refined accent.

"He's assisting with the investigation," Ormsbee retorted.

"An interesting case, gentlemen." The coroner kept his voice low. "Is there a place where we could speak privately?"

"I've been using the dining room to conduct my interviews," Ormsbee told him. "Let us go there."

The three of them proceeded to the dining room and Ormsbee closed the door behind them.

"I take it you will provide me with a list of potential witnesses," Alton said, one black brow arched.

"By the end of the day," Ormsbee assured.

"It shouldn't be difficult, since it seems the only possible suspects were here on the grounds at the time of the murder." Alton looked at each of them and then settled his gaze on Gideon. "Wouldn't you agree, Inspector Pierce?"

Gideon felt odd to be the coroner's focus. He could feel Ormsbee bristling. "I've only spoken to one resident of the house and one staff member since I arrived, sir." He turned a look the sergeant's way. "I do think Mr. Winters' clothing should be assessed based on the piece of evidence you found. The two individuals I spoke to indicated Lord Lockhart and Winters argued on the day of viscount's death."

"I've had similar information," Ormsbee told him, "and Constable Withers is overseeing the search of his clothing now with one of the footmen."

"No sign of the murder weapon?" the coroner asked.

"Not as yet. The grounds and outbuildings are still being searched," Ormsbee confirmed. "The doctor seemed to indicate we're looking for a club of some sort."

"That sounds reasonable," Alton said, "but I did find two things that Dr. Brownlow may have missed."

Gideon and Ormsbee both snapped their heads toward Alton, focusing on the older man.

Alton reached into his pocket and drew out what looked like a shard of glass, holding it in his palm. "I removed Lord

Lockhart's suit coat, waistcoat, and shirt to see if I could detect any further wounds. When I did, this fell out."

Ormsbee took the shard and lifted it up to the light. "It's thicker than window glass, and seems to have broken off of something."

"Mmm, but whether it's related to his death is the real question," Alton said. "You may retain it until the inquest in case you must match its broken edge against something."

Gideon stared at the shard of glass and thought immediately of Electra. If she touched it, might she be able to tell them whether it was indeed involved in Lockhart's murder or where it came from? It was a mad and disturbing thought because what he truly wanted was to board a train with Electra and take her far away from the tangle of Lockhart's murder.

"Did you find further injuries?" Gideon asked the coroner.

"I did." Alton looked at Gideon and then Ormsbee. "I found scratch marks on his upper chest and neck, and a bruise on his shoulder. The scratches were quite deep but scabbed over."

Ormsbee looked both perplexed and intrigued.

"And regarding blood. Do you believe the assailant's clothing would be stained?"

Alton took a moment to consider the question. "Possibly. I believe much of the bleeding was internal, though the weapon did pierce the skin and cause the stains you saw on his shirt and waistcoat. Dr. Carter, who's performing the autopsy, will have his results to me this evening."

"Very good," Ormsbee said. "I'll have a report on the investigation and a witness list to you this evening too, Alton."

"And I'll see you at the inquest. Good afternoon, gentlemen."

After Alton left, Gideon turned to Ormsbee. "I'll speak to other staff members and transcribe my notes of all of the interviews."

"What did you learn from those you've conducted?"

"The lady's maid confirmed that Lady Alice was in her room until shortly before the murder, and Miss Poole has confirmed that she arrived in the drawing room a quarter hour before midnight."

Ormsbee nodded grimly. "And what did Lady Alice have to say?"

"She confirmed the conflict that several people, including the lady's maid, witnessed between herself and Lord Lockhart in the morning, but she claims they took lunch together amicably in the conservatory."

"We'll need to confirm that."

"I can ask a staff member," Gideon told him. "But she did say another person had a conflict with Lockhart in the hours before his death."

"Based on what you said about searching Winters' clothing, I'm guessing it was him," Ormsbee concluded.

"Yes. The viscount had loaned Mr. Winters a great deal of money, apparently."

Both of Ormsbee's dark brows shot up at that revelation. "The fact that Miss Poole says Winters was the last person to be seen with the victim has put him at the top of my list, I must admit."

"He'd be at the top of mine too."

"Then let's have him in for a chat." Ormsbee strode to the dining room threshold and called for a passing footman. "Please locate Mr. Winters and send him to the dining room."

Gideon was in the process of pouring himself a cup of tea while they waited when Mr. Winters swaggered into the room. It was the only way to describe the way the man presented himself. Chin up, chest out. Shoulders squared.

He looked like a man who wore a chip on his shoulder with pride.

"Shall we get this over with, gentlemen, so that my sister and I may depart? I have business meetings to attend to in London. I cannot stay in this house."

Ormsbee stood a few beats longer after Winters took a seat, his arms crossed as he looked down at the slightly older man. "Didn't you come for a house party, Mr. Winters, that would have continued for several more days?"

"I've already been here for a week, Sergeant. And now that I've lost a dear friend, I have no desire to stay where I am faced with constant reminders of him."

"Tell us about your friendship, as you say, with Lord Lockhart," Ormsbee said as he pulled a chair around to arrange it in front of where Winters sat.

"We've been friends for almost a decade. My sister is quite close to his fiancée. They were at school together." Winters shot a look at Gideon. "With Miss Poole."

"Were there any entanglements between you as friends?" Gideon asked.

"Entanglements?" Winters looked more irked by the question than perplexed.

"Obligations sometimes strain a friendship," Ormsbee pointed out.

Winters narrowed his eyes. "What are you getting at, Sergeant?"

"How much money has he loaned to you over the course of the last year?"

Alex Winters' smug expression faltered into something like shock. "That is an impudent question, Sergeant Ormsbee."

"I'm conducting a murder investigation, Mr. Winters. I'm afraid that questions will sometimes be indelicate and may seem impudent."

"What was the sum you owed Lord Lockhart?" Gideon pressed.

Alex Winters shot him an icy stare. "It wasn't a loan. It was a kindness from a friend, and I was appreciative."

"How much, Mr. Winters?" Gideon pushed again because Winters resisted.

"Approximately five thousand pounds."

Gideon clenched his teeth to stop from reacting. It was an enormous sum of money for anyone, even a viscount, to give to a friend.

"And when was it due?"

"It wasn't—" Winters started, then shook his head. "Yes, all right," he said more cooly, "he wanted the money back, but he also understood..."

"Understood what, Mr. Winters?"

"That my mother and sister rely on me. They must be kept in a respectable home with fine clothes and a fine carriage. Ophelia may never marry. My mother expects to live in luxury."

"Did he give you a date by which the money was to be repaid?"

Winters gave Gideon a long, narrowed-eye look. "He wanted it all resolved before his nuptials."

"When was the wedding set for?" Ormsbee looked first at Gideon, as if he might have gleaned that detail from Lady Alice, and then at Winters.

"In a month or so. In early June."

"You didn't have much time left." Ormsbee spoke the words softly, almost giving the impression of sympathizing with Mr. Winters' plight.

"And you argued about the matter yesterday, did you not?" Gideon put in.

Winters' eyes widened the merest bit, but then he scoffed. "Where did you hear such a ridiculous claim?"

"Did you not row with him yesterday?" Ormsbee leaned

forward a bit on his chair and stared unblinking into Winters' eyes.

"It wasn't an argument. More of a heated discussion." He glared at Ormsbee. "And he would be appalled to know Carthorpe staff tittle-tattled about it. Lockhart relied on discretion more than most."

"So you had a *heated* discussion in the afternoon and then spoke with him again in the evening prior to the séance?" Gideon asked. "Can you pinpoint the last time you saw Lord Lockhart that evening?"

"Ask Electra. She saw me out front as she re-entered the house. She and Lockhart were having some sort of tussle."

"Tussle?" Ormsbee's whole focus sharpened on Winters.

Gideon swallowed hard. "What do you mean?"

"He grabbed her arm, and she pulled away from him."

"What were they saying to each other?" Ormsbee asked.

"I'm not an eavesdropper, Sergeant. I only know that Lockhart sounded irked and Electra looked displeased when she passed me on her way back inside."

"And yet by several accounts, you didn't enter the drawing room until near midnight. Did you speak to Lord Lockhart while you were both outside?" Gideon asked.

The man had motive and opportunity to kill Lockhart, and Gideon loathed the way he called Electra by her given name.

"He stalked off into the hedge maze."

"That doesn't quite answer the question, Mr. Winters," Ormsbee noted. "Did you speak to him?"

"I asked him what was between him and Electra."

Gideon clenched his hand where it lay on his thigh.

"He told me to mind my own business." Winters said with a smirk. "Henry rarely minced words."

"Where is the suit you wore last evening?" Gideon asked.

Ormsbee shot him a quizzical look, then understanding seemed to dawn.

"My suit?" Winters smiled at him, baring his teeth. "I am doing my best not to take offense at your implication, Inspector. My suit is in among the other garments I brought to Carthorpe."

Ormsbee nodded and gave Gideon a quick glance.

"But if you mean to search for bloodstains," Winters said archly, "you *will* find them."

He looked at both men, no longer smiling and yet showing no signs of fear or distress either. "I helped carry Henry's body into the house, gentlemen. If you find blood, it would have gotten onto my clothing then."

The sergeant cast a questioning look Gideon's way, and Gideon gave a slight shake of his head. He had no other questions for Winters. The man could not be excluded as a suspect, and the only alibi he could offer was the victim himself.

"That will be all, Mr. Winters," Gideon said. He was eager to be out of the abrasive man's company.

Alex Winters stood and adjusted the lapels of his suit. "I'm departing for London, Sergeant Ormsbee. You did say I'd be welcome to do so once you'd finished with your questions."

"Circumstances have altered, Mr. Winters." Sergeant Ormsbee stood and approached to stand toe to toe with Winters. "You will be called as a witness at the inquest. Until further inquiries are complete, I would ask that you remain at Carthorpe."

Winters made a scoffing sound, and looked at each of them as if they were mad to command him to do anything. Then he stormed from the room, letting the door crack against the wall as he shoved it open.

"Will you remain while I question Mrs. Markland? We allowed her to return home because she has an infant who needed her care, but Mr. Jenks tells me she's returned."

"Of course." Gideon nodded.

"We also need to look further into Mr. Winters," Ormsbee said as he took up his pen again and began adding details to his notebook.

"You think he could be the killer?" Gideon asked.

Ormsbee kept his head bent but lifted his eyes to the dining room threshold before finally turning to Gideon. "He has sufficient reason, does he not? But what we need now is more evidence."

Chapter Nine

Mrs. Cora Markland carried herself with a kind of ethereal air that Gideon could not quite work out for himself. He suspected it was nothing more than a theatrical performance, meant to match her professed abilities. She kept her chin slightly elevated, her shoulders ramrod straight, such a slight smile on her lips that one could almost convince oneself that she wasn't smiling at all. She wore an elegant black ensemble covered in glittering faceted jet beads that clicked against each other as she entered the room. Yet, even once she was seated, unmoving, looking at himself and Ormsbee expectantly, Gideon felt a ripple of unease.

Electra's otherworldly quality felt right to him because it had been part of her from the moment he'd met her. She was unlike any woman he'd ever known and unique in the best of ways.

To Gideon, whatever Mrs. Markland wished them to see in her, think of her, seemed much more practiced, like a mask she had donned.

"Thank you for returning as requested, Mrs. Markland,"

Ormsbee began. "Can you tell us why you came to Carthorpe Hall last evening?"

Her eyes flickered with what seemed like surprise at the question. "I was asked to come, Sergeant Ormsbee, for the purpose of conducting a séance."

Gideon heard the defensiveness in her tone, along with a bit of patronizing lilt that Ormsbee should ask a question that he clearly knew the answer to.

"And when were you asked and by whom?"

Mrs. Markland stretched up even taller in the chair and licked her lips. "Lady Dalrymple sent me a note and requested my presence."

"Did she mention the purpose of her request?"

Mrs. Markland scoffed, her shoulders and neck still tensed. "Of course, Sergeant. She knew I am a medium and requested that I conduct a séance because of the belief that a ghost troubled the grounds of Carthorpe Hall."

"And you decided the event must occur at midnight?"

She nodded. "That is, I've found, an optimal time for communing with those beyond the veil."

Ormsbee eyed her with undisguised derision. "I see."

"So the timing was your choice and not a preference of Lady Dalrymple?" Gideon asked.

Mrs. Markland flicked her gaze his way, and said tightly, "Yes, it was my choice, Inspector."

"When did you arrive?" Ormsbee asked.

"About an hour before the event was to begin. I need time to prepare the space."

"Did you meet Lord Lockhart during that hour?"

Mrs. Markland's composure seemed to slip, but it was so quickly recovered that Gideon was impressed with the lady's ability to control her reactions.

"I did not meet Lord Lockhart. The guests were gathered in

the parlor prior to the séance, but I believe many remained in their room until close to the time we commenced."

"Who did you speak to?" Gideon pressed. "Prior to the séance, I mean."

"Oh." Mrs. Markland shifted her gaze, as if trying to recall. "I spoke to Lady Dalrymple certainly. I also spoke to Lady Alice, who greeted me when I arrived. Then I had a few words with Miss Electra Poole." Mrs. Markland looked straight at Gideon as soon as Electra's name left her lips. Her gaze was so searching, so direct, it was if she was pinning him in place. It was as if she knew what Electra meant to him somehow.

"And what was the substance of that conversation with Miss Poole?" Ormsbee inquired.

"Well, I'd heard about her abilities from Lady Alice and I'd also read about her in the papers. I sensed her power immediately, and I suspect she sensed mine. I chose for her to be seated next to me, thinking perhaps our joint abilities might serve the sitting well."

Ormsbee frowned and tapped his pencil against his notepad. "But Miss Poole did not participate in this séance, did she?" His blond brows had arched high.

"No." Mrs. Markland smiled. "Not in any overt way, but I suspect she sensed things, as did I from those seated around the table."

Ormsbee exchanged a look with Gideon. He swallowed so thickly, his Adam's apple bobbed in this throat. Gideon felt a bit of sympathy for Ormsbee's predicament. He'd felt the same when he'd begun asking for Electra's assistance during the Becknell case. Whatever Mrs. Markland claimed she sensed from others would never stand up as evidence in an inquest or any sort of judicial setting. And her senses might be nothing more than fabrication, though it struck Gideon in that moment that he'd never suspected the same of Electra. He trusted her entirely.

Finally, Ormsbee seemed to come to some sort of decision and nodded. "Go on then, Mrs. Markland, tell us what you sensed from others at the séance."

"A spirit came through to speak to Alex Winters. I only heard her name as Mary, and she was determined for him to stop his intended course of action."

Ormsbee frowned. "What course of action do you refer to?"

Mrs. Markland smiled. "That is something Mr. Winters would know, but it was not revealed to me. And though Mr. Winters made light of the message I conveyed, I sensed that he knew exactly what the spirit of Mary was referring to."

Ormsbee turned another look Gideon's way, looking confused. But Gideon had no clarity to offer him. Mrs. Markland's statements were vague enough to provide them with precisely nothing.

"And what else?" Gideon asked, as Ormsbee looked confounded at that moment. "What else did you ascertain during the sitting?"

Mrs. Markland arched one auburn brow. If nothing else, she seemed an intensely perceptive woman, and he knew she could detect Ormsbee's unease, but perhaps she sensed his own reticence too.

He had no basis of trust with her as he did with Electra.

"The late countess came through."

Ormsbee shifted as if he might actually rise up from his chair. "Lady Carthorpe?"

Mrs. Markland nodded. "Indeed. She was most concerned for her eldest daughter, Lady Alice."

Gideon leaned forward. "Concerned in what regard?"

"For her safety, Inspector. Lady Carthorpe felt Lady Alice was in danger."

"From?" It felt to Gideon that she was purposely saying less, almost forcing him to pull the information from her. It wasn't unusual during an interview with a witness, but it felt more practiced with Mrs. Markland for some reason.

For the first time since walking into the room, Mrs. Markland seemed less than confident. She dipped her head, drew in a long, deep breath. "The spirit did not tell me who, but I sensed it like an invisible cord between the two of them." She lifted her head, notched up her chin. "Between Lady Alice and Mr. Winters."

Ormsbee had now placed a hand over his mouth, staring at Mrs. Markland. Finally, he rolled his head on his shoulders and straightened against the back of his chair.

"Did you personally witness anything, Mrs. Markland, with your own eyes and not your purported abilities to indicate that Mr. Winters intended to do something reckless or that he posed any sort of threat to Lady Alice?"

"No, Sergeant. As I never met Mr. Winters prior to the moment when he walked into the drawing room prior to the séance's commencement."

"And when was that?" Gideon asked.

Mrs. Markland took a breath as if she intended to say something and then fell silent. "Miss Poole entered first, and that was at about quarter to midnight. Then Lady Alice and Lady Dalrymple came soon after. Only minutes later, I should think. Then Miss Winters and Mr. Winters sometime later—"

"How much later?" Ormsbee cut in.

"Perhaps five minutes? Maybe a bit more."

"Go on," Gideon urged.

"Mr. Lockhart came in soon after the Winters, and then Lady Honoria arrived last, almost at the moment the clock struck midnight." She swallowed and glanced at each of them.

"Lord Lockhart never arrived and it was decided that we should proceed."

Ormsbee flipped the pages of his notepad. "A Mr. Hobbes, footman, was sent to look for him, yes?"

"Yes, and he was found some time later, causing Hobbes to break up the séance. He said…" She hesitated. "He said his lordship was bleeding and he thought he was dead. It was all very shocking."

Gideon watched her say the word "shocking" with perfect poise and satisfaction, as if she knew she'd used the right word, and yet he couldn't see any indication that she felt any lingering shock about what had transpired the previous night.

Ormsbee glanced over at him expectantly. Gideon shook his head. He had no other questions for the medium.

"Thank you, Mrs. Markland, for answering our questions," Ormsbee said as the lady got to her feet. "If we have further questions, we will contact you at that time."

"Of course, Sergeant." She turned a look Gideon's way. "Inspector."

After she'd gone, Ormsbee sank into his chair with a sigh. "That was certainly unsettling. Do you think she's a fraud or that she actually believes the things she says?"

"I can't say," Gideon told him. He wasn't certain of everything Electra said she sensed, and yet he believed her. But something felt off about Mrs. Markland, and it disturbed him because he couldn't quite put his finger on what it was that unsettled him.

"But you are thinking something, Pierce. It's written all over your face."

Gideon didn't like being so transparently readable and worked to smooth his features.

"You must know the instinct that tells you, whether you can

prove it or not, that someone is not being entirely forthcoming with you?"

"Of course."

"I got that sense from Mrs. Markland, and yet it maddens me because I cannot point to any single cause. What she said sounded reasonable."

Ormsbee chuckled. "Except the bits about the *séance*."

"That seemed like speculation, I admit." And vague speculation at that.

"Let's hope something more emerges with the staff interviews," the sergeant said.

"I'll report back later in the day."

Ormsbee nodded. "I'd like to bring something solid to the coroner so that this inquest provides us with a viable suspect. As of now, there's a tension in the air in this house, and very likely a murderer walking about right under our noses."

Chapter Ten

"Do you know if Lady Alice is in her room?" Electra asked one of the maids as the young woman strode toward her in the upstairs hallway.

"Yes, miss. She's taking a nap and said she did not wish to be disturbed until dinner time. But I was sent to find you, Miss Poole."

"Well, then can you tell me which room is Lady Dalrymple's?"

"She's waiting in your room, miss. She's the one who sent me to find you."

"Oh, thank you."

Electra walked down the hall and opened her door to find Lady Dalrymple standing near the fireplace. She turned the moment Electra entered the room, looking even more disheveled than she had after her fall the night they'd met. Today, her hair hung loose from its pins, her gray-blue eyes were wide, and she wore a shawl half on one shoulder and drooping down her arm on the other side.

She appeared frightened and extremely anxious.

"There you are, my dear. I've been trying to find you for the last half hour. Where have you been?"

Electra approached and Lady Dalrymple immediately reached to take her gloved hands. This was how she'd often been greeted when she'd visited the noblewoman's London residence.

Electra didn't need to remove her gloves to sense that Lady Dalrymple was shaking. The removal of Lord Lockhart's corpse had seemingly rattled her deeply.

"I was with Inspector Pierce."

"The Scotland Yard man who's come? I do hope he can find the fiend who did this before he gets to someone else under this roof. The local sergeant is so young. He seems out of his depth."

"I'm certain he will. Inspector Pierce is excellent at what he does. You may remember me mentioning him. Gideon."

Lady Dalrymple's eyes lit with affection and amusement. "The young man your father took in. Yes, you spoke of him in quite heroic terms."

"Did I?"

"Oh, yes, my dear." Lady Dalrymple lifted a hand to the center of her chest. "If you think so highly of him, it puts me quite at ease to know he's assisting with this case."

"Shall we sit?"

Once they were settled into the arm chairs arranged near the fireplace, Electra tipped her head, studying the older woman, trying to sense something beyond her obvious distress.

"Is there anything I may do for you, Lady Dalrymple?"

Turning to face her, Lady Dalrymple assessed Electra for a moment. "My dear, I am going to admit something to you that I rarely admit to anyone. Indeed, it is something I have no need to admit because it is rarely part of my life."

Electra noted how Lady Dalrymple leaned heavily to one side as she put her weight on a cane clutched in her right hand.

"Forgive me," she said, drawing in a long breath. "Dr. Brownlow gave me a sleeping draught, and I feel muzzy-headed. As if I've been asleep for days. Yet the moment I stepped out of my room, I saw poor Henry. Bloody clothing..." She shook her head and pressed her lips together. "I've seen death many times, Miss Poole. You don't reach my age without attending your fair share of funerals. I also nursed my mother in her illness and sat with her as she took her last breath."

Her ladyship took a deep breath herself, lifted her chin, and let it out slowly. "Death never frightened me. I thought I'd made my peace with it, even as I am nearing my own. But now I must acknowledge that it does frighten me. Perhaps that explains my interest in spiritualism." She lifted her pale eyes to Electra. "I am afraid now and fear for my life."

Electra leaned closer. "Who do you fear?" A chill rippled through Electra. The noblewoman's fear was potent and palpable. Did Lady Dalrymple know who'd killed the viscount?

"That night you arrived, I thought I'd stumbled. I did fall, of course." She gestured to her cheek. "Scratched my face on the hedges and then fainted dead away. But there was a part of it I didn't recall until now."

"What part is that?"

"I didn't stumble on the gravel. The path in the hedge maze is well tended. The groundskeeper at Carthorpe is a fastidious man. He always has been. Julia took care with the staff she hired."

"Julia?"

"The late Lady Carthorpe. She was not only my sister-in-law but also a dear friend." She smiled, and her eyes took on a faraway look as if she'd gotten lost in a memory. "But yes, the hedge maze path is well maintained. The gravel is raked, weeds are pulled, and any overgrown roots are removed. I didn't trip, dear Electra. I was pushed."

"By whom?"

"I saw a figure of a young man. That's why I went into the hedge maze. I thought it was the specter, you see. The wandering man of Carthorpe."

"A specter." Electra's pulse had sped at the prospect that Lady Dalrymple might have witnessed something, or someone, who might help Gideon and Ormsbee solve Lockhart's murder, but now doubt swept in.

"Do you not believe in ghosts, Electra? You must. Do you not see them?"

"I can't say that I do, my lady. Perhaps Mrs. Markland does."

Lady Dalrymple reared back as if affronted. "That is most unusual if you have the abilities the newspapers say you possess. You've truly never seen a ghost before?"

"Not that I'm aware of, no. But I don't seek to see them either. Perhaps if I tried, I would."

"But why wouldn't you try, my dear?" Lady Dalrymple tipped her head. "To reach those beyond seems a great gift. Do you fear seeing someone you've lost?"

"No." Though Electra suspected part of what the noblewoman said was true. She never wanted to see a specter of her father or mother, as it would be proof that they did not rest peacefully.

"Well, I have seen them off and on for most of my life. My family lived in an old manor house in Derbyshire. So I wasn't afraid, you see, when I followed what I thought was an apparition of a young man into Carthorpe's hedgerow maze."

"Did you see the figure after you entered the maze?"

"I did. In the distance. Then I wasn't certain. He seemed to...disappear. Perhaps I took a wrong turn, but I did summon the spirit back once or twice, calling out for him to show himself." The noblewoman swallowed hard and licked her lips before adding, "I turned back, thinking to retrace my path to where I'd seen him, and that's when someone shoved me from behind. I remember now. The tickle along the back of my neck. The presence behind me. The hands at the center of my back." The older woman shivered and adjusted her shawl to pull it up closer around her neck. "Do you believe me, Electra?"

The question emerged on a whisper, full of emotion.

"I cannot argue with your memory, my lady. But why tell me and not the sergeant or Inspector Pierce?"

"Because you can help me recall more." Her expression softened a bit. "I read about your involvement in the Becknell case. And now it seems fortuitous that you came to Carthorpe as Alice and I hoped you would."

Electra didn't feel anything about her arrival or time spent at Carthorpe was fortuitous, though perhaps being the cause of Gideon arriving and assisting Ormsbee, would prove fortunate in the end.

"As I understand it, you can see things when you touch a person. Memories or visions of future events."

"It doesn't always work." Electra felt resistance well up, just as it had since the press coverage of the Becknell case.

"You cannot control it?"

"Not as well as I would like. I admit I'm a bit of a novice, my lady."

"So your gifts are newly acquired?"

"No, they are not, but I did not acknowledge or attempt to wield them for a very long time."

"But you do now, so will you do a sitting with me, my dear? I will compensate you, of course."

The impulse to refuse rose up in Electra, but her desire to make sense of what had happened at Carthorpe in the previous forty-eight hours proved greater. She did not have all of the accoutrements she would usually bring when preparing for a psychical sitting. But she had one part that meant the most to her—a moonstone gifted from an aunt in Ireland. Her mother's sister insisted the stone would enhance Electra's second sight. Though she had no notion of whether that claim was true, the stone did provide comfort, and she considered it a talisman of sorts.

"We could use this table." Electra pointed to a round table with a chair on either side.

While Lady Dalrymple settled into one of the chairs, Electra collected her black velvet traveling cape and arranged it over the table's surface, then collected a candlestick from the mantel and matches from the drawer of the table near the bed.

While she lit the candle, she drew in and released a few deep breaths. It had been months since she'd done a sitting. Yet it felt surprisingly right to be doing so again.

She sat, removed her gloves, and then drew the moonstone from her pocket, placing it on the table beside her.

"May I take your hands, my lady?"

Lady Dalrymple reached out and allowed Electra to clasp her hands.

"I'd ask you to think back to what you saw that night," Electra said softly.

Then she closed her eyes and tried to focus her mind and open it to whatever images or feelings might come through.

Suddenly, she wasn't in her guest room at Carthorpe. She was walking through the grass, looking out toward the fields beyond the estate on a moonlit night. A movement caught her eye. A man—dark clothed, dark haired—was striding toward the hedge maze purposefully. He carried something that glinted in the moonlight.

"He's holding something," Electra said quietly.

"Was he? I don't recall that." Lady Dalrymple sounded a bit dismayed.

Electra felt a chill rush through her as Lady Dalrymple's memory unfolded. The sight of the figure frightened her, and moments passed before she moved again, heading for the hedge maze that he'd stepped into.

She'd moved hesitantly, reaching out a hand to draw her fingers against the trimmed waxy leaves of hedge's wall.

"There..." Electra said.

"What is it?" Lady Dalrymple whispered.

But Electra heard her ladyship's voice as if she was far away rather than sitting across from her. Her mind was too focused on the sharper images of a man's figure crouched down. The distant figure wiped his hands on what looked to be a white handkerchief.

She could see only a profile of a man; his collar was pulled up around the lower half of his face. Electra couldn't make out anything about him other than dark hair and pale skin.

Then he stood, strode forward as if stepping into the wall of hedges themselves, and was gone. He seemed to disappear, as Lady Dalrymple had said.

"Do you see him, Electra? Tell me what you see."

At Lady Dalrymple's insistent queries, the images in Electra's mind began to scatter.

"I saw him. He was no spirit. He was very real." Electra opened her eyes. "Just as you said. I saw him crouching down. Do you recall that?"

Lady Dalrymple shook her head slowly. "No, I do not. It's all a bit muddy in my mind, but I recall the feeling of those hands at my back, pushing me down." She lifted a worried gaze to Electra's. "Did you see that occur?"

"No, it faded from my mind. I could try again."

"Oh, please do. I have a dreadful notion that someone wants

to do me harm. And the next night, a man died. Now Sergeant Ormsbee insists we remain in this house together, which means a murderer walks among us."

The thought disturbed Electra too.

"Let's try again." Electra drew inward, trying not to force anything, yet allowing her mind to open to whatever she might see.

Images rushed in, but they weren't of the hedge maze or any shadowy figure of a man. What she saw was in daylight. Sun streamed into the Carthorpe conservatory, greenery filled her field of vision, and whispered voices echoed up to the high ceiling.

Lady Dalrymple, whose view Electra saw through, walked toward the raised voices, then reached up to push a palm leaf aside to see Lady Honoria and Alex Winters conversing. They stood close to each other.

"Have you told James?" Winters asked.

"How could I?" Honoria shook her head. "I don't know what to do."

"Well, I might," Winters said, then snapped his head toward where Lady Dalrymple stood.

Electra felt a spike of fear tense the muscles of her body as they must have done with Lady Dalrymple. She dropped the palm leaf and immediately stepped back.

"You look frightened." Lady Dalrymple tightened her hold on Electra's hands. "What do you see?"

The images flickering in Electra's mind faded, and she looked up at Lady Dalrymple.

"Good heavens, did you foresee my death as you did with Lady Becknell?"

"No, not at all." Electra gave Lady Dalrymple's hands what she hoped was a reassuring squeeze. "I saw a conversation you overheard in the conservatory."

Lady Dalrymple's face fell. "Why, yes, between Honoria and Mr. Winters."

"Do you recall when that was?"

With a sigh, Lady Dalrymple tipped her head. "I think...the day before the séance."

The day before Lord Lockhart's murder.

"But that has nothing to do with what I wish you to help me discover, my dear."

"As I said, I can't truly dictate what comes through and what does not."

"The man who accosted me—" She shook her head. "No, I suppose I do not know if it was a man or woman, only that I followed a man into the hedge maze. But whoever pushed me down, do you think that same person still means me harm?"

"I cannot say, my lady." Electra shook her head, knowing that even if she tried again, seeing another person's motives was unlikely. Whatever she saw while holding the noblewoman's hands would be Lady Dalrymple's thoughts or feelings.

"Please, my dear. Let us try one last time."

"Very well." She couldn't bring herself to refuse someone who'd only ever been kind to her. Electra laid her hands out, palms up. "One last time."

The subtle jolt that signaled the coming of a vision rippled through Electra's body. This feeling was like that night when Lady Becknell had embraced her last November. As if what she was seeing was something beyond sensing the feelings or reading the memories of another. In her mind, she saw what looked like a bedchamber with an elderly man laid out upon it. The bedchamber faded and she saw the conservatory's interior again, but this time a white wrought-iron table with a tea service laid out atop it.

A lady approached. As if through a haze, Electra saw that it was Lady Dalrymple herself. She turned to look up at someone approaching. "I'm glad we're doing this," Lady Dalrymple said. And then the images faded like smoke blown by a breeze.

Electra's head ached and her chest felt odd. Her heart raced wildly and her pulse fluttered in her throat.

"I saw the conservatory again," Electra told Lady Dalrymple, who stared at her expectantly.

"And what else?"

"I saw you in the conservatory preparing to take tea with someone."

Lady Dalrymple frowned. "I do so quite frequently."

"I couldn't see who was joining you, but I did see you." Electra laid a hand on her chest where her heart still thudded fiercely. "I know it may not sound particularly ominous, but I believe it was a vision of something yet to happen."

When she'd seen the vision of Lady Becknell's death, she had seen the lady herself, much as she was seeing Lady Dalrymple now. It was different from seeing someone's memories through their own eyes. And Electra's whole body felt different, as if the visions took hold of her more completely. She felt slightly dizzy and a bit nauseous.

"Are you saying that someone will try to harm me in the conservatory?" Her ladyship gripped the neckline of her shawl, pressing it against her throat.

"I didn't see anyone trying to harm you. Not all visions I have are of danger."

Lady Dalrymple let out a sound very like a harumph. "Well, I shall avoid the conservatory and hope that since you did not foresee my death, it is not imminent."

She gave Electra a tremulous smile.

"I certainly hope not." Electra clasped her hands a moment longer, not to see anything more, but to offer any comfort she could.

AFTER FINISHING with a handful of staff interviews, none of which garnered Gideon more information than the fact that Lord Lockhart was occasionally sharp-tongued with Lady Alice and with Carthorpe's staff. A footman called him "exacting" and then blushed furiously at his honesty.

One of the housemaids, Lydia, mostly wanted to report that she had seen the infamous Carthorpe ghost. She also reiterated that Lord Lockhart could make the staff ill at ease with his moods.

Rather than start again with staff interviews, Gideon went out into the hedge maze. Based on Ormsbee's description, he found the section of maze where the murder had occurred. It wasn't deep into the maze, yet it was more than a few strides and turns into the structure.

A spot in the hedges looked as if someone might have fallen against them. Branches were bent back, but he couldn't detect any blood. He walked ahead of the spot, then back again, scanning the ground. If one button was recovered, perhaps something more had been deposited during the attack. That shard of glass Alton found intrigued him. If it was chipped from some object that was used to strike Lord Lockhart, perhaps there were more shards on the ground.

Though clouds hung in the sky, he thought a broken bit of glass might glint enough for him to spot it. Yet he saw nothing along the pathway.

At the sound of footsteps, he stilled. For a moment, he considered ducking back into one of the hedge's alcoves.

It was surprisingly common for one who'd committed a crime to return to the scene, often for the very purpose Gideon was out scanning the ground. If there was a possibility some evidence was left behind, a cunning criminal would want to retrieve it.

"This second turn…" A feminine voice mumbled quietly, as if to herself.

A voice he'd recognize in his sleep. Gideon stepped out from the alcove to see Electra approaching.

"What are you doing out here?" he asked, though he could never be sorry to see her.

"I wanted to have a look at the spot where it happened." She clasped her hands in front of her and dipped her head, then added, "More than a look, if I'm honest. I wanted to see if I could sense anything."

Gideon drew in a sharp breath, but he couldn't deny that he was curious what would happen if she used her *gift* to touch the ground or the hedge where Lockhart fell. If Ormsbee would allow it, he'd have her touch the shard of glass or even the button that had been found.

"Where's the spot?" she asked as she'd stepped closer.

Gideon gestured to the area in front of him. "See those broken branches? I believe he fell there." A bit of the gravel was disturbed. As he crouched down, Gideon noticed blood covering a few of the gravel pieces at the edge of the path. "There. He bled there."

Electra came closer and knelt down, surprising him by getting on her knees. She gathered the edges of her skirt closer so as not to disturb the ground overmuch.

She glanced at him once, then closed her eyes, reaching out to place her hand on the ground.

It felt as if he'd been given the same privilege her clients experienced when they sat across from her and waited to see what her abilities would reveal.

A frown pulled her black brows closer, and she shifted her hand, moving it across another patch of gravel. One finger alighted on a stone that looked to have a spot of dried blood on it.

When she let out a gasp, Gideon bent closer, wanting to reach for her. He resisted.

"He heard their approach," she said quietly. "But they moved quickly."

Her eyes sprang open, those bright blue-green depths arresting him for a moment. She swallowed several times, then lifted a hand and ran it over her head.

Gideon thought he saw a sheen in her eyes, and it made something in his chest ache.

"What did you see?" he whispered.

"I couldn't see who did it because he did not see them." For a moment tears seem to well in her eyes. "He was terrified. I felt that. Whoever it was, they moved quickly and struck fast. After that, it all faded."

"Do you...?" He didn't know quite how to ask about her gifts without letting his lingering doubts creep into his tone. "You said you felt as he did at the moment of his death. I'm not sure I understand."

She gave him a grim look. "I'm not sure I do either. Sometimes I only see images, but perhaps if the emotions in that moment were powerful, I feel them too."

It made no sense to him, and it unsettled him that she was at the whim of visions and feelings that were not her own.

He got to his feet and reached down for her. "Allow me to help you up?"

She ignored his outstretched hand and fixed her gaze a bit farther down the hedgerow. "What is that?"

Gideon swung back and squinted. "What is what?"

Electra got to her feet on her own and took a few steps past him, then knelt again. "This earth has been disturbed."

Gideon joined her, lowering to his haunches.

Under one of the hedgerows, he saw a depression in the ground and loose soil around it. It looked as if something had been buried or dug up from the spot, then dirt had been hastily pushed back into the hole without much finesse.

"What was buried?" he voiced the question aloud, though he was mostly talking to himself.

Electra reached out and sank her hand into the overturned dirt, then closed her eyes.

Gideon watched her, the profile that was so familiar, the determined set of her jaw. When she opened her eyes, she glanced over and shook her head as if disappointed.

"I don't sense anything." She stared at the overturned soil.

"Could Lockhart have been out here searching for something?" Gideon never could quite understand why Lockhart was walking the hedge maze near midnight. "Or was he hiding something?"

"Possibly." Electra said the word excitedly. "Lady Dalrymple saw someone. She told all of us it was a specter, but I…had a sitting with her, and I saw it in her mind. It was man of flesh and blood, and he crouched down in the hedge maze."

"At this spot?"

Electra let out a little sigh. "I can't say for certain."

"And when was that?"

"The night before Lockhart's murder."

Gideon stood and reached out a hand again. This time Electra took it and got to her feet, then bent to brush dirt off the skirt of her gown.

He couldn't resist asking, "Did you see anything else during your sitting with Lady Dalrymple?"

"Lady Honoria," she said with an arched brow. "I saw her when I touched Alice during the séance too. I think we should speak to her."

"We?" Gideon's chuckle emerged half-strangled. "Ormsbee

must certainly have her on his list and may have already spoken to her."

"But—"

Before Electra could finish saying whatever she'd intended, a scream rang out. Men's raised voices followed. Gideon and Electra glanced at each other and took off, rushing toward the sounds.

Chapter Eleven

lectra spotted them as soon as she and Gideon exited the hedge maze. The three stood at the far edge of the garden: Alex Winters, James Lockhart, and Lady Honoria.

Alex had his hand wrapped around Lockhart's lapel, and Honoria had her hands up, trying to dislodge him. The men were shouting at each other, their voices carrying across the distance.

"Gentlemen," Gideon called as strode over quickly and pushed at Winters' hand. "Stop this." He planted himself between the two men, hands out to keep them apart from one another.

As she drew closer, Electra noticed a trickle of blood on Alex Winters' white shirt.

"Tell him, Winters. Tell the Scotland Yard man what you did," Lockhart shouted at him. His eyes blazed with fury, and he pushed so close his chest brushed Gideon's hand. Electra suspected he'd launch himself at Winters again, if given the chance.

"You have no bloody idea what you're talking about."

Winters tugged at his lapels, then brushed off the fabric, as if cleaning away Lockhart's audacity. "You're a fool and always have been."

"Cease!" Honoria cried, eyes beseeching as she looked at one man and then the other. "Both of you. This is unbearable. James has just lost his brother. Of course you would defend him."

"I'm not defending anyone," Lockhart all but snarled.

"There's been a tragedy here," she said more quietly, though her voice broke as if she fought to hold back tears. "Neither of you are making this any better by going at each other so viciously."

"And if he did it, Honoria?" James said to her, his tone suddenly softening the merest bit as he looked at her. "Have you considered that?"

Honoria's face, which had been full of anguish, went slack as she turned to look at Alex Winters.

"Did you, Alex?" she said quietly, lips trembling. "Did you do this for—?"

"Enough!" Winters shouted, swiping a hand through the air. Then he turned on his heel and stalked back toward Carthorpe Hall.

"It can't be true," Honoria said. Her voice had dropped to whisper. "James..."

Lockhart turned to her and drew her into his arms. They embraced, and it seemed so tender and so easy between them that it almost seemed to Electra as if it was something they'd done before. But Honoria soon broke free and bowed her head, pulling a handkerchief from her pocket.

Tears streamed down her face, and she dabbed them away. Honoria seemed a lady given to letting her emotions free, and Electra could almost admire it, since it was so unlike her own instinct to keep her feelings reigned.

"Lady Honoria," Gideon said in a shockingly gentle tone, "I have some questions to put to you. Would you accompany me and Miss Poole back into the house?"

"I'm not sure she's in any state to answer questions, Inspector," James Lockhart bit out.

"I'm afraid there's little time to be delicate in this matter. I have questions that must be answered before the inquest so that the corner may conduct the most effective inquiry as possible."

"He's right," Honoria said, her voice stronger. "I will come with you and Miss Poole, Inspector Pierce." To James she offered a simple nod as if to reassure him. "I'll be all right. Let us speak later if you wish."

James Lockhart shot a glare at Gideon and turned a cooler look Electra's way, but he finally focused on Honoria and said, "Of course." Then he turned on his heel and strode back toward Carthorpe.

"Would you mind if we spoke in the library, Inspector?" Honoria asked. "I understand you're speaking to others in the dining room, but it's easy for others to overhear what's said in that room."

"Please lead the way, my lady."

Honoria led them to the library near the back of the house. Thick velvet drapes of forest green covered its windows and shelves of neatly aligned books covered its walls. Thick carpet on the floor muffled the sound of their footsteps as they walked into the room.

Honoria gestured toward the door. Gideon seemed to understand and closed it behind them. Then she immediately walked to a settee and sat, pointing to the two chairs arranged opposite it.

Electra had no discussion with Gideon about whether or not she would sit in on the interview. He was allowing it, and she was going to take the opportunity to observe Honoria's demeanor and hear her account regarding Lord Lockhart. She was grateful for it. So she took a seat first. He waited for her to do so, then settled into the chair beside her.

Rather than launch into questions, he pulled out his notepad and pencil from his pocket. Finally, he looked up at Honoria expectantly. "Thank you for taking the time, my lady."

"Of course," she said. She smiled warmly, and it was a striking contrast to how upset she'd been moments ago, Electra thought. "I realized this is necessary. I knew it was coming. Though I did speak to Sergeant Ormsbee, I suspected you'd have questions too." She huffed out a soft laugh. "Despite what you saw outside, I am well, and I am prepared to tell you whatever you'd like to know."

She was so calm now. So composed and forthright that Electra couldn't help but wonder about the change and how quickly it had come on. Men sometimes thought ladies cried to gain sympathy, yet nothing about her tears in the garden had seemed false. And yet this other utter poise didn't seem like pretense either.

"Tell me how you knew Lord Lockhart, Lady Honoria."

"Well, as you know, he was my sister's fiancé. So I've known him for quite some time." She looked between Gideon and Electra as she spoke, and on her second glance toward Electra, the oddest thought came to Electra.

Honoria didn't like Lord Lockhart. Electra sensed it from her, a pulse of anger, a flash of disdain as soon as she spoke of the man, though she immediately seemed to tuck it away. It was there and gone as Electra's eyes met Honoria's honey-brown ones.

"How long?" Gideon prompted.

"Oh, I suppose he first met Alice about two years ago."

"That is a long courtship."

She grimaced, then dipped her head, tucking a lock of her

blonde hair behind her ear. When she looked up again, her expression was serene. "Yes, it was a long courtship," she admitted.

"Was there a reason for that lengthy courtship?"

"My father's illness certainly played a role. Alice has tended to him devotedly, and the thought of leaving his side to go away with Henry to his ancestral home never sat well with her."

"And yet she eventually agreed to marry him."

Again, the flicker of a frown. "Yes, but they had an agreement that she could return to Carthorpe whenever she was needed. Henry had even offered to bring Papa to his estate, but none of us liked that idea."

"Why?"

"We knew he'd be much happier here."

Electra shifted in her chair, eager to question Honoria herself, but knowing it was Gideon's role to do so. Still, he glanced over at her, and she took it as an invitation.

"What was your impression of Lord Lockhart when you met him?" she asked Honoria.

Honoria blinked as if surprised to have a question put to her by Electra. Then her eyes looked a bit glassy, as if she was holding back tears. But again, she took a moment, reined it in, and gave Electra a half-smile.

"He seemed amiable enough. Fine looking. Could be charming. He..." The first true crack in her composure came as she tried to draw on memories of Lord Lockhart.

Electra focused her efforts, trying to reach out to Honoria in her mind, but she couldn't get a perception of any one feeling from her clearly. It was as if her emotions were a churning pool. Electra recognized anger, sadness, and fear. And finally, the oddest of all, a feeling of hopefulness.

"He could be very blunt at times, and that could be offensive to people," she added, almost as an afterthought. "Alice, I think, liked it. She prefers someone who is straightforward and without pretense."

"So they were a good match in that regard," Gideon said, picking up the thread. "Did you ever observe your sister and Lord Lockhart in any sort of conflict with each other?"

Honoria reached up and patted the artful knot of braided hair at the nape of her neck. "I believe every couple probably has an argument once in a while. They disagreed at times about where father would reside and when Alice would be prepared to actually wed and exchange vows."

"How did Lockhart respond during those arguments?" Electra asked.

She recalled the image she'd seen when she'd touched Alice at the séance. Lockhart on his knees cradling Honoria. What had provoked that sort of intimacy?

Honoria looked at her, her eyes suddenly harder than she'd yet seen them. "He liked things to go his way, so he would sometimes shout. He was insistent, I suppose you could say."

"You observed him shouting at your sister?" Gideon asked.

Honoria nodded. "I believe there was at least one occasion when I do recall them raising their voices, but no more than you observed just now with James and Mr. Winters."

"James," Gideon repeated. "You speak of him familiarly."

"Well, yes. He's the brother of my sister's fiancé. We would have eventually become siblings via their marriage. I suppose we became close on that account."

"So you're close friends with Mr. Lockhart." Gideon's persistence on the point intrigued Electra.

"Yes, we are."

"More than a friendship?" Electra had seen the looks they exchanged.

Honoria blushed, the color rushing over her high cheekbones. "I don't want to be presumptuous, Miss Poole. You know how these things are. Gentlemen can be inscrutable at times."

"And what about your relationship with Alex Winters?" Electra asked, now that it seemed clear Gideon wasn't going to stop her inquiries. Based on what she'd seen in Lady Dalrymple's recollection, the two had been in a heated discussion in the conservatory.

"He is a friend of Henry's and has been to Carthorpe many times, and as you know, Ophelia and Alice have been friends since finishing school."

"Do you think he's a man who's capable of violence, my lady?" Gideon's voice had turned grave.

Honoria looked suitably unsettled by the question, laying a hand over her chest and staring at the carpet a moment. Whether she was considering the question or deciding what to confide, Electra couldn't tell.

Finally, she looked at Gideon with a sheen in her eyes. "I cannot say, Inspector."

Gideon frowned at her, clearly frustrated with her reply. "We came upon you and Mr. Lockhart and Mr. Winters in a rather heated exchange. Mr. Lockhart seemed to think Mr. Winters may have harmed his brother. How did that argument start?"

For the first time, all her poise seemed to abandon her. "Must I divulge a personal matter when it has no relevance to what you're investigating?"

"May I ask that you tell us and allow us to determine whether it's relevant, my lady?" Gideon asked.

She stared at him, swallowed thickly, and then ducked her head. Electra noted that the faint blush in Honoria's cheeks deepened.

"It started because James believes that Alex has...inappropriate designs on me," she said quietly. "I have assured him it is not true." She lifted her head and fixed Gideon with a direct stare. "He does not." Then she turned to Electra. "I swear it."

"I believe you," Electra told her. And she did. She sensed Honoria's unease, that she was struggling to speak of something that made her deeply uncomfortable.

Honoria offered her a soft smile. "Thank you, Miss Poole." Her smile deepened a bit. "Electra." Cocking her head, she studied her. "Can you read my mind now, as we sit here?"

"No," Electra told her honestly. "I can sense some of your emotions, but I cannot see any of your memories. Mostly, when I can see someone's thoughts or memories, it is because I am touching them."

Honoria looked down at her gloved hands. "Is that why you wear them?"

"It is. Yes. They can...mute my abilities."

Honoria drew in a sharp breath. "I would not want to see others' memories. There are even some of my own that I don't wish to revisit."

"What memories?" Electra said quietly. There was more Honoria was not saying, and though she'd said they were memories she did not wish to recall, Electra sensed that something in her wanted to be unburdened.

Honoria lifted her shoulders. "Oh, that glimpse of them carrying Lord Lockhart through the hall, for instance. Watching my father suffer."

"Of course," Electra said quietly.

"Do you think Mr. Lockhart will be pleased to inherit his brother's title, Lady Honoria?" Gideon asked.

Honoria flinched back.

Electra thought the question was a bit blunt too.

"James will do his duty, but I assure you he did not want the title, Inspector Pierce." Her voice had turned brittle.

"May I ask a question?" Electra queried. She directed it at Gideon.

He nodded.

"You were observed in the conservatory with Alex Winters, my lady. Only a couple of days ago. Do you remember what that conversation was about?"

Honoria blinked and glanced away, lips pursed as if in contemplation. "I don't recall that conversation. We very well could have conversed. He's been at the house for nearly a week. Sometimes we all take tea in the conservatory."

Electra pondered how much to disclose about what Lady Dalrymple had seen. "You were observed referring to Mr. Lockhart. Mr. Winters asked you if you'd told Mr. Lockhart something."

Honoria became very still, her eyes locked on Electra's. "You weren't here at that time, Miss Poole. How would you know what we discussed?"

"As I said, you were observed." Electra had a strong sense that she should not mention Lady Dalrymple. A protective impulse, perhaps.

Lady Honoria lifted a hand and tugged at the high neck of her gown. "If you must know, it was regarding the same topic."

"Same topic?" Gideon asked.

"That caused the argument you observed and broke up, Inspector. Mr. Winters knew of James's suspicions and wanted me to set things straight with him." She lifted her lips in the semblance of a smile. "In truth, I didn't want to discuss the matter at all, either with James or Mr. Winters. Because there was nothing to discuss," she said with a forced lightness, then shrugged her slim shoulders again. "In my mind, Mr. Winters was overreacting, as was James. You saw the culmination of that today."

"I must ask a difficult question, Lady Honoria," Gideon said.

"Another one?" Honoria asked tightly. "Go on then, Inspector."

"Do you have any notion who might have wanted to kill Lord Lockhart?"

Honoria shook her head immediately, then dropped her eyes to the carpet. "I won't point fingers at anyone, Inspector."

Gideon shot a look at Electra, as if the answer surprised him.

"Surely," Electra started in a soft tone, "you do want the person responsible to be found, especially considering that he is likely here at Carthorpe at this very moment."

At that, Honoria began to tremble. "Yes, it's as you say." She tucked a gold-blonde lock of hair behind her ear. "He is still among us."

"So is there someone you suspect?" Electra asked.

Honoria drew in a long breath and then sat up a bit straighter, pushing her shoulders back, looking Electra squarely in the eyes. "The only person I ever saw having a true row with Lord Lockhart was Mr. Winters. They argued quite a bit, but they were also friends. I cannot imagine..." She shook her head. "No, despite what James said during their argument, I cannot imagine Mr. Winters doing such a thing. James was angry. That is why he accused Mr. Winters."

"So the argument was more about jealousy than any genuine accusation?" Electra pressed.

"Precisely," Honoria said with a half-smile at her, almost as if grateful to have someone understand.

"Thank you, Lady Honoria," Gideon said.

Electra sensed that he was preparing to end the interview, but Electra couldn't get the vision she'd seen when she'd touched Alice out of her mind.

"Pardon, Honoria. May I ask one more question?"

Honoria gave Electra a look that said she was not pleased with the prospect. "Of course, Miss Poole."

"Did you find Lord Lockhart to be a kind, comforting sort of person?"

"Comforting?" Honoria's brows arched up as if the very word confused her.

"Yes, if you were...overcome or in distress, would he be the sort to offer comfort?"

Anger filled the air around Honoria, a shimmer of red. In Electra's experience, that only happened when another's emotions were at a peak and difficult for them to control.

"I would not seek comfort from Lord Lockhart for any reason," Honoria's warm voice had turned decidedly hostile, "so I could not say."

Lady Honoria had not only disliked Lord Lockhart; she loathed him. Electra sensed it, felt the certainty of it like an object hanging the air between them.

"Where were you prior to the séance, Lady Honoria?" Gideon asked.

"In my room preparing to go downstairs, of course."

"Did you avail yourself of Alice's lady's maid."

Honoria looked pensive. "No, I don't believe I did that night. Madeline had assisted me to dress earlier in the day, and she would sometimes help me with my hair, but that night I did not require her."

"Thank you, my lady," Gideon said after making a few notes in his notepad. "You've been very forthright."

"Of course, Inspector." She offered Electra a soft smile. "And you, Miss Poole. I hope you will find who's done this. None of us can feel at ease at Carthorpe until you do."

"We will, my lady," Gideon said, and it sounded very much to Electra like a vow.

Chapter Twelve

James Lockhart was still trembling with frustration by the time he took a seat in the dining room. Gideon suspected if they gave him the chance or the slightest provocation, he would have been out of his chair and on his way to continue his row with Alex Winters.

Gideon couldn't help recalling the fury in the young man's face as he stood with his hand wrapped around Alex Winters' lapel. His cheeks had been red, his eyes glowing with anger. No, it had been more than anger. It seemed more akin to hatred, and Gideon had seen it in the eyes of many men over his years of police work.

He had a dozen questions in his mind that he wanted to ask James Lockhart, but it was Ormsbee's prerogative to begin the interview. Gideon had filled the sergeant in on what he and Electra had observed in the Carthorpe garden and also what they'd found in the hedge maze and learned from Lady Honoria Kirkham.

"You seem quite upset, Mr. Lockhart," Ormsbee began in a calm, clear voice. "Can you tell us what has provoked your temper this evening?"

Lockhart unlocked his crossed arms and pressed his hands against his thighs. He drew in a deep breath and exhaled as if struggling for equanimity. "May I ask you a question first, Sergeant Ormsbee?"

Ormsbee waved his arm as if to urge Lockhart to ask his question.

"Have you or Inspector Pierce made any progress in determining who killed my brother? We are all trapped here, while whoever did this is in the house." Lockhart flicked his hand out toward the closed dining room door. "Even Winters is still here despite you giving him permission to hie off."

"Mr. Winters was not given permission to 'hie off' as you say. He's been asked to remain to be called, as you all will be, at the inquest."

Gideon cleared his throat to let Ormsbee know he had a question. The sergeant turned to him in acknowledgement.

"You sound, Mr. Lockhart, as if you do not think Mr. Winters should not be allowed to leave."

Lockhart pursed his lips. "I hope you are investigating him thoroughly and you will not jump to some hasty conclusion before you do consider him."

Ormsbee's expression eased into something defensive. "We are currently gathering evidence, Mr. Lockhart. I am not in the practice of doing my work in a *hasty* manner." Ormsbee shot Gideon a look. "I am assuming the same can be said for you, Inspector."

"I have drawn no final conclusion," Gideon said, eyes fixed on James Lockhart.

"With our combined efforts, I am confident we will bring this case to a successful conclusion," Ormsbee told him. "If you have anything to offer that will assist us, I urge you to provide it. Hold nothing back, sir."

James Lockhart gave each of them a crestfallen look and

then pinched the skin between his brows. "I never would. We are talking about the murder of my brother, Sergeant. No one wishes to have answers more than I do."

"Are you implying that you believe Alex Winters is responsible for your brother's death?" Gideon couldn't hold back the question anymore. He'd seen the animosity between the two earlier and heard the question Lockhart had put to Lady Honoria.

Ormsbee's brows quirked. "If you have some evidence or testimony to offer against Mr. Winters or anyone, we need to hear it, Mr. Lockhart. And it will be presented at your brother's inquest."

Lockhart eyed Ormsbee, then crossed his arms. "If you've spoken to him, and he's been honest, then you will know that Alex Winters owed my brother an outrageous sum of money."

Ormsbee was as still as a stone, neither acknowledging nor denying Lockhart's supposition.

"The funds were not given to him as a gift, though I've heard him make that claim. Henry told me himself that Winters had always vowed that he would pay him back."

"But he did not," Ormsbee said.

"No." Lockhart scoffed. "Henry was a fool and gave away money too freely. He was forever loaning funds to this friend or that. Draining the family's coffers with too little thought as to how they'd be refilled."

"You thought your brother was a fool, Mr. Lockhart?" Ormsbee asked quietly.

Lockhart's jaw clenched, and he gave the sergeant an icy look. "Forgive me. I don't wish to speak ill of my brother. I am mourning him as are we all. But, yes, at times he was frivolous and impulsive and made choices that I wish he had not."

"What was the cause of your altercation in the garden just now with Mr. Winters?" Gideon asked.

Lockhart swept a hand along his jaw. "As you may know, I have been courting Lady Honoria. We have an understanding between us. I care for her very deeply. I have asked her to be my wife, and she has agreed."

The young man's expression turned almost wistful. "Honoria is beautiful. I understand that. And I know that others have sought her attentions. Mr. Winters is quite renowned for his interest in the attracting ladies' attention."

"Has he been inappropriate with her?" Ormsbee asked.

A muscle tensed along Lockhart's jawline. "Honoria is one of the kindest ladies you'll ever meet. Soft hearted, gentle. And when she sees someone in need, she wishes to help. I believe he has played upon her sympathies."

"So jealousy provoked you today?"

"I needed to make it clear to him that his attentions to Honoria and his involvement with the sisters needed to cease. Henry is gone now. There is no reason for Winters to continue to visit Carthorpe Hall."

"Did he pursue Lady Alice too?" Gideon asked.

Lockhart tossed back his overlong hair and clenched his hands into fist. "Prior to her betrothal to my brother, Lady Alice and Mr. Winters carried on in a way that made many of us think she would receive a proposal from him."

Gideon arched both brows. The relationships between those at Carthorpe were nothing if not tangled.

"Not that her father would have approved," Lockhart added. "There was competitiveness between Winters and Henry. When Winters saw Henry succeeding at something or wanting something, he suddenly wanted it too."

"But you said Mr. Winters pursued Lady Alice first," Ormsbee pointed out.

"Henry had expressed interest in her before Winters began his stratagems." Lockhart looked at each of them in turn.

"Thankfully, Alice is discerning. She put an end to his nonsense very quickly."

Gideon felt that itch at his nape that always came when the facts being conveyed to him conflicted. "So Mr. Winters pursued Lady Alice, then she rejected his attentions, and she ultimately chose your brother?"

"Indeed," Lockhart affirmed. "Very firmly. Alice was polite to Winters, and then she wasn't. He's a persistent lout."

"Yet Lord Lockhart remained friendly with him and Lady Alice saw fit to invite him to this house party. Why?"

"Henry couldn't hold a grudge to save his life." Lockhart's eyes widened as he seemed to recognize what he'd said. "God rest him." Lockhart let out a sigh. "It is a grave thing to accuse a man of murder, and I have no solid proof to offer you, Sergeant. But if either of you were to come to me and tell me that you'd found evidence that Alex Winters did this dastardly thing, I would not be surprised."

"Have you ever seen him act in a violent manner?" Gideon asked.

Lockhart shifted in his chair, then admitted, "No, I have not, Inspector."

"Were you angry with your brother?" Ormsbee put in.

Lockhart shot him a quizzical look.

"You mentioned that he"—Ormsbee consulted his notes—"'gave away money too freely,' as you put it. Did that anger you?"

"It didn't please me," Lockhart bit out, but then he lowered his shoulders as if trying to calm himself. "But he was heir and steward of the Lockhart title and estate. I could not gainsay him."

"Did that displeasure provoke arguments between you?" Ormsbee seemed to notice what Gideon did. Lockhart was struggling to contain his emotions and a push might reveal more truth than he'd intended to let out.

"I advised him not to trust men like Alex Winters. I urged him to be more circumspect." Lockhart shrugged. "He did as he pleased."

"And where were you on the night of your brother's murder between eleven in the evening and midnight?" Gideon asked.

Lockhart licked his lips, looked down at his hands, and then turned to Gideon. "I was preparing for the evening's event, then took a brief walk outdoors with Honoria before we joined the others in the drawing room."

"I spoke to Lady Honoria and she did not mention your outing together," Gideon interjected.

"Perhaps she thought it indelicate to mention," Lockhart suggested.

"She did not mention that you proposed to her either," Gideon admitted.

Lockhart licked his lips and looked momentarily pensive. "We did both agree not to speak of it until we could secure her father's approval, but he's been so ill. She didn't wish to press him until he felt better."

Gideon made a note of the discrepancy, not sure if Lockhart's reasoning rang true. It would have been just as easy for Lady Honoria to admit such a thing when they questioned her, but she had not. She'd indicated that she wasn't certain of Lockhart's true intentions.

Ormsbee seemed eager to move on. "Based on your admission about a walk with Lady Honoria, the two you were likely outdoors when the events in the hedge maze unfolded. Did you hear anything? See anything?"

"Do you not think I would have come to one of you immediately if I had?" Lockhart shook his head. "No, I saw and heard only Honoria. And we were on the east side of the house, near the conservatory, not the west side where the hedge maze is located."

A tremor seemed to rush through Lockhart. "I wish I'd been on the other side," he said quietly. "I wish I'd been able to do anything to prevent what happened to Henry. Despite it all, he was my brother."

Gideon and Ormsbee exchanged a look. Gideon believed Lockhart's emotion was genuine, yet he still sensed there was something the young man was holding back. Perhaps someone else he was trying to protect. Yet he didn't think Mr. Lockhart would be pushed into confessing anything more.

"You and Mr. Winters assisted to carry your brother into Carthorpe Hall," Ormsbee began. "What did you observe when you found him and after he was brought inside?"

Lockhart's brow drew down. "He was lying on his back and there was..." Lockhart lifted his hand and gestured toward his neck and head. "A great deal of blood on his collar. Only when we lifted him did I see the blood in his hair."

Lockhart's eyes took on a glassy sheen and he stared at the wall, his expression shifting as if he was experiencing the memory again. "Once we got him upstairs, it was clear he was gone. His eyes were half open, unseeing, and his hands were already growing cold."

"He said nothing?"

Lockhart shook his head. "No. Nothing at all."

"Alex Winters assisted you to carry him in," Ormsbee said, "yet you now suspect he may have been responsible for the crime. Did you see any evidence of guilt that night? Did he behave oddly? Nervous? On edge?"

"No, I cannot say that I did."

"Then what do you base your suspicion on, Mr. Lockhart?"

"The money," Lockhart said, in a tone that made it seem as if both of them should think it an obvious motive. "Henry had finally begun pressuring him to pay it back, and Alex had promised and lied and prevaricated. Henry even threatened to bankrupt him at one juncture, though I don't know if he would have gone through with it." Lockhart shrugged. "Perhaps there was lingering jealousy over Alice too."

Ormsbee let out a thoughtful hum, then nodded. "Thank you, Mr. Lockhart. We will see you at the inquest tomorrow."

Lockhart looked at both of them before standing and leaving the dining room.

Once he'd gone, Ormsbee settled back against his chair and ran a hand over his beard. "We should convene after the next interviews so that I may be as complete as possible in my report for Coroner Alton."

"Of course," Gideon agreed. "Have you drawn any conclusions about—?"

Before he could finish his question, Constable Withers rapped on the half-open dining room door before stepping into the room.

"We've completed the search of Mr. Winters' and Mr. Lockhart's clothing and could find no match to the button that was found at the site of the murder."

Ormsbee let out a groan.

"But..."

Ormsbee sat up straight. "But?"

"The housemaid that assisted with the search believes one of Mr. Winters' coats is missing. An overcoat that he arrived to Carthorpe in last week and that she brushed several times in the course of her work that week. It had a purple lining that stood out to her and that's why she recalled it."

Ormsbee got to his feet and braced his hands on his hips. "We should initiate another search of the property and the hall. Dusk will fall soon, so please start now, Withers. Ask the footmen and housemaids to assist you."

"I could lend a hand," Gideon said as he got to his feet.

"We have one last house guest to speak to, Pierce," Ormsbee said. "Have a housemaid send Ophelia Winters to the dining room," he told Withers.

The constable nodded and departed.

"Tea, Pierce? Have you eaten?" Ormsbee's question surprised him.

"I'm all right. I'll grab a bite later."

"Suit yourself," the sergeant said before going to the urn on the sideboard, pouring himself a fresh cup of tea, and collecting a biscuit from a tray the staff had laid out.

"Miss Poole and I found something in the hedge maze."

Ormsbee swung around to face him, scattering biscuit crumbs. "Evidence? Why didn't you give it to me immediately."

"It's nothing tangible I could bring to you, but I'm telling you now." Gideon tried to dispel the irritation from his tone. After five years, he was used to leading his own investigations, yet he tried to remind himself of how it might feel if he were in Ormsbee's role. "We found a hole. It was crudely dug underneath one of the hedges."

"Did you record the dimensions?"

"No, but I'd estimate around ten inches long and perhaps half as wide."

Ormsbee cocked his head. "A hole under a hedge doesn't sound terribly unusual. A rabbit or some other garden beast must have dug it."

"It wasn't a rabbit hole, nor deep enough for any other animal to burrow in it. Perhaps six inches deep, at most."

"I see." Ormsbee sounded utterly perplexed. "Perhaps I should have a look after we speak to Miss Winters." He lifted his pocket watch from his waistcoat pocket, then crossed to the threshold. He called to a footman. "Where is Miss Ophelia Winters?"

"I believe one of the maids is looking for her, sir. She was not in her room."

Ormsbee cast a worried look back at Gideon over his shoulder.

"Which room is hers?" Ormsbee asked the footman.

"Third on the left, sir."

Ormsbee swept past the young man, boot heels clattering quickly across the house's marble hallway. Gideon decided to follow, curious as to why Ormsbee should be so impatient to speak to the young lady.

He climbed the stairs a few paces behind Ormsbee and followed him down the hall to the room the footman had indicated. The sergeant rapped three times, waited not more than a few seconds, and rapped again more forcefully.

Without saying a word, he twisted the doorknob and pushed inside.

Gideon was taken aback by the man's lack of tact.

But once Ormsbee stepped into the room and glanced back at Gideon, he felt the same tremor of unease he saw reflected in the younger man's eyes.

"She's gone," Ormsbee said ominously.

"What do you mean?"

"See for yourself." Ormsbee pointed and Gideon took a few steps to follow his line of vision.

The wardrobe against the far wall stood with its doors open and a few pieces of clothing lay on the carpet beneath it. Otherwise, the space was empty.

"We need to find Alex Winters and speak to the staff."

Half an hour later, Alex Winters sat in the dining room, looking supremely irritated that they'd interrupted a conversation he'd been having with Lady Dalrymple in Carthorpe's drawing room.

"Mr. Winters, where is your sister?" Ormsbee made no attempt to hide his irritation. His baritone voice had lowered to a near growl, and he didn't sit. He seemed unable to and had been pacing back in forth in front of Winters for several minutes while Gideon waited for him to begin the questioning.

Winters lifted his shoulders as if the whereabouts of his sister didn't interest him in the least. "She should be in her room. Or perhaps she's taking a walk. I know that we're not allowed to leave this blasted estate, but Carthorpe lands are quite extensive, and she's visited often enough to know them well."

"It's nearly dark, Mr. Winters, and we have yet to apprehend the individual responsible for Lord Lockhart's murder. Would your sister truly walk out on her own under such circumstances?"

Gideon understood why Ormsbee was drawing this out, but they were also losing time, and the inquest would go forward tomorrow, whether they had no information to provide to the coroner or not.

"I don't know where she is, Sergeant," Alex Winters finally said, then cocked his head as if in challenge.

Ormsbee shot Gideon a look and gave him a nod.

"She's gone, Mr. Winters," Gideon said. "Her clothes have been removed from her wardrobe. Her traveling trunk is missing."

"I know nothing about that." Winters' reply was too quick, too flippant.

"We've spoken to the staff," Ormsbee said, his voice low, almost menacing. "You were seen, Mr. Winters, strutting down the carriage drive with your sister. Who then boarded a carriage and departed down the lane." Ormsbee took a step closer to Winters. "Where did she go? Where did you send her?"

"I won't say."

"You realize this doesn't look good for you or your sister, Mr. Winters," Ormsbee bit out.

"Where is your overcoat that you wore when you arrived at Carthorpe?" Gideon asked.

Winters shot a frown at Gideon. "I'm assuming the staff have collected my winter coat and it is in my wardrobe. Have you asked them?"

"We have," Gideon told him. "It is missing, Mr. Winters. It was not found in your wardrobe, and the maid who's been tending to you room said she has not seen it since the night of Lord Lockhart's murder."

Winters shrugged as if entirely uninterested in the revelation. "Then someone took it. I'm sure it's not the first time a staff member filched an item of clothing."

Ormsbee took a step closer, standing directly in front of Winters. "You are a proven liar, Mr. Winters. Not two minutes ago, you told me you didn't know what happened to your sister, then you admit that you do know but won't reveal her whereabouts." Ormsbee notched his chin up as haughty as any aristocrat. "Now you say you do not know what happened to your overcoat, but I believe you do know."

"Believe what you like, Sergeant."

When Ormsbee took yet another step closer, Gideon shifted, preparing himself to stop Ormsbee before he might do something he'd regret. "I'm very close to taking you into custody, Mr. Winters. I need but another sliver of proof, and I will have you from murder. Consider that before you lie to us again."

Alex Winters had the audacity to smile. "As you like, Sergeant. But you'll find no proof because I've committed no crime."

Gideon leaned forward, forcing Winters' attention to him. "You did assist your sister to leave the grounds when everyone was asked not to."

"She was not under arrest, Inspector. Nor am I. Nor is anyone here. We've all been patient with your requests, but my patience, and my sister's, are at an end."

"Was it a personal matter that she needed to attend to?" Gideon asked more quietly, hoping to bring the conversation back to a less emotional keel.

"Yes," Winters admitted.

"Where is she?" Ormsbee pressed again. "Miss Winters has been requested to appear at the inquest tomorrow. Therefore, I must find her."

"If she received a summons," Winters told him, voice sharp, "then she will be there as requested, I'm certain."

"For her sake, I hope that's true," Ormsbee said, then spun away from Winters.

He seemed so perturbed that Gideon half expected to stride out of the room. But he stopped near the threshold, chest rising and falling as if he was attempting to steady himself.

Winters lifted his gaze to Gideon, then glanced back at Ormsbee. "Even with your Scotland Yard man here, you're out of your depths, Sergeant. Both of you are. This is far more tangled than either of you can imagine."

"Well, then you must help us untangle it. We need to find who did this, Mr. Winters," Gideon said, his voice taking a pleading tone he did not like.

"I wouldn't want an innocent man to go to prison, Mr. Winters," Ormsbee said coldly.

"How many times must a tell you? I had nothing to do with Henry's death."

"We'll see you at the inquest tomorrow, will we not, Mr. Winters?" Gideon asked.

"Certainly, and I will tell them everything that I've told both of you."

"Except for the whereabouts of your sister," Ormsbee snapped. Then he swung his arm, waving Winters away. "Go on, back to your room. Do whatever you plan to do. I'll continue looking for your overcoat and your sister."

Alex Winters stood and couldn't quite hide a satisfied little grin. "Do as you must, Sergeant," he said before striding from the room, head high.

"Oh, I will," Ormsbee murmured.

Chapter Thirteen

As evening descended, Gideon set out to find Electra.

He decided to start with her guest chamber and then visit Lady Alice's chamber, who he guessed Electra may have checked on or perhaps shared a meal with.

Gideon's stomach growled, but he ignored it. He was used to being so busy with work that he forgot to eat. He'd go down to the kitchen for a bite later, but he was worried about Electra. She was unsettled in a way he'd never seen her before.

When they'd met again last year, she'd been seemed so self-possessed. It was one of the characteristics he admired most about her. Electra did not balk at challenges. In fact, he'd learned some of his own self-possession from her.

As if he'd summoned her with his thoughts, she approached from the opposite end of the upstairs hallway, looking fatigued. The lightest half-moon shadows hung under her vivid blue-green eyes.

"I was just coming to find you," she said.

His first thought was that they should return to her chamber and have the staff send up dinner trays for each of them, but he was due to convene with Ormsbee in ten minutes. Though perhaps that presented an opportunity.

"I'm to convene with Ormsbee in the dining room. Perhaps you could join us. The staff could bring all of us a simple repast there."

"Nothing extravagant." She laid a hand across her middle. "Bread and cheese. Maybe some pickle."

It was the kind of simple meal they'd shared when they were younger and Erasmus worked late nights.

"Nothing extravagant," Gideon agreed. "Will you come join us?"

"Will Ormsbee want me there?"

Gideon shrugged, too eager to speak with her and spend time with her to worry overly about Ormsbee. "We can eat first. All I intended was to speak to him about the interviews I conducted in preparation for tomorrow's inquest. You attended some of those interviews and could provide your insights."

She hesitated. "There are things I've seen, Gideon. Not... with my physical senses, as you might say. I can't tell him any of that, can I?"

He thought of Mrs. Markland and how reticent Ormsbee had been to give credence to any of her claims.

"What you asked Lady Honoria about," Gideon surmised. "You wouldn't tell her who'd seen her and Alex Winters in the conservatory."

Electra nodded. "Lady Dalrymple saw them, and I saw it during a sitting we conducted together."

And Lady Honoria hadn't denied it. What Electra had seen through Lady Dalrymple's memories was accurate. The notion of such powers was still uncanny to Gideon, but he couldn't deny that Electra seemed to have insights that it made more than logical sense for her to possess.

"I don't know how much you trust my abilities," she said, as if she could hear his thoughts.

Maybe she could.

"I'm not demanding that you accept them or tell me that you believe me. But I will just say that I have seen things that are odd." She glanced behind her, as if worried someone might overhear them.

"Let's go downstairs," he urged.

They descended the stairs together and entered the dining room. All of Ormsbee's notes and documents were laid out on the table, but the staff were laying out plates and cutlery at the edge of them. A footman carried in a terrine of soup, then poured glasses of wine.

"Could we add a place setting?" Gideon asked the young man, who nodded, left the room, and returned with another plate, glass, and cutlery set.

Ormsbee hadn't arrived yet, but Gideon and Electra took seats at a corner together.

"You've seen things, you say," Gideon asked, ignoring the glass of wine and getting up to pour himself a cup of tea.

"Would you bring me one too?" Electra asked.

Gideon smiled as he stood at the tea urn with his back to her.

"Do you want to hear?" she asked with a bit of uncharacteristic uncertainty.

"All of it. Yes, I do." He did not say *I may not believe it,* didn't even add *I will try to believe,* but he would always listen to whatever Electra wished to tell him.

During the case they were involved in together in November, her insights had been crucial. Her feelings, senses, visions, whatever she called them. So, yes, he wanted to hear them now.

At this moment, he didn't know who'd killed Lord Lockhart.

His suspicions veered between several possibilities. Alex Winters was the one who was being put forward by everyone that he'd spoken to, it seemed. Yet something didn't sit right with him about that answer. It was an easy answer. Even a seemingly reasonable one. But it didn't feel right. Like a key meant to fit a lock, yet once you twisted it, you found it to be a similar key missing certain grooves. It was the wrong key after all.

"During the séance..." Electra began.

Gideon felt himself stiffen and told himself not to, but Electra noticed and arched one dark brow. He still wasn't comfortable with that word. Still wasn't comfortable with the idea of trying to contact spirits. It seemed distasteful to him somehow. Shouldn't the dead be allowed to rest in peace?

"Go on," he encouraged. "I'm listening."

"During the séance, I sat next to Alice. Initially, she'd hoped that I would sit next to Henry."

Gideon's brow furrowed. "Why did she want that?"

"She asked me to look into Henry's mind and see if I could detect his true intentions toward her."

"She doubted his intentions? In what regard? To marry her?"

Electra shook her head. "I think she doubted him altogether. After I walked in on their altercation, she denied that he'd ever truly harmed her, yet I suspected she wasn't being entirely forthcoming. Perhaps she feared him too much to reveal everything."

"It sounds as if she didn't trust him."

"She wanted to know if he wished to marry her for her dowry. Her father was fond of him, she said, and she seemed disinclined to end the engagement, despite the way he treated her."

Gideon took a swallow of tea. "So she wanted you to find something to give her a reason to end the engagement?"

"I made her promise she would if I learned anything that might put her in danger."

"But Lord Lockhart never came to the séance."

"No, and so I joined hands with Alice instead, as she was sitting nearest on my left-hand side. When I touched her, I saw an image of Alex Winters in her mind."

Gideon set his teacup down and turned more fully toward her. "And what was he doing?"

Electra licked her lips, hesitating. "He was in her bedchamber. He looked...arrogant."

"Does he ever look any other way?" Gideon couldn't help but ask.

Electra scoffed. "Alice seemed displeased with him. It was a brief flash, but I got the sense that there was conflict between them."

"Something romantic?"

"I can't say."

"But he was in her bedchamber alone with her?"

"Perhaps she feels a comfortable familiarity with him," she mused.

Gideon couldn't help but recall that Electra had invited him into her bedchamber without a second thought. He swigged down more tea rather than let his mind wander down that path.

"Did you see anything else?" he asked in a quieter tone.

"The images shifted to what I can only presume was another memory. A different day and place. Alice observed Lord Lockhart with someone. He and the lady were on their knees as he embraced her."

Gideon leaned in, intrigued. "A lady? Who?"

Electra lifted her teacup and sipped, as if she wished to delay telling him the rest. "It was Lady Honoria."

Gideon's jaw dropped unbidden before he snapped it shut. "Your question about whether Lord Lockhart was someone who'd offer her comfort. That's what you were getting at."

"Yes, I thought she might reveal something, but all I sensed is that she did not like Henry much at all. In fact, I sensed that she hated him."

Gideon tapped the table, thinking about the connections between the various people at Carthorpe Hall. "Have you spoken to Lady Alice about what you saw?"

"No. I considered doing so, but she seems fragile right now."

Ormsbee strode into the room and looked taken aback to find Electra sitting with Gideon.

"Forgive me for the delay, Pierce." He flicked his gaze between them. "I see Miss Poole is joining us."

Gideon turned to the sergeant. "Miss Poole sat in on a few of the interviews I conducted. Namely with Lady Alice, the lady's maid who provided her alibi, and Lady Honoria." Gideon gestured toward her. "Her insights proved crucial when we worked together in the past."

Ormsbee stared at Electra a moment, then nodded. "Very well."

He took a seat where a third place setting had been laid out and immediately used the ladle near the soup tureen to fill his bowl. Gideon and Electra did the same, taking a bit of the bread that had been set out for them too.

"Well, carry on," Ormsbee said, reaching for his wine glass. "What insights do you have to share, Miss Poole?"

Electra flicked a look Gideon's way, dabbed her mouth with a napkin, then said, "I had a private conversation with Lady Dalrymple."

Ormsbee stilled a spoonful of soup halfway to his lips. "Did you indeed? And what did you learn from her?"

"She's frightened. The night before Lord Lockhart's murder—"

"Yes," Ormsbee said, interrupting her. "She fell in the hedge maze while seeking a specter she claims to have seen." Ormsbee scoffed. "She seems rather preoccupied with such nonsense."

Gideon watched Electra bristle at that characterization. When it was clear Ormsbee was finished, she drew in a breath.

"She did fall," Electra continued, ignoring Ormsbee's comment, "but she has now recalled that she didn't simply lose her footing. She was pushed."

Ormsbee stilled again. "She didn't mention that when I questioned her."

"I believe it's a memory that she's only just recalled."

"Does she have any idea who might have pushed her?" Gideon asked.

"No, except that..." Electra turned a look his way. Gideon suspected she was hesitating because what she knew was a detail she'd extracted from Lady Dalrymple's memories. "She's quite certain it was a man with dark hair."

Ormsbee tightened his hold on the napkin near his plate. "Like Mr. Winters."

"Mr. Lockhart's hair would look dark in dim lighting as well," Gideon pointed out. "And several of the footmen have dark hair as well."

Ormsbee drew in a breath and smiled grimly. "Any notion why a footman would wish to push an elderly lady to the ground in the middle of a hedge maze, Pierce?"

"No," Gideon admitted. "Why would Mr. Winters wish to do so?"

Ormsbee shrugged. "Perhaps he was planning what happened the following evening, finding the perfect spot."

Electra let out a little gasp, almost too quiet to hear, but Gideon heard it. He shot her a questioning look.

"We found a depression in the soil." Electra looked at Gideon expectantly, as if urging him to pick up the thread.

"Yes, Inspector Pierce told me he found a hole that seems to have been dug in the hedge maze." Ormsbee sounded as disinterested as he'd been when Gideon told him.

"It's very near where Lord Lockhart was murdered," Electra pointed out.

Ormsbee's brows bent low. "And you said the size was...?"

"Perhaps eight to ten inches long and about half as wide," Gideon told him. "I think perhaps something was dug up there."

"Or buried and then dug up again," Electra murmured.

Ormsbee's dark eyes took on a shiny glint and his mouth twitched under his mustache. "So it was a plot all along. Someone buried what? The murder weapon? To have it at hand after luring Lord Lockhart into the hedge maze?"

"Why bury a murder weapon?" Gideon asked. "Seems easier to slip it into your pocket on your way to perpetrate the crime."

"Maybe they only had access to it at a certain moment and didn't want to keep it with them or risk it being found in their possession."

Ormsbee settled back against his chair, crossing his arms. "And we still don't bloody know what *it* is."

Gideon's pulse quickened. "The shard," he said to Ormsbee. "Do you still have it?"

"Of course." Ormsbee flicked the edge of his suit coat aside and slid two fingers into his waistcoat pocket. He pulled out the chunk of glass and laid it in his opposite palm, holding it out to Gideon.

Gideon glanced at Electra.

"Might I see it, Sergeant?"

Ormsbee offered it to her. Electra took it into her bare hand, examining it, then placed her fingers around it. She stared at the polished grain of the dining room table, saying nothing.

"It's…" she started, but her voice died off.

Gideon wondered if she was seeing something he and Ormsbee could not. If the glass had a story to tell, they needed to know what it was.

"Yes?" Ormsbee prompted when she said nothing more.

"Heavy," she finally replied. "It feels heavier than glass somehow. It's odd." She passed the shard to Gideon.

She was right. It was heavier than the glass of a wine bottle or a vase. Leaded glass, perhaps. Or crystal.

"I wonder why we didn't find more of it," Ormsbee mused. "Withers had spoken to the footman, Hobbes, on the first night. The young man who initially found Lord Lockhart. He never mentioned seeing any glass, yet this was found within Lockhart's clothing."

"Lockhart says his brother was not alive when they found him," Gideon said. "He said the viscount's eyes were open and unseeing once they got him inside. James Lockhart says his brother never uttered a word."

"If he was alive, it was by the merest breath," Ormsbee said with a grimace. "And, no, he said nothing discernible to Hobbes either. Moaned a bit, he said, then fell silent."

"Who do we have without alibis for the time of Lord Lockhart's murder?" Gideon asked.

"Most of them claim they were up in their rooms preparing for the séance," Ormsbee said. "And you verified that Lady Alice was via her lady's maid. None of the other guests were assisted by a maid or valet, except for Lord Lockhart, earlier in the evening."

"James Lockhart did admit to us that he and Lady Honoria were out having a stroll, though she never mentioned that detail when we questioned her. And Electra saw Winters outside with

Lord Lockhart when she went inside. He didn't enter the house until ten or less minutes before midnight." Gideon clarified.

Ormsbee's mouth tipped in a half-smile. "Last man known to have seen Lockhart. Known to have rowed with him hours before his death. Owed him an enormous sum. He has motive."

"Is debt a sufficient motive?" Electra asked.

Gideon and Ormsbee both turned her way.

"What could Lockhart have truly done?"

"Bankrupted him," Ormsbee snapped.

"I think there's more to it," Gideon said, voicing that nagging doubt that plagued him about Winters' guilt.

Ormsbee let out a frustrated sigh. "In what regard, Pierce?"

"It all seems too simple."

Ormsbee barked out a laugh. "Nothing about this lot of individuals seems simple to me, Inspector." He drew a circle on the table with his fingertip and then tapped the spot. "The séance seems key to me."

"How so?" Electra asked.

"Whoever did this thing knew the séance would distract almost everyone." Ormsbee pointed at Electra. "You say that several participants were in the room fairly early. Lady Alice. Lady Dalrymple. When I spoke to Lady Dalrymple, she told me that Lady Alice had arranged for the séance on quite short notice—"

"Alice?" Electra cut in. "No, Alice told me that Lady Dalrymple arranged for Mrs. Markland to come."

Ormsbee frowned at her and pulled out his notepad, flipping through the pages. "When I questioned Lady Dalrymple, she told me that Alice arranged for Mrs. Markland to come. She'd consulted her previously, apparently."

"But Mrs. Markland told us that Lady Dalrymple had written to her," Gideon pointed out.

Gideon noted Electra's confusion, the way she shook her

head as if the two divergent claims from the two ladies made no sense to her.

"Why would either of them lie?" she asked.

"It doesn't seem as simple as a misunderstanding," Gideon said, not wishing to call either lady a liar, yet knowing that one certainly was. "We have a strange discrepancy."

"Perhaps Lady Dalrymple asked Alice to handle matters," Electra said softly, more to herself than either of them.

"Lady Honoria came into the room a bit later, you said, Miss Poole?" Ormsbee asked, changing the subject.

"Yes."

"Can you remind me of the order of arrival of each guest?" he asked.

"Alice and Lady Dalrymple came when Mrs. Markland and I were in the room. Then Ophelia Winters came. Her brother a short time later. Then James Lockhart soon after. And finally Lady Honoria arrived at almost the midnight hour."

Ormsbee arched his brows as he looked over at Gideon. It comported with what they'd already heard from other witnesses, as he would expect. Electra had no reason to lie.

"I don't think Lady Honoria would be physically capable of taking down a man of Lord Lockhart's size with a single blow," Gideon opined.

Ormsbee nodded. "Nor Miss Winters, so we must consider the gentlemen. Lockhart and Winters. And Winters is the more obvious suspect."

"Yes," Gideon said. He could not deny it, despite a persistent sense that Alex Winters, if he struck the blow, was not alone in perpetrating Lord Lockhart's murder.

Chapter Fourteen

The inquest was set to convene at ten in the morning at the local meeting house, and Electra followed Gideon out to the Carthorpe carriage that would carry them into town.

Ormsbee, who'd been provided a guest room at Carthorpe the previous night, had journeyed into the village early. Then the Carthorpe coachman had taken those gathered in the house. Alex Winters and Lady Dalrymple went first. Ophelia Winters had still not been located, and her brother refused every attempt by Ormsbee and Gideon to persuade him to reveal her whereabouts. Alice, Honoria, and James Lockhart traveled over together next, and then the carriage returned to convey Gideon and Electra.

Though there were two benches in the carriage and room for at least four, after Gideon handed her up, he settled on the bench next to her. It reminded her of their time spent in a hansom cabs the previous autumn during the Becknell investigation.

She told herself she shouldn't like being close to him as much as she did.

"There's little doubt about the verdict, is there?" Electra asked as they waited for the coachman to return and start them on their journey.

He'd been staring out the window on his side of the carriage as if lost in thought.

At her question, he looked over and his expression lightened. "No, there's no doubt they will return a verdict of murder." Tapping his fingers against his leg, he added, "Ormsbee is keen to arrest Mr. Winters." He watched her intently, as if to gauge her reaction.

Electra realized he was under the impression that Alex Winters meant far more to her than he did.

As they looked at each other, a rap against the carriage door made her jump, and they turned to find one of the footmen standing nearby.

He opened the door and directed his gaze at Gideon. "There's something you must see, Inspector."

"What is it?"

"Mr. Jenks has it secured in the dining room. He thought he might catch the sergeant, but he'd already gone."

Gideon climbed out of the carriage and then offered a hand while Electra stepped down. The footman took off at a quick clip and they followed. An anxious tension twisted in her middle as they stepped inside Carthorpe Hall. It reminded Electra of the way the air had felt the night of the séance. There was a portentous sort of weightiness to the air.

The footman didn't enter the dining room, but stood outside the door for them to go in first.

"We found it hidden in the stable's tack room," Mr. Jenks said.

"I swear we'd already searched the stables, sir," the footman who'd entered behind them added.

They'd laid out the overcoat on the dining room table.

Gideon approached and immediately checked the lining, which Electra could see was a dark purple satin. Then he ran his hand along the line of buttons on the front, then picked up each sleeve. Electra saw his shoulders stiffen.

"Can we get the housemaid in here who tidied the guest rooms, particularly Mr. Winters'?"

"She's here, sir," the footman said from the threshold.

"Hello, Annie," Gideon said, "we spoke a bit yesterday. I asked you about Mr. Winters' overcoat that he wore when he arrived at Carthorpe." He gestured at the coat. "Could you take a look at this one and tell me whether you think it's the same one he was wearing that day?"

The maid stepped forward and examined the piece of clothing carefully, lifting the arm, examining the cuff, and then running her fingers along the collar to look at the lining and the stitching at the collar's edge.

"It looks very much like the same one, sir," she said finally, hands clasped in front of her. "The same notched collar, the same plum satin lining, the same stitching pattern as the one I brushed off in Mr. Winters' room last week."

"Thank you very much," Gideon said. Then he slid an object out of his pocket, lifted the arm of the coat closest to him, and compared what Electra could see was a button in his hand to the ones on the coat.

Even from a distance, Electra could see that they matched.

He looked back at her, every muscle of his face tensed. "We should take this to Ormsbee."

"The coat?"

"He'll want to see it with his own eyes, I believe."

"I can bundle it for you, sir," Annie offered.

Gideon nodded, and she sprang into action, folding the coat neatly until it was a manageable size, then handing it to Gideon like a parcel she'd just prepared for shipping.

He carried it out to the carriage, and climbed inside again. Gideon laid the overcoat on the bench opposite them and sat beside Electra again.

"We'll be cutting it close," he said, lifting his pocket watch out for a glance.

"Will Ormsbee take him into custody now?" Electra asked.

"I think he will, but he may wait until the inquest is concluded." There was a sharpness in his tone. He wasn't pleased by the new piece of evidence. He stared across the carriage at it as if it was a loathsome thing.

"What's troubling you?" Electra asked softly.

At first, he gave no reply, just braced his hands on his knees and glowered at the finely made men's overcoat.

"What if you touched it?" he said in a low tone, almost a whisper. "Could you discover who put in the stables?"

"Possibly."

"Would you be willing to?"

"Of course." She inched forward on the bench and reached out her hand to lay it on the fine wool of the coat. Closing her eyes, she summoned whatever it might tell her, trying to focus on the question of who may have touched it last.

At first nothing came. That familiar tingle along her spine or at the nape of her neck that often served as a harbinger of images arising never came. She smoothed her hand along the fabric and laid it flat against the lapel.

An image flashed, then lingered. Alex Winters stepping inside the front door of Carthorpe Hall, then being greeted by Mr. Jenks. The butler took the coat from him, and a figure approached behind him. Lord Lockhart. Winters turned to greet him with a smile. But when Lockhart turned to lead Winters across the hall, Winters' face became a mask of barely concealed loathing.

Her own chest filled with a fiery ache and she felt an echo of the hatred behind the look on Winters' face.

"Electra?"

Gideon's voice pulled her back, like a rope thrown when she' gone in too deep. He laid a hand gently on her arm.

She opened her eyes, removed her hand, and settled back against the carriage bench. Sliding her fingers against the fabric, breathing in the enclosed air filled with the scent of Gideon's shaving soap, she pulled all of her focus out of the feelings, the images.

"Are you all right?"

"Yes, I'm fine."

"You don't...look fine."

"Do I not?" Electra turned to look into Gideon's eyes, the light brown like amber in the sunlight.

"You were trembling and you grimaced as if you were facing your worst enemy." Gideon tipped his head, studying her. "You're flushed. Does it always cause you distress to do it?"

"No, not at all. It was that I felt someone's feelings. Alex Winters' feelings, I think."

"Did you see who put his coat in the stables?"

"No, I'm sorry. I didn't." It felt terrible to disappoint him when she'd been so pleased that he'd asked her at all. "I saw Alex Winters though. Maybe it was the day he arrived at Carthorpe last week. The butler greeted him and then Lord Lockhart approached."

Electra paused to catch her breath. A wave of that loathing she'd felt washed through her again. "Alex hated Lockhart."

Gideon flinched. "How do you know that? Did he say it?"

"No, I felt it, and in the vision, I saw his face. The one he didn't show to Lockhart."

Gideon shook his head. "I cannot shake the sense that none of it is right. Does it feel right to you?"

Electra stared at the overcoat with the missing button. "The footman did say they'd searched the stables previously."

"And everyone we've spoken to has little good to say about Alex Winters."

"Shouldn't that all add up to his guilt?" Electra knew Gideon was much like her father and often trusted his "gut" to guide him during a case, often allowing him to push aside obfuscation and false leads from witnesses.

"You'd think it would feel as satisfying as a puzzle piece fitting into place." Gideon's jaw tightened in a way that told her nothing about it felt satisfying to him. "Ormsbee will take him into custody and call the case solved, no doubt."

"But that doesn't mean we have to stop inquiring."

Gideon lifted a brow and looked over at her with a half-smile. "You agree with me then?"

"I trust your instincts."

He leaned toward her bit so that their shoulders brushed.

"Thank you, and I yours."

"Even my gifts?" Electra said it with a bit of cheek, but his answer mattered to her a great deal.

"I trust you," he said earnestly.

And that was enough.

THEY ARRIVED at the meeting house with only minutes to spare before the commencement of the inquest, and Electra was surprised to find the space nearly overwhelmed with spectators. Yet it was smallish room, and two tables took up a good deal of it. One was where a silver-haired man, who she assumed was the coroner, sat and the other held the body of Lord Lockhart, covered in a pristine white sheet. To the left of that table, the gentlemen of the jury were assembled in their seats.

At the only other inquest she'd ever attended, the body of the deceased had been laid out in an ante room, but having Lockhart there in front of them added a morbid sort of solemn gravity to the proceedings. Few people spoke, and the room was quiet but for footsteps as people found their seats.

Almost as soon as she found two chairs empty situated side by side, she sat down, placing her reticule on the other chair to save it for Gideon. She pivoted in her seat, trying to spot the others from Carthorpe. Lady Dalrymple sat next to Alice and Honoria, with James at her side. Alex Winters sat separate from the others, his face grim, jaw tight. She didn't, however, see Ophelia Winters.

A moment later, the clock struck ten and the coroner knocked a gavel against the oak table where he sat. Gideon had approached Ormsbee to speak to him. Electra watched as he held the folded coat up, no doubt describing how it had been found by a staff member and that he'd matched it to the button found in the hedge maze. He slipped said button from his pocket and handed it over to Ormsbee.

Ormsbee leaned toward Gideon and seemed to whisper something in his ear. Gideon nodded and then found her in the crowd, coming over to claim the chair beside her.

"Ormsbee wants to handle Winters after his testimony and doesn't want anyone to alert him, in case he tries to flee like his sister did."

With the inquest called to order, the coroner first called Constable Withers, who spoke of being called upon by a messenger sent by Mr. Jenks. He'd been roused from his bed to answer the door and the note informed him that Lord Henry Lockhart had been found bleeding in the hedge maze of his estate.

"What did you observe when you entered the house, Constable?"

"Most everyone was gathered in a particular room." The young man paused, look at the juryman, and said, "I was given to understand that they were all attending a séance in the drawing room."

A little titter went around the room. People leaned in to whisper to those sitting next to them. The house's infamy about its ghostly inhabitants would make such a detail even more intriguing.

"Where was Lord Lockhart when you arrived?"

"He'd been brought in by several gentlemen, two of the guests, and one footman, who carried him up his bedroom where he was meant to convalesce, but unfortunately, he was deceased." Withers gave a look that was appropriately regretful at that declaration.

"Did you examine the hedge maze where the deceased was found?"

"I did, sir."

"And did you collect any evidence or find any indications of what had occurred?"

Withers paused and then said, "The shrubbery was bent, as if perhaps someone had fallen into it. It was past midnight and difficult to see by lantern light, but I did touch the hedge and caught a bit of blood on my fingers. I found no weapon. I did, however, find a button."

"Yes, I believe Sergeant Ormsbee will testify regarding the button. That will be all, Constable."

Ormsbee was called next and succinctly recounted all he'd discovered during his time at Carthorpe Hall, including details of his interviews with staff members and its various inhabitants and guests. What he did not mention was the suspicion and evidence that seemed to be gathering around Alex Winters, but he did discuss and display the button found at the site of Lord Lockhart's attack.

After he'd finished his testimony to the coroner and jury, Ormsbee gestured to Gideon to follow him. Electra followed, though Gideon hadn't explicitly invited her to do so, and they made their way through the row of chairs, trying to cause the least disturbance to others observing the proceedings.

Ormsbee led them to a small, dusty side room and turned to Gideon expectantly, not even sparing Electra a glance. His eyes fixed on the bundle in Gideon's hands.

"Let's have a look," Ormsbee said, then reached into his pocket to pull out the button.

"It's the same," Gideon affirmed, lifting the overcoat out to Ormsbee. "I've confirmed that it belongs to Alex Winters. The housemaid who saw to his garments during his stay will testify to that."

"I believe you, Pierce," Ormsbee said as he found the sleeve where the button should have been and compared it to the matching one on the opposite sleeve. "You know how it is. Sometimes one must see a thing for oneself."

"Of course." Gideon said, then shot Electra a look that said Ormsbee's insistence irked him only a little.

Ormsbee drew in a sharp breath, slipped the loose button back into his coat pocket, and turned to face them both. "We've got him. I'll speak to Withers. We'll take him quietly as soon as he's finished his testimony. Better than doing so back at Carthorpe with the whole household as an audience."

"And you feel confident about Winters being the culprit?" Gideon asked the question with a lightness Electra knew he did not feel.

"I do," Ormsbee said, almost defensively. "We have multiple witnesses who say he and Lockhart were in conflict. There is the matter of the enormous sum he owed Lockhart and could not repay." Ormsbee locked eyes with Electra for the first time. "Miss Poole places him out of doors with Lockhart within the timeframe when the viscount was murdered." Ormsbee patted his coat pocket with the flat of his hand. "And we now have a piece of evidence that links him to the site of Lockhart's murder. Not to mention that the coat itself was hidden, though Winters made no mention of the garment ever being missing. We had to learn that from the staff."

Rather than express any of his reservations, Gideon asked, "Do you need my assistance at all?"

"No." Ormsbee assessed him a moment and then stuck out his hand to shake Gideon's. "But I do thank you for your aid in bringing this case to a successful close. Once we're back at Carthorpe, we can convene about final details before you return to London."

"Very good."

Ormsbee gave Electra the briefest of nods before leaving her and Gideon alone.

"Well, that's that," Gideon said, his tone unusually taut.

"Should we go out and watch the rest of the proceedings?" Electra asked him.

He nodded, but before any of them moved toward the door, Lady Honoria pushed it open. "Miss Poole, will you please come and help Alice?"

"Of course." Electra had time for one glance back at Gideon before Honoria took her hand and tugged her out into the inquest proceedings. She led her along the edge of the room quickly, and not a few gazes turned their way with interest.

Finally, they left through the meeting hall's door and stepped out into the sunny morning light. Alice stood with her back to the building as if bracing herself against it.

She looked frighteningly pale and tears streaked down her cheeks.

"Alice, what's happened?"

"They lifted the cover on Henry's body," Honoria said

quietly beside her. "It was a quite a shock." Honoria's voice quivered a little, but she was not sobbing as she had been the night Lockhart was found.

"We should get her to the carriage," Honoria urged. "Will you accompany her back to Carthorpe, Miss Poole?"

Electra nodded, wrapped an arm around Alice's narrow shoulders, and led her to Carthorpe carriage, which waited only a few steps away at the edge of the pavement.

"Let's get you home, Alice," she said in a soothing tone.

Alice seemed almost senseless, letting Electra guide her the way a child might, and Electra could feel the tremors racking her body. When they reached the carriage, Alice looked back at her sister. "Are you not coming, Honoria?"

"I'm going to stay. I'll accompany James back after the jury's verdict. I don't think it will be long."

"Very well," Alice whispered the words, then turned to climb up into the carriage. She gripped the vehicle's frame and wobbled a bit as she placed her boot on the step. Once she was inside, she settled heavily onto one of the benches. Electra took the one opposite her.

"The verdict will be murder," Alice said, her voice low and reedy. "But we still don't know who. Likely someone in that room we just walked out of."

"Alice..." Electra licked her lips and considered ways to tell Alice what Ormsbee would be doing, even as the carriage started into motion to carry them back to Carthorpe. "Ormsbee is..." She wasn't certain why she hesitated. Perhaps because she wasn't at all certain what was truly between Alice and Winters. Did she care for him?

"Yes?" Alice's blinked, and her eyes looked suddenly less listless.

"He's taking Alex Winters into custody for Lord Lockhart's murder."

Alice's eyes blew wide and every muscle in her body seemed to sag as she lifted a hand to her mouth. Tears welled in her eyes. "Why would Alex do such a thing? Henry was his friend. *I* was his friend."

Electra reached out to lay her gloved hands atop Alice's. "I'm sorry, Alice. But now perhaps everyone at the hall can feel safe again." Even as she spoke the words, trying to offer solace, Gideon's doubts whispered in her mind.

"He really is gone then," Alice said, her expression bleak. "Some part of me could hold on to denying it until I saw him lying there. Colorless. Lifeless. And now to hear that Alex—" She turned a terrified look toward Electra. "Is it my fault?"

"How could it be?"

"I insisted we invite the Winters. I wanted Henry and Alex to reconcile. I wanted to see Ophelia."

Alice lifted both her gloved hands, slipping free of Electra's gentle hold, and clasped them over her mouth.

"Do you know where Ophelia is?" The question was out before Electra could consider whether it was poorly timed. If Ophelia was in the meeting house, she hadn't seen her.

Alice shook her head. "I do not. I cannot think why she left as abruptly as she did, except out of fear. Remaining at Carthorpe, knowing that someone we know, that we trusted... I did trust Alex, as cutting and difficult as he could be. I wouldn't have invited him if I'd known."

"You cannot blame yourself," Electra insisted, and the vehemence of it touched something in her—her own guilt about her mother's death, that she couldn't have kept her from the awful fate she'd suffered.

"I think I needed to see him as I did, laid out on that table." She reached down and patted the reticule she carried. Its seams were stretched into a squarish shape, and Electra suspected her ever-present sketchbook was inside. "I've been working on a drawing of him, one I started months ago. That's how I shall remember him."

"Would you allow me to see?" Electra recalled her being rather shy about sharing her artwork with others, but occasionally she'd convinced Alice to give her a peek. She hadn't done so once since Electra had been at Carthorpe though.

To her surprise, Alice lifted the sketchbook from her bag and flipped to a page at the far end. She held the pages open and showed Electra a very rough sketch that even in a few lines was a clear representation of Lockhart's slicked back hair and wide-set eyes.

"It will look much better when it's finished, of course."

"You've already captured him well," Electra said honestly. "You're very talented."

Alice gave a half-hearted half-smile at the compliment and then turned to look out the carriage window. "I must focus on those I have left. I worry about Father. I worry about my aunt. She's been so fretful since her fall that night you arrived. We should have brought her back to Carthorpe with us. I never wanted her to attend the inquest."

"Perhaps we should have."

"I understand she spoke to you privately," Alice said with a curious edge to her voice. "I knew she'd be fascinated with you because of her current preoccupation with spiritualism."

"Yes, I did speak to her." Electra knew Alice was close to her aunt and she considered telling Alice of her ladyship's fears. Yet if she'd wanted Alice to know, certainly Lady Dalrymple would have told her.

"She's not ill, is she?" Alice looked suddenly terror-struck. "It would be just like her not to tell any of us she's close to, especially in the present circumstances."

"If she is ill, she didn't confide that to me." Electra clasped her hands together and admitted. "She wanted me to do a psychical reading for her."

Alice looked suddenly intrigued. "Did she indeed? Were you able to divine anything for her?"

"I think her fall that night had her feeling a bit shaken."

"Yes, I imagine it did. And she'd worked herself up so with her talk of the Carthorpe ghost." Alice looked out the window again, smiling now as she spoke of Lady Dalrymple. "I doubt she saw anything at all out there that night and simply stumbled on a root or bit of gravel."

It was precisely what Lady Dalrymple insisted had not happened.

"I think she may have seen someone," Electra said quietly.

"Oh, you do believe in ghosts after all?" Alice teased.

"I don't think it was a ghost."

Alice cocked her head. "You mean someone was on the grounds?" She looked pensive a moment. "Perhaps it was Eggers, the groundskeeper."

Electra shrugged. "Perhaps." Yet she couldn't help thinking of the depression in the earth that she and Gideon had found and its proximity to the spot where Lockhart had been attacked by Alex Winters. Maybe it had been him Lady Dalrymple had seen crouching down in the maze that night, but doing what? Hiding something? The weapon he'd use the next night?

"Did my aunt mention that it was an older, burly man? Eggers has a beard too."

Electra shook her head. "No, it seemed to be a young man."

Alice looked pensive for a moment. "Goodness, maybe she really did see the Carthorpe ghost. They say he's a young man with dark hair."

Electra knew the man she'd seen in Lady Dalrymple's memories was not a specter. His breath had puffed out in front of him in the cold night air. It *could* have been Alex Winters.

Glimpsing him in Lady Dalrymple's memories, shrouded in darkness, it was simply too hard to tell.

"When my aunt returns, let us all take tea together by the fire," Alice suggested softly.

"That sounds lovely." Yet even as she said the words, an odd tension rushed through her, a feeling of doubt. As if Gideon's own doubts had settled inside her.

What if Winters wasn't the killer? What if, once all the guests and servants returned, the killer still walked among them at Carthorpe?

Back inside the hall, Mr. Jenks informed Alice that her father had been asking for her.

"Has he worsened? Have you sent for Dr. Brownlow?"

"We've sent for him, my lady."

Alice clutched at Electra's gloved hand. "Will you accompany me? I suddenly feel dizzy."

"Of course." Electra held onto her arm, clasped around her own as they ascended the stairs side by side.

Once inside the earl's bedchamber, they found him lying with his eyes closed. He seemed to be sleeping peacefully.

"Father," Alice said, as she shed the cloak she'd not had time to take off. She handed both the garment and her reticule to Electra, who settled them on a chair not far from Lord Carthorpe's bed.

"Father, it's Alice," she said a little more loudly. "I'm here now."

The nobleman's eyes fluttered open and he smiled to see her. "Ah, Alice. I was asking for you."

"Are you feeling worse?" she asked as she perched on the edge of his sick bed.

"No, my dear, only wondering where you all went off to. Where's Honoria and the young man?"

"They all had a matter to attend to in the village, Father. I went too, but I decided to return early to see you. I had a feeling you needed me," she said with a soft smile.

Electra knew it wasn't true. Alice had left the proceedings because she'd been overwrought, but her father looked so pleased to be the reason for her return that she could understand why the little fib emerged so easily.

Alice stood and began fluffing her father's pillow and rearranging his blankets.

Electra recalled seeing Alice's memory of being in her father's room and feeling such disappointment and anger. But none of that seemed visible on her face or in her demeanor now.

Electra felt suddenly superfluous. "Is there anything I may do?"

Alice turned back and shook her head. "I'll sit with him for a while," she said quietly. "I shan't keep you, but thank you for accompanying me to his room."

"Of course." Electra turned to make her way out of the room and caught her gown on the edge of Alice's cloak. The garment shifting, sending the reticule underneath tumbling off the chair. "I'm sorry," Electra murmured as she bent to retrieve the reticule. When she did, the sketchbook, which had been sticking out, slipped onto the carpet.

Electra let out a little huff at her own clumsiness and scooped up the sketchbook too, its pages fanning out and flipping past as she righted it. She glimpsed a series of sketches that covered page after page. All of the same face, but with varying expressions. A man's face, but not the one she was expecting to see.

She settled the cloak, sketchbook, and reticule back on the chair, then she made her way out of the room. In the hall, she stood unmoving for a moment, a hand resting at her throat, feeling the racing of her pulse.

She needed to speak to Gideon.

Chapter Fifteen

Electra didn't intend to go down to tea until she spoke to Gideon. She knew that one of the maids would likely come for her if she missed the hour Alice told her they would sit down in the drawing room with Lady Dalrymple. Yet Electra remained upstairs, pacing her guest chamber and watching from her window that looked out on the front of the house and its carriage circle. Lady Dalrymple returned first, alone. Of course, she'd traveled to the inquest with Alex Winters, but he would now be in the constabulary's custody.

Still, there was no sign of Gideon. She sat and opened the journal he'd gifted her at Christmas, noting down her experiences since arriving at Carthorpe, including what she'd observed and sensed with her abilities.

At one point, she heard voices in the hall and stuck her head out, but it was merely Dr. Brownlow, who'd come to check on Lord Carthorpe.

Finally, another carriage arrived, and she took a relieved breath when Gideon stepped down from it. She rushed downstairs and found that he'd beelined for the dining room. He was already inside conferring with Ormsbee. The moment he spotted her on the threshold, he'd seemed to understand that she wished to tell him something important.

Initially, she considered asking to speak to Gideon alone, but he would likely tell Ormsbee everything afterwards. So, instead, she closed the dining room door and approached the two of them.

"You've discovered something," Gideon said.

It wasn't a question. He could read her well. He had always been able to.

"I might have." In Electra's mind, she sifted through everything she'd observed and sensed since she had arrived at Carthorpe.

"I recall your words," she said to Gideon. "That you thought it all seemed too easy. But now I've begun to believe that it hasn't been easy at all." She turned to look Ormsbee's way. "I think someone concocted an elaborate plan, and so far, everything has unfurled very much as they'd intended."

Ormsbee frowned. "So everything is not as it seems?"

"The relationships are tangled." Electra hesitated.

Ormsbee exchanged a look with Gideon, who shrugged.

"I don't understand." Gideon rarely admitted such a thing to anyone. He liked being in control of facts and his own thoughts. But he was looking at Electra as if she might have answers, insights, that he couldn't. That bolstered her to say the rest, despite the feeling that she was betraying a friend.

"Alice is an artist. She sketches. From the time I've known her, she's always had a sketchbook with her. She watches people to observe them because she prefers sketching portraits."

She thought back to the rage she'd sensed from Alice, for her father, for Lord Lockhart. She'd sensed her fear of Lockhart but anger towards him.

"Before you all returned, I was upstairs in the Earl of

Carthorpe's bedchamber with Alice. She'd brought her sketch-book with her. In the carriage, she'd shown me an unfinished drawing of Lord Lockhart. It was unfinished. Just a very rough sketch."

Ormsbee's looked at her expectantly. "And?"

"The sketchbook fell off of a chair while we were in the earl's chamber. I saw several pages. All containing portraits of one person. But it wasn't Lord Lockhart. It was his brother, James."

"Pardon me," Ormsbee interjected, "but isn't he engaged to Lady Alice's sister?"

"We don't know that for certain," Gideon told him. "He claims that he asked her and that she agreed, yet Lady Honoria never mentioned an engagement at all."

"That never made sense," Electra said.

"So you believe Lady Alice is enamored with James Lockhart?" Ormsbee asked.

"I can't think of any other reason that she would have multiple pages of sketches of him. There were more than few. Dozens of pages. Indeed, I saw nothing else but his face."

"Would a man kill his own brother to get his fiancé?"

Gideon tapped his fingers against his thigh. "Seems a potential motive to me. Mr. Lockhart would have to do it before she married his brother, but it seems an enormous risk. If Lady Alice ever discovered what he'd done..." Gideon shot a look at both of them. "Though he also gets a title, and he did express disdain at the way his brother handled the family's funds."

Electra nodded.

"But all the evidence points to Alex Winters," Ormsbee insisted.

"Yes, exactly," Gideon agreed, "but what if that's because it was meant to point us there?"

"You believe your friend and James Lockhart framed Mr.

Winters, Miss Poole? Are you saying you believe that Lady Alice is involved?"

"No!" Electra's voice rang to the gilded ceiling. "No," she repeated, trying to control her emotions. "I don't want to think she is involved at all. I knew her well once, and she was not a liar." Electra looked to Gideon as if he might help her, and he leaned forward, as if eager to.

"You did say she was in the drawing room during the period when Lord Lockhart was killed," he pointed out.

"No one is suggesting she struck the blow," Ormsbee countered.

And, of course, that was what made Electra's heart ache in the center of her chest. Even if she had not struck the killing blow, if Alice had arranged the séance, if she had conspired to arrange Lord Lockhart's murder, she would be certain to secure her alibi.

At a knock on the dining room door, Electra jumped. Her nerves had been wound tight since the moment she'd arrived at Carthorpe Hall.

Ormsbee stood, crossed the room, and opened the door.

A maid stood on the other side, offering him something on a silver salver. Ormsbee picked up the folded note.

The sergeant turned back to them, eyes wide, then laid the piece of paper on the dining room table. The note was written in block letters.

OPHELIA WINTERS IS AT THE CARBERRY ARMS

While Electra and Gideon examined the note, Ormsbee called the maid back.

"Who brought this note?"

"I found it, sir."

"Where?"

"On the front hall table, just inside the front door. Was just lying there, sir. I picked it up, read it, and thought I should bring it to you."

"You did right," Ormsbee told her. "Thank you."

Ormsbee turned back and collected his suit coat from the chair where he'd hung it, donning it and straightening his cuffs as he looked at Gideon. "We should go and speak to her. You'll accompany me, Pierce?"

"Of course." Gideon glanced at Electra. "Perhaps Miss Poole should accompany us."

Ormsbee scoffed. "Have you been hired by the Metropolitan Police, Miss Poole? I was not aware." There was more amusement in his tone than anything else.

Electra gave him a smile, but Gideon didn't give her a chance to defend herself from such provocation.

"Electra was friends with Miss Winters at finishing school, Sergeant. If Miss Winters left Carthorpe and dodged the inquest to avoid answering questions, she is likely going to be resistant to doing so when we show up."

Ormsbee grinned as he buttoned his suit coat. "It is a compelling argument. Perhaps we should send Miss Poole in first to disarm Miss Winters."

"I wouldn't mind," Electra said. "No one wishes to be cornered. She fears something, it seems. I might be able to get her to confide that to me."

"She is the sister of the man I have in custody. I will speak to her myself, Miss Poole, but do accompany us, if you will."

Electra nodded.

"I've asked Withers to remain at the hall for now, especially considering the information you've provided to me about Lady Alice and Mr. Lockhart. Who knows what's going to happen next with this crafty lot."

Almost as if on cue, shouting echoed in the house.

Electra recognized Alice's voice, crying out for Dr. Brownlow.

Electra rushed out of the dining room door, stepped out into the hallway, and saw Brownlow descending the stairs, a worried frown on his face.

Alice stood on the threshold of the drawing room, tears streaming down her face. "I don't know what's happened to her," she said, her voice a strained rasp. "She was perfectly fine one moment, and then... Please."

Electra crossed to her and heard Gideon and Ormsbee's footsteps behind her.

Lady Dalrymple was half lying, half sitting on the far settee, her body slumped, hand clutched in the shawl around neck, eyes staring wide, unblinking.

"I don't know what's happened to her," Alice repeated as Brownlow brushed past all of them to approach Lady Dalrymple.

The doctor reached for Lady Dalrymple's wrist, clutching it between his fingers, saying nothing. Then he returned her arm gently to her side and reached up to push the high collar of her gown down. He pressed his fingers along her neck. After completing his examination, Brownlow stood, his brow furrowed.

When he turned back to face everyone assembled, he gave a short, insistent shake of his head.

Reaching out, he took care to lower Lady Dalrymple's eyelids.

Electra's stomach dropped as she stared at her ladyship. Some part of her could not fathom that she would not suddenly revive and open her eyes. Her ladyship had been so frightened, and now she was gone.

"Can you tell us what happened, Lady Alice?" he said, his voice low and grave, his accept clipped and precise.

Alice was shaking. Instinctively, Electra approached to wrap an arm around her shoulders, and she let out a little relieved breath as if grateful for the comfort.

"We were chatting, and then she…seemed to faint away." Alice looked around at each of them. "She clutched at her chest…" Her voice broke and tears began to slip down her cheeks. "Is she gone? She can't possibly be gone."

"I am afraid I must confirm that she is, my lady. I offer my deepest condolences," Brownlow intoned. Then he approached, his expression full of what appeared to Electra to be genuine concern. "After what you've endured the past few days, this must be a terrible blow."

Alice nodded.

"You say she clutched her chest," Ormsbee said quietly. "Her heart seized perhaps." He directed the last toward Dr. Brownlow.

The doctor looked at the sergeant, then down, as if pondering that possibility. "I have treated Lady Dalrymple for some years, and there has been no sign that she was in poor health or that her heart troubled her." He heaved a deep sigh. "But it is possible for one's heart to seize unexpectedly. It is not out of the realm of possibility."

Brownlow glanced at Alice, then stepped away from her to convene with Ormsbee. "A postmortem will need to be conducted to determine anything definitive," he whispered to Ormsbee.

The sight of the elegant lady who'd been so kind to Electra brought tears to her eyes. Her throat burned, and she couldn't help but wonder if it was more than a natural death.

Her own grandfather's heart had given out on him suddenly only the winter before her mother's death. She knew such occurrences did sometimes come on most unexpectedly. But something about Lady Dalrymple's face, the shock in her unseeing eyes, the grimace on her lips.

"What happened?" she heard herself whisper to Alice.

Alice stepped out of her embrace and turned to Electra. "As I said, we were taking tea. We'd hoped you might join us. Indeed, I was on the cusp of having a maid send for you." Alice looked at Electra steadily. "We did invite you. Did you forget?"

"No, but I got caught up speaking to Gideon. Inspector Pierce," she corrected.

"Good heavens," Alice said suddenly, lifting a hand to her mouth. "She's really gone."

Almost as soon as the words were out, Alice swooned. Electra reacted too slowly and couldn't prevent her from going down. Brownlow immediately approached and knelt beside her.

"Could someone please fetch my medical bag?" he called out.

As he'd done with Lady Dalrymple, he gently lifted one of Alice's arms and pressed two fingers to her wrist to check her pulse.

Moments later, a footman entered the room and sat the doctor's medical bag on the carpet beside him.

Brownlow lifted out a vial with a cork stopper. He pulled out the stopper, then placed the vial near Alice's nostrils, waving it lightly.

Alice's eyes blinked open, and she looked around her, blinking as if confused. "What happened?"

Ormsbee and Brownlow each took one of Alice's arms and helped her to stand. Brownlow guided her to a chair far away from Lady Dalrymple's body. Then he returned to collect his medical bag. Electra noted that he seemed to linger over the bag, as if searching for something.

Electra went to sit on an ottoman near Alice. "Are you all right?" she whispered to her friend.

"My head aches. I might have bumped it when I fell." She peered into Electra's eyes, looking genuinely dazed. "Why did I fall?"

"You were overcome, which is understandable." Electra's own throat burned, but she tried to hold back her own grief. "You fainted." Electra glanced back at where Gideon had lifted a cloth that someone had retrieved for him over Lady Dalrymple's body. "Do you remember what happened?" she asked her friend.

Alice swallowed thickly, then met Electra's gaze again. "My aunt is dead, isn't she?"

Electra reached for her then, taking her hand. "She is, Alice. I'm so very sorry."

Alice bowed her head and let the tears flow, sobbing quietly.

Behind her, Electra heard Dr. Brownlow ask to speak to Ormsbee.

A maid hovered nearby, as if unsure what to do with herself, and Electra nodded to get the girl's attention. "Would you sit with Lady Alice a moment?" she asked quietly.

"Of course, miss." The young lady immediately circled the chair and collected a small lap blanket that had been warming by the fire. She settled the blanket around Alice.

Electra released Alice's hand and stood, gesturing toward the ottoman. The maid immediately took her meaning and sat in the seat Electra had just occupied.

Electra crossed to where the two men stood conferring. Gideon joined them too.

"I hesitate to say this," Brownlow began, "but when I went to replace my vial of smelling salts, I noticed one of my medicine bottles is almost empty."

"And why is that significant?" Ormsbee asked.

Brownlow looked slightly affronted and then said, "It is a medication I always have on hand and access regularly when I come to Carthorpe. I use it to treat Lord Carthorpe, who has an ongoing heart condition. I used a bit just last night and the vial was nearly full at that time. I'm very careful with this particular medication."

"What is the medication?" Gideon asked.

"Digitalis," Brownlow told them. "In a proper dosage, it can be quite helpful in treating maladies of the heart. But in higher doses, it will stop the heart entirely."

"Can it be detected during a postmortem?"

Brownlow shook his head. "It would be difficult. I suppose a physiological test could be conducted."

Ormsbee swept his gaze around the room. "And if it was detected in liquid?"

"Again, I would think collecting a sample and determining the presence of digitalis might be difficult."

"But you could try?" Ormsbee pressed.

"Of course," Brownlow returned immediately.

Without saying another word, Ormsbee crossed the room and pulled the bell pull, despite the fact that one of the maids still sat attending to Alice.

A few minutes later, the blonde housemaid, Lydia, appeared in the doorway.

Ormsbee directed the girl quietly, pointing to the teapot and cups set out on the low table near Lady Dalrymple.

The girl nodded, departed, returned moments later with a wide tray, and collected both before leaving the room again.

Electra hadn't realized that Constable Withers had entered the room and positioned himself near the doorway until she'd watched the young maid depart. Ormsbee approached the constable and whispered under his breath, "Collect the tea and cups. They must be sent to the doctor who performs the postmortem."

Withers nodded, then departed the drawing room.

Gideon came and stood by Electra's side.

"When could someone have accessed the bottle of medication?" she whispered to him.

"An excellent question," Gideon said. "He was here last night and Withers says he arrived about three hours ago at Carthorpe."

"And he spent that time with Lord Carthorpe?"

"That's my understanding. The staff told Withers that he often says for some period of time with the earl. They've been friends for decades."

Electra let her gaze slide across the room to fix on Alice. She looked truly distraught, and Electra felt a surge of sadness that her friend had lost so much in but a few days. Guilt swept in. Moments ago, she'd suspected Alice of conspiring to kill her fiancé.

Ormsbee finally approached the two of them.

"We've sent for the coroner. I should remain at Carthorpe. May I rely on the two of you to manage the Ophelia Winters interview? I don't think we should delay speaking to her."

"Of course. We'll depart now." Gideon looked at Electra as soon as Ormsbee stepped away. "I understand you were acquainted with her ladyship. If you feel you're not up to this or would prefer to stay with Lady Alice—"

"No, I'm all right. I want to go with you." She did feel a hollowness at the loss of Lady Dalrymple, but until she knew whether her death was natural, as Electra's grandfather's had been, or due to malfeasance, her energy was best spent on discovering the truth of what had happened to Lord Lockhart.

Electra glanced at Alice once more, then followed Gideon out into the hall. She had a strong feeling that Ophelia Winters might shed light on facts that would clarify whether the wrong man was now being held for the murder of Lord Lockhart.

Before they departed, they strode past the dining room, and Electra spotted the teacups that had been collected.

"Gideon," she said to stall him. "I want to attempt something."

When she glanced back at him, he nodded. Electra strode into the room where Ormsbee was convening in a corner with Constable Withers. Gideon moved to join them, seeming to sense that the distraction would be helpful.

Electra laid her fingers against the handle of one of the teacups, kept her back to Ormsbee, Withers, and Gideon and closed her eyes. She concentrated her mind, attempting to draw up any images that might come, any indication of who'd touched the cup.

She knew she had only a moment and the low murmur of the gentlemen's conversation proved unsettling, but images emerged. Murky at first. Alice's hands. She recognized a ring she often wore as she prepared the tea for each of them, placing a strainer over each teacup and pouring out before handing a cup to Lady Dalrymple.

Electra felt anxiousness as the noblewoman reached for the cup.

Lady Dalrymple tipped her head, looking back questioningly.

Even as she focused, hoping she might hear what either Alice or Lady Dalrymple might say, the images faded. She let go of the teacup.

Electra turned back to Gideon, who'd positioned himself so that he could watch her as he spoke to his fellow policemen.

"Shall we be off?" he asked her.

Electra nodded and he immediately excused himself.

As they headed out to the carriage circle, he shot her a look.

"Nothing. I saw Alice and Lady Dalrymple taking tea, which we already knew."

Gideon leaned a little closer and said, "It's all right. Hopefully, we'll learn something from Miss Winters."

Chapter Sixteen

The inn where they found Ophelia Winters was tucked away from the high street in the local village, sitting in little corner with fields stretching out behind it.

Though the innkeeper was reluctant to divulge whether Miss Winters was staying at the inn, Electra tried persuading the man by telling him that she was a friend of Ophelia's and needed to see her urgently. When he still hesitated, Gideon managed to convince him by providing his title and name, emphasizing that he was on official police business. It seemed that Mr. Carberry did not wish for any trouble with the law.

As they walked up the stairs to her room, Electra wondered who'd sent the note the housemaid had found and whether someone might have alerted Ophelia too.

Standing in the hall outside the door of the room they'd been directed to, Gideon leaned a bit closer.

"Do you think you should try speaking to her alone first?" he asked.

Electra had been considering it on the carriage ride over. "No, let's do it together. It's worked for us in the past."

He smiled and nodded. "I'll still let you take the lead, since you know her."

Electra knocked once, got no response, and tried again. Soft footsteps on the other side of the door indicated that somebody was in the room.

When the door opened a few inches, Ophelia gazed out, eyes wide, hair down around her shoulders.

"I didn't think you'd be the one to come find me," she said quietly, eyes fixed on Electra.

"I'm not alone." Electra turned toward Gideon, who stood off to the side, perhaps far enough that Ophelia hadn't seen him.

"Ah, yes, Detective Inspector Pierce, you're the one I expected. Or Sergeant Ormsbee." She took a few steps back and opened the door wider. "Come in, both of you."

Electra entered the low-ceilinged room and Gideon followed. Ophelia wore a simple day dress, and she looked utterly exhausted. Her green eyes were ringed with shadows and were red, as if she'd been crying.

After Electra and Gideon took the wooden chairs at a small round table in the room, Ophelia perched on the edge of the bed and faced them.

"You said you expected someone to come," Gideon began. "Does that mean you arranged for Sergeant Ormsbee to be presented with the note?"

"Yes," Ophelia said. "I received word, I won't say from whom, of what happened at the inquest." She pressed her lips together and her eyes welled with tears. "I was told what happened to my brother and decided it was time that I confide in someone."

No tears fell, but Ophelia sniffed as if they had, then lifted her chin. "Where should we begin? Ask me what you will, and I will answer."

"Why did you leave Carthorpe?" Electra asked.

"Because I couldn't bear to go to the inquest. I knew that I would have to swear to tell the truth, and I couldn't bring myself to say...certain truths publicly."

"What truths?" Electra prompted softly. "What were you afraid to say, Ophelia?"

"If I was asked about my relationship with...Lord Lockhart." She'd paused before speaking his name, and when she did, those two words came out differently than all the others. They emerged filled with a bitter sharpness.

"If I may, Miss Winters, what was your relationship with Lord Lockhart?" Gideon asked.

Ophelia turned her attention on Gideon. "As I'm sure you know, he was a friend of my brother's. They'd been at school together. He came to visit our house on occasion. And we also went at times to visit Edgemont, his family's estate."

"So you've known him for many years?" Gideon clarified.

"Yes, we'd visit each other often, even at Christmas time, if that gives any indication of how close our families were. Then..." She paused again and seemed to collect herself. "At a certain point, he showed an interest in me."

"How did your family and his respond?" Electra asked, realizing that often noble families would not tolerate a gentry family like the Winters joining with their own.

"Oh, he expressed his interest in me surreptitiously. No one in my family knew, nor in his. He said he didn't think that Alex would be comfortable with it or approve."

"Did you welcome his attention?" Gideon asked.

Ophelia winced. "I was young and silly. And, yes, I suppose I liked the attention, even though I knew I wasn't in love with him. I didn't quite understand what love was, but I knew I should feel more than I did for Henry. But he was my brother's friend, and I trusted him." She smiled a crooked, pained smile at that.

"Henry could be persuasive, and when he couldn't persuade, he was demanding. And when his demands weren't met, he was forceful."

Electra's gut twisted as the realization hit her of what Ophelia would say next.

"He seduced me, I suppose one could say. He began taking liberties, physically touching me. Holding my hand. Putting an arm around me. I tried to be comfortable with it because I told myself that my family would be pleased if I married my brother's friend. He was to inherit a viscountcy."

When she fell silent, Electra sensed that Gideon was preparing to nudge her with another question, but she stilled him with a quick squeeze of his hand under the table's edge.

"He said Alex would disapprove, but he wouldn't have. He would have approved because he did, at one point, love Henry." Ophelia turned her gaze from theirs and stared at the opposite wall. "There was a garden party. Henry got me away from the rest of the guests. I thought he meant to propose, but he didn't. He...forced himself on me."

Tears began to slip down Ophelia's cheeks and she swiped at them. Gideon immediately produced a handkerchief and she took it with a half-smile.

"Even afterwards," she said, "I tried to rationalize it. We would likely get married. What difference did it make? But then...he shifted his attentions to Alice." She inhaled sharply. "It was clear that he did not intend to do right by me, and yet I still told no one what had happened."

She smiled at both of them. "I felt like a fool."

"You are not," Gideon told her firmly.

"Yes, well, he acted as if nothing had happened. For a while, I thought I would go mad because I felt as if I could not trust my own memory of what had happened. I began to doubt whether it had been wrong, began to convince myself that it had not hurt me as it had." She shrugged. "Eventually, I decided to pretend it had not happened. I tried to go on like I was the same person, but I wasn't."

"Did Alex notice?" Electra guessed, speaking softly.

"Yes, of course he did because he's my brother." A genuine, sweet smile softened her pretty face. "Alex knows me better than anyone, and he wore me down until I told him the truth. He was incensed. He wanted to harm Henry, but I begged him not to. I knew the Lockharts were powerful and our family was not, though our families were friendly. I wasn't certain anyone would truly care about what he'd done to me because soon Henry was Lord Lockhart." She drew herself up, straightening her shoulders. "And then my father died, and his debts were enormous. Alex worried for me and our mother."

Ophelia fell silent and twisted Gideon's handkerchief in her fingers.

"We know that Lord Lockhart loaned him a good deal of money," Electra said quietly.

Ophelia lifted her head and her eyes ballooned wide. "Oh, I see. Yes, well, that may be what he told you, or what Alice claimed, but it's not true. Alex decided that the solution to our family's financial woes was to blackmail Lord Lockhart."

Gideon made a little sound that Electra knew indicated he'd just found a thread that intrigued him.

"You might have heard it referred to as loans. That's how Henry referred to the payments anytime he was asked about them by James or his solicitor. To save face, he would say he loaned Alex money."

"When Henry blamed him for failure to repay, why didn't Alex expose him?"

"In truth, I don't think Alex ever would have under any circumstances. His main concern was always protecting me." Ophelia drew in a deep breath. "He might have made Alex out to be a reprobate who did not pay his debts, but I suppose I was the real culprit because I told someone a horrible, secret thing, and Henry didn't like being reminded of it."

"You aren't to blame," Electra reminded her, "for any of it."

"Regardless, Henry didn't want to face any consequences. And why should he? It was years ago and our families still carried on as friends."

"That must have been awful," Electra said, "that you were still forced to be in his orbit. Was this near the time when I visited that summer?"

Ophelia tipped her head as she looked at Electra. "It had happened the summer before."

Electra felt an ache in her chest to know that Ophelia had endured such a violation, and she'd been unable to tell anyone, to tell her. And why hadn't she noticed or sensed her pain?

But, of course, she understood how one could keep secrets. She'd perfected the ability to pretend as if she was not heartbroken over her mother, terrified of her own abilities. And Ophelia had been in all of their finishing school's plays along with Alice. For some reason, the notion of being on stage terrified Electra. It felt far too exposing. But Ophelia and Alice had been marvelous in every Shakespeare production their school put on.

"I'm sorry," Electra finally said, "that I didn't—"

"What could you have done, Electra? I enjoyed that visit. Truly, I did. And I was always sorry that Alex behaved the way he did toward you."

Electra shook her head, trying not to look at Gideon, whose eyes were on her. "It was nothing."

Ophelia licked her lips and said, "Do you wish to know the hardest part? It wasn't just what happened, it was the knowledge that I was the means of supporting our family via the blackmailing. I became very good at pretending, but the hardest part was pretending as if it was all right. That I had survived unscathed and that we could go on as friends. Sitting in the parlor together. Taking meals together at Carthorpe during this house party."

"It must be like torture," Gideon agreed.

"At times, it is." Ophelia lifted a hand and laid it across the back of her neck, then looked up at them again. "So that is why I am here, and the reason I wanted to speak to you, Inspector, or Sergeant Ormsbee. Alex is many things, but he is not a murderer."

Electra could feel the tension in Gideon's body as he sat beside her. She looked over to see him seeming to struggle with what to say next.

"May I be honest with you, Miss Winters?" he finally asked gravely.

"Of course. I'd like you to be."

"Before you told us this very difficult story, the motive I assumed for Mr. Winters related to the purported loans from Lord Lockhart. But you must understand that, to some, this will seem an even more compelling motive." Gideon glanced at Electra. "If a man did such a thing to someone close to me, a sister if I had one—"

"Revenge makes no sense as a motive, Inspector, because without Henry, there would be no payments. Nothing to support our family. The incident I confessed to you happened many years ago."

"They were heard arguing the day of Lord Lockhart's murder," Electra pointed out.

"I don't doubt it," Ophelia said, her mouth softening into a slight smile. "But no matter how angry Alex became, he wouldn't harm Henry because his money was paying for our mortgage, to keep horses and carriages, and to fill our larder."

Electra considered the matter and had to agree with Ophelia. She couldn't imagine what would provoke Winters to kill Lockhart after so many years. Perhaps if Lockhart refused to continue paying, but in such a case, Winters' tangled relationship with Lockhart would be exposed, just as it was being now. And that had led to his sister being forced to expose her secret too.

"Alex is innocent," Ophelia said emphatically.

"This may seem an unfair question, Miss Winters, but do you have any notion who might have killed Lord Lockhart?" Gideon asked.

Ophelia didn't answer straight away, which indicated to Electra that she may have had someone in mind but was reticent to admit as much.

When she remained silent, Electra couldn't resist asking, "Who?"

Ophelia looked at her, then turned more fully to face her. "I can only say this, Electra. I don't think that I was the last woman that he did this to."

"You're saying he took advantage of someone else?" And Electra knew. In that moment, the image she'd seen when she touched Alice at the séance arose in her mind. "Lady Honoria?" she whispered, almost wishing Gideon wasn't there so that she could speak to Ophelia about this part privately.

"Yes." Ophelia said the word so low, it was little more than an exhale.

"Did she tell you that?"

"No." Ophelia shook her head. "She never told me outright. But one day, when we were all taking lunch together in the conservatory, she somehow sensed my unease whenever Henry spoke. Whenever he walked by my chair."

Ophelia pressed her lips together and let out a breath. "Afterwards, she caught me alone in the hall. She leaned in and whispered in my ear. She said, 'I understand.' Just those two words and we never spoke of it again."

Electra wondered if Honoria's fury might be enough to inspire James Lockhart, who seemed to be a beau of hers, to attack his own brother.

"Will you return to London? I take it you won't return to Carthorpe," Electra said, "but there is still the matter of the summons."

"I won't leave Oxford while Alex is awaiting his fate." Ophelia lifted her gaze to Gideon. "Now that I've told you everything, is there any possibility the summons could be rescinded?"

"I can speak to Sergeant Ormsbee. I will not have much influence with the coroner, but he might."

"Thank you, Inspector. And you too, Electra."

Gideon got to his feet, and Electra did too. When Ophelia stood to usher them out, Electra felt a strange, uncharacteristic impulse and reached for Ophelia's hand with her gloved one.

Ophelia immediately clasped hands with Electra.

"Thank you for sharing what must have been very difficult to say," Electra told her quietly.

"Will you help Alex?" she asked, tightening her hold on Electra's hand. "Matters may have been awkward between the two of you once, but he's not a killer, Electra. I know him."

"I'll do all I can," Electra vowed, and she felt the gravity of making such a promise.

After Gideon and Electra made their way outside the inn, and Gideon had helped her up into the Carthorpe carriage that had transported them, he settled on the opposite bench and studied her.

Electra didn't need her abilities to know what Gideon was thinking.

"What is it?" she finally said. "I can tell you have something on your mind."

"What is between you and Alex Winters?" He sounded unusually hesitant, as if he didn't truly want the answer. Though she'd never known a time when Gideon's curiosity didn't overcome his reticence. They were alike in that regard.

"I already told you. That summer I went to Essex, he was at the Winters' estate too. He showed me a bit of attention, and I..." Electra still felt foolish for how easily she'd been taken in. "I liked it for a bit, and then as soon as he'd won my attention, he didn't desire it anymore."

Gideon's only response was to look out the carriage window as they rolled toward Carthorpe. Finally, he said quietly, "Even if he is not a murderer, it seems he is a fool."

Electra tipped her head down and smiled. "We don't know that he is innocent," she pointed out. "He is a blackmailer, if nothing else. Though I am beginning to come around to your way of thinking. This is more tangled than one man attacking another in a hedgerow."

Gideon finally turned back to her. "Agreed."

"I have an idea."

"Tell me."

"I'd like to hold that shard again. Could you get it from Ormsbee?"

"I can try, yes. Did you...sense anything the first time?"

"No, I need more time. Ormsbee was watching me. Nothing came." Electra tugged at the edge of her glove. "I also think that their rooms should be searched. Lord Lockhart's, James Lockhart's, Alice's, and Honoria's."

Gideon's brows arched. "That would alert all of them that something we've learned has cast further suspicion on them."

"True, but I'd still think those rooms should be searched. I'd like to have a look."

"No," he said with a sort of scoffing laugh. "Ormsbee would never allow you to be involved in such a manner, and I would not wish to put you at risk."

"You wouldn't know what to look for."

He looked offended. "And you would?"

"I could touch things."

"Electra..."

"Gideon, please."

For a long moment, he studied her. So long that Electra saw a warmth in his gaze that made her cheeks heat.

"No," he finally said. "Ormsbee is leading this investigation and he would never allow it."

Electra clenched her teeth. "Very well."

Chapter Seventeen

Upon returning to Carthorpe, Gideon conveyed to Ormsbee all they'd learned from Ophelia Winters. As Gideon expected would happen, the details of Lord Lockhart's treatment of Miss Winters only confirmed to him that they had the right man in custody. Alex Winters, he insisted, had more than enough motive. There were now several options to choose from.

"Then we've well and truly got him," Ormsbee said, with not a small amount of satisfaction.

"I think there's more to discover," Gideon insisted.

Ormsbee looked at him like he'd lost his head. "Shall we further investigate two young ladies who've lost their beloved aunt and a gentleman who's grieving his brother?"

Gideon knew, as he trusted Ormsbee did too, that such concerns could not, should not, impede an investigation. Still, Gideon could not deny that nothing Miss Winters told them implicated James Lockhart. If anything, it could have given Lady Alice motive to be rid of Lord Lockhart. Learning that her fiancé had defiled a friend and potentially her own sister should have ended any potential match between them, not to mention how the man was depleting his coffers by paying blackmail payments. *If* she knew.

But, of course, Lady Alice had the most solid alibi of any of the guests and residents of Carthorpe.

"I think we should look further into James Lockhart." It seemed likely that one of the gentlemen attacked Lord Lockhart, and if it wasn't Alex Winters, that left only the viscount's brother.

Ormsbee ran a hand over his neatly pomaded hair. "It seems to me, Pierce, that you are willfully ignoring the facts we've gathered. The evidence points to one man and one man acting alone." He swore under his breath. "I will not condone further investigation into Lord Lockhart's murder when we still have the matter of Lady Dalrymple to contend with."

"I'd like to speak to Lady Alice and Lady Honoria one last time," Gideon said. "With your permission, of course, Sergeant."

The other police officer lifted his hand to pinch the skin between his brows.

"One final time, Pierce." He looked up, bracing a hand at his hip. "Then will that satisfy you that the right man is in custody?"

"I hope so." Gideon dipped his head once in leave-taking and turned to depart, then remembered his conversation with Electra and turned back. "May I have the shard of glass that was found, if you still have it in your possession?"

Ormsbee frowned. "I still have it. I'm preparing the final reports and will include all evidence when they are handed over to my superior at the Oxford Constabulary." He cocked his head. "Why do you want it?"

"Have either of the Kirkham sisters been asked about it?"

"No." Ormsbee drew in a breath, then turned to the dining room table where his documents and writing implements were neatly arranged. From an envelope, he extracted the shard, which had been wrapped in paper. "You'll return it forthwith?" he asked.

"Of course."

Only after that agreement did Ormsbee place it in his hand.

"I must go into town to meet with the doctor who'll be conducting Lady Dalrymple's postmortem. I shouldn't be longer than an hour or so. I'll tell you what he found when I return."

Gideon nodded, then left the dining room, found a maid, and asked her to request that Lady Alice and her sister join him in the parlor in thirty minutes, and then he set out to find Electra.

Electra found one of the maids tiding her room when they returned from questioning Ophelia.

The young woman, Lydia, informed her that Lady Dalrymple's body had been removed by the coroner and Constable Withers.

That had put a lump in Electra's throat, and tears stung, threatening to fall. She carried the grief of her mother's loss deep inside, but this grief was fresh and it seemed to prick at the older, deeper sadness too. She'd spoken to Lady Dalrymple only yesterday, and she'd been so frightened. Electra swallowed at the memory of the noblewoman's face, those clear eyes, and her certainty that someone meant her ill.

That vision she'd seen. Lady Dalrymple had been taking tea in the conservatory, but she'd never made it to the conservatory. She'd been found in the drawing room. None of it made sense, and Electra's head had begun to ache.

She thought back on her brief conversation with Gideon. He'd forbidden her from getting further involved in the investigation, but that hadn't stopped her during the Becknell case.

"Who's at the hall now?" she asked the housemaid as the young woman cleaned the fireplace grate.

"Mr. Lockhart is the only guest who remains, miss, and Lady Alice and Lady Honoria, but Mr. Lockhart went out a bit ago and has not returned."

"Oh." A little frisson of excitement made Electra take a step closer. "Do you think he's returned to London or his family home?"

"I don't think so, miss. I tidied his room before yours"—the maid gestured to the south wall of Electra's room—"and all his clothes and traveling case remain."

"So you've no notion when he'll return?" she asked.

"No, miss. I was told I'd be bringing a dinner tray up to him as usual, so I suspect he'll return in due course." The maid pushed a wisp of hair from her brow with the back of her hand and glanced back at Electra. "Were you needing to speak with him, miss?"

"I'd hoped to, yes," Electra fibbed.

"If you write out a note, I can push it under his door. It's just the one next to yours."

"I'll just wait until he returns."

Lydia nodded and then turned back to her work.

"Did you push the note under my door from Lady Alice on Wednesday morning?"

Lydia nodded, face still turned toward the task at hand. "Yes, miss. Though she'd given it to me the previous morning before you'd arrived. Had to remember to keep it safe all day." Lydia let out a light laugh, then stood and dusted off her hands on a rag before turning back to Electra.

"So she wrote it out and gave it to you the previous day? You're certain?"

"Yes, miss. Very certain because I had to remember it was in my apron pocket, and I didn't want to dirty it or forget it. She said I should slip it under your door the morning after your arrival, and I did."

"You did, yes. Thank you, Lydia."

"Anything else I can help you with, miss?"

"No, that is all."

When the maid departed, Electra stood staring out the window onto the Carthorpe's carriage circle. The morning she'd walked in on the conflict between Alice and Lord Lockhart, the morning she'd found the note under her door, Alice told her that she'd left her the note because she wanted to speak to her about the séance that evening.

Had the séance been planned before she'd even arrived?

Electra's impression had been that Lady Dalrymple had arranged it rather precipitously after her incident in the hedge maze, but then Ormsbee insisted Alice had arranged it. Perhaps she had done it much earlier.

Electra turned toward the door, determined to risk a look around James Lockhart's room, now that she knew he was out, but someone knocked on her door first.

She opened it to find Gideon on the threshold.

"May I come in?"

Electra stepped back to admit him, and he immediately turned to her, reached for her hand, and placed an object on her palm.

She still had her gloves on, but she knew instantly what it was.

"Do you want me to go?" he asked quietly.

"No, but I'd ask that you don't speak until I do."

"I can do that."

Electra went over and sat in a chair by the fire. Gideon followed and sat across from her.

She removed her gloves, set them aside, then clasped both of her hands around the shard. Closing her eyes often helped her, so she did that, feeling safe to do so in Gideon's presence.

At first nothing came, but she concentrated on that night, on her brief interaction with Lord Lockhart earlier in the evening. She thought of the hedge maze and the spot where they'd found the depression in the soil.

The jolt in her body, the tensing of her muscles that foreshadowed a vision, came just before the first images flickered in her mind.

She saw a bedchamber with pale green wallpaper. Alice's room was papered in the same shade and one other room Electra had been in—Lord Carthorpe's suite.

The person whose memory she saw felt uncomfortable in the room. They paced a rug near the fireplace, then glanced toward the window where night had fallen. The images shifted, and they faced the mantel, reaching for an object that sat atop it, glinting in the firelight. It looked like a very short-handled mallet, smaller but similar to a mallet one might use to play croquet. But the two sides of the mallet's head were faceted like a jewel. It reminded Electra of the Waterford crystal dish her aunts in Ireland had gifted to her when she visited.

The person whose memories she was seeing was a man. Their hands were masculine in size and shape as they wrapped their fingers around the grip of the mallet, lifted it from the mantel, and hefted it in their hand, as if testing the weight. Something startled them, and they dropped the object from their hands.

Electra gasped. She could hear a sound, soft, growing stronger, like a faraway echo.

"What are you doing in here?" a voice called, the sound emerged distorted but recognizable.

Electra opened her eyes. Gideon leaned toward her, a look

of concern etched on his features, his hand extended like he wanted to reach for her.

"Gideon," she breathed, feeling suddenly drained and unnervingly shaken.

"I'm here," he said in a soothing tone. "Are you all right?"

"I heard a voice."

He gave her a fierce frown. "What did the voice say?"

Electra reached her palm out, offering the shard back to him. Gideon took it immediately and slipped it into his pocket.

"Nothing of consequence, but it's not what was said, it's that I heard it at all. I have never heard anything in my visions before." Electra's hands shook a bit when she pressed them into her lap, trying to steady herself. "Most importantly, I recognized the voice."

Gideon's head snapped up at that. "Who?"

"It was Honoria."

"And who was she speaking to?"

"I don't know. A man. He was in a chamber here at Carthorpe." She swallowed and looked into Gideon's eyes. "I believe it was the earl's chamber. The man in my vision took something from the mantel. It was strange. A decorative mallet made of crystal, I think."

"The murder weapon?" Gideon said the words quietly, though they were alone behind the closed door of her guest chamber.

"Possibly, but he dropped it when Honoria called out."

Gideon scrubbed a hand across his face. "You could not identify the man?"

"No. I'm afraid not." Electra stood and felt so woozy she reached out, her hand landing on Gideon's shoulder.

"Easy," he said, instantly getting to his feet and wrapping his hands around her waist.

Electra closed her eyes and drew in some deep breaths.

She could smell Gideon's spice and citrus shaving soap and the unique scent that seemed to be his alone. It comforted her.

"I'll be all right," she said quietly.

The feel of his hands on her waist offered a soothing heat, a sense of security her jangled nerves craved. She let her hand drift down to his chest, resting just over the top of his waistcoat. Electra felt the strong but rapid thump of his heart beating against her palm.

He was worried about her, and it felt far different than Cordelia's fussing or her father's sometimes overbearing ways. It felt lovely.

When she looked up at him, he stared into her eyes as if they fascinated him.

"What?" she said, her tone emerging far breathier than she intended.

"You have the most striking eyes I've ever seen."

Electra chuckled, feeling instantly lighter and not a little embarrassed at the earnestness of his compliment. "Is that so?" she teased.

Gideon lifted his hand and gently cupped her cheek. "And I never felt so seen as when those lovely eyes of yours are on me."

It felt extraordinary to be looked at with such affection, such admiration, and she felt it in return, so deeply that it frightened her.

Gideon seemed to sense it, as he always sensed shifts in her mood, and lowered his hand. "Feeling better?"

"Yes," she said quietly. "Thank you." Electra smiled up at him. "For the compliment and for coming here because you care."

He lowered his hands from her waist, but stayed close, their chests almost brushing.

"I do," he said, his voice deep and warm. "Very much."

Electra licked her lips and turned her eyes away because looking at Gideon was suddenly overwhelming.

"James Lockhart is out. A maid told me." Her voice was husky, and she drew in a breath to steady herself. "She also told me that the note Alice had her deliver to me, the one that caused me to go to Alice's room, where observed her altercation with Lord Lockhart, was written prior to my arrival."

Gideon's brow furrowed in that pensive way she was so familiar with. "That is odd, is it not?"

"It is, especially since I spoke to Alice the night I arrived. She might have asked me to visit her room the next morning herself if she wished for me to do so." Electra thought back to that night. "But, of course, she was quite distracted because Lady Dalrymple could not be located."

Gideon nodded but didn't seem quite satisfied with that explanation. Electra found it left her with questions too.

Still, her mind remained set on one objective.

"We should search James Lockhart's room while he's out."

Gideon blinked. "*We* are not searching his room. Ormsbee wouldn't want me to do so either, but he has agreed that I may further question Lady Alice and Lady Honoria." He lifted his head and stared at the far wall. "You're certain you saw the interior of the earl's chamber when you touched the shard?"

Electra nodded. "I was in it earlier with Alice when I saw the sketchbook. I feel certain it's the same room."

"Brownlow is with him now." Gideon glanced at the clock on her room's mantel. "I have a few minutes before I'm to meet with the sisters. Let's go to Carthorpe's room, and you can determine whether it was indeed the room you saw."

"You believe me?" Electra heart did an odd little dance in her chest.

"I think we should test it. See if that object you saw is on the mantel."

"And then you'll let me join you when you speak to the sisters?"

Gideon arched one dark brow. "We'll see."

They walked down to the earl's suite, not encountering anyone in the hallway, and Gideon rapped twice.

The doctor opened the door, his eyes flickering with surprise when he took the both of them in.

"What can I do for you, Inspector?" He glanced at Electra. "And Miss Poole."

"May we come in for a moment?"

Brownlow glanced behind him. "I'm afraid the earl is resting and would not be in a condition to answer any questions. The news of his sister's death has struck him quite hard," he said more quietly.

"We won't disturb him, Dr. Brownlow, but it's imperative that we take a look around his chamber."

Brownlow seemed on the verge of refusing, but he studied Gideon's expression. Something there must have convinced him, for he ducked his head, stepped back, and ushered them in with the wave of his arm. "As quietly as you're able," he said in a low tone.

Gideon placed a hand on Electra's lower back, urging her to precede him.

Electra stepped inside and knew instantly that she'd been right. This was the room she'd seen in her vision.

While Gideon pulled Brownlow aside and spoke to him in a near whisper, Electra strode toward the mantel. In the spot where she'd seen the faceted object, a polished wooden square sat with a carved-out dip and a golden plaque affixed to its face. On the metal plaque, a few words were etched. *In thanks to our founder, Lady Carthorpe. Oxford Ladies' Croquet Club.*

Electra reached up and touched the plaque, then ran her

fingers over the depression where the crystal mallet had likely sat. A gift, it seemed, for Alice and Honoria's late mother.

"He took it," a small, creaking voice said.

Electra whipped around.

Gideon and Brownlow turned their attention toward the earl too.

"Who took it?" Gideon asked.

Brownlow put a hand on Gideon's arm as if to forestall more questions.

The earl, thin and pale, covered to his neck with blankets, turned his attention to Gideon with surprisingly sharp blue eyes.

"Lockhart," he said, his voice little more than a rasp.

"Lord Lockhart?" Brownlow asked.

The Earl of Carthorpe turned his head back and forth on the pillow. "The brother," he said, his voice a bit stronger. "Honoria asked him not to, but he wouldn't listen."

At that, the earl began to cough, and Brownlow immediately rushed to his side. He laid a hand across the earl's forehead, and the nobleman seemed to settle again.

"He has the slightest of fevers," Brownlow informed them. "I shall do my best to bring it down." The doctor turned back to them. "Best leave him now, Inspector."

Electra headed toward the suite's door, and Gideon followed behind her.

Out in the hall, Gideon looked around to ensure they were alone, then leaned close.

"He was talking about the mallet, I think," Electra told him.

"We don't know for certain that it was the murder weapon."

Electra ground her teeth.

"You didn't see that, did you?" he asked. "The mallet being used as the murder weapon?"

"I certainly would have told you if I had. But if it was, and James Lockhart was in possession of it, then this may have nothing to do with Alex Winters after all."

"I'll need to speak to James Lockhart." A muscle jumped at the edge of his jaw. "But first I need to go downstairs and interview the sisters again." He glanced away from her and then back.

"May I come too?" Electra asked, sensing something had shifted between them. He seemed almost irked with her, but she wasn't certain why. "I could be a comfort to them. They've both experienced so much loss in the last few days, and they're likely both shaken by Lady Dalrymple's death."

"Very well. But I'll do the questioning."

"Of course, Gideon."

He narrowed his eyes at her, as if to determine whether she was sincere. He was worried about her. She rarely tried to read him. It felt like something she should not do without his express permission, even if she had no trouble doing so with others without theirs.

But now, standing so close, she felt it.

"Shall we go?" she said when he continued to stare at her silently.

"Yes, all right."

They proceeded down the stairs together, and as they went, he whispered, "I do want to know if you sense anything from either of them, with your...abilities."

Electra felt a little surge of pride, but simply nodded.

As they rounded the bottom of the staircase, Electra could see Honoria and Alice sitting close on one of the settees in the parlor.

Before she could proceed into the room, Gideon reached down and laid a hand lightly on her arm.

"I may say things that are not true to provoke a response," he said quietly. "Will you follow my lead?"

"You can trust me," she told him.

He said nothing more, and she followed him into the parlor.

Chapter Eighteen

The two sisters sat side by side, holding onto each other's hands.

Lady Honoria looked devastated. Tears glistened on her cheeks under puffy, red-rimmed eyes. But Lady Alice, as Gideon had experienced with her since coming to Carthorpe, seemed much more composed, though her eyes still held a look of pain and her brows were drawn together. She hunched a bit, curling inward, almost as if her pain was physical.

As he took a seat on the settee across from them, he felt a bit like a brute to have to question them when they were in such an understandable state. They'd just lost their aunt, Lady Alice had lost her fiancé, regardless of what a blackguard he was, and their father was lying ill upstairs. From the look on Dr. Brownlow's face, he sensed that the doctor did not hold out much hope for the earl's prognosis.

Still, he felt certain that one, or both, of the sisters was somehow tangled up in Lord Lockhart's death, and perhaps Lady Dalrymple's, if it was proven to be unnatural.

From the inconsistencies between their statements and those of others he'd questioned, from who arranged the séance, to whether Lady Honoria and James Lockhart were truly engaged, he believed the sisters knew more than either had been willing to tell.

If the crystal mallet Electra had seen had been taken by James Lockhart, as the earl claimed, then it seemed likely he was tied up in the murder. But in order to prove that or even begin to convince Ormsbee of that fact, he would need to understand why a young man would strike down his own brother.

Electra perched on a chair near the edge of the settee where Lady Alice sat, and Gideon noticed that she'd removed her gloves. It was the perfect place for her to view the sisters' reactions to his questions, and he suspected she might use her bare hand to reach for, ostensibly to offer comfort, Lady Alice during the course of his questioning.

"Thank you for coming down to speak with me, Lady Alice and Lady Honoria. I know it is a quite trying time, and I will make this conversation as brief as possible."

Lady Honoria offered a shaky nod of her head.

"I have no wish to add to your distress in any way," Gideon added, trying to soften his tone even further.

Lady Alice finally bristled. "What is this about, Inspector Pierce? Sergeant Ormsbee has quite efficiently solved my dear Henry's murder. What more could you possibly ask of us?"

"Is it about our aunt?" Lady Honoria asked softly.

"No. It is not, my lady. It is about the death of your fiancé, Lady Alice."

The sisters exchanged a look, which Gideon thought appeared to be worry.

"Surely, you have all your answers after the inquest," Lady Alice said. "Or at least the sergeant does. He had a man arrested and taken into custody. Are you just collecting more evidence to strengthen the case against Mr. Winters?"

"You could say that I am, yes, my lady."

"Well, then we'll be as helpful as we can be," Lady Alice continued, "but I've already spoken to Sergeant Ormsbee, and I know you've spoken to Honoria too."

"What could we possibly add?" Lady Honoria said, her voice pitched high, almost a plea.

"Perhaps nothing," Gideon said, shifting his gaze between them, "but I do have some questions, so I hope you'll bear with me."

After a moment, Lady Alice gave a single regal dip of her chin.

"I do appreciate it, my lady." Gideon took a breath, sifting what he'd learned from his interviews, clues, the inquest, and separated it from what Electra had told him based on her special abilities.

Then he consulted that inexplicable gut instinct that drove him.

"I spoke to Ophelia Winters today."

Lady Honoria gasped.

Lady Alice merely quirked one brow. "I thought she'd gone back to London."

"She is not in London, my lady, and I did speak to her, as I said. She told me that Lord Lockhart forced himself on her several years ago and that Alex Winters was blackmailing his lordship regarding that fact."

Lady Honoria's tear-splotched face seeped of color and her eyes grew wide. Lady Alice notched up her chin and narrowed her gaze at him.

"That is an outrageous accusation, Inspector," she bit out, her jaw tight.

"It is indeed an outrageous thing for any lady to endure. I take it you were not aware of the incident or of the payments he was making to Alex Winters."

"I was not aware of it, and I do not believe it. I don't know why she would dare to say such a thing." She turned a look her sister's way. "Do you know why she would say such a thing?"

Lady Honoria dipped her head. Gideon couldn't tell if she was weeping. He regretted the bluntness of his question if she too had experienced what Miss Winters had, but he'd hoped mention of it might cause either or both of them to speak plainly.

"This is not an appropriate topic, Inspector. Shall we call for Sergeant Ormsbee?"

"Forgive me," Gideon said quickly. "Let us move on then." He pulled his notepad from his coat pocket and flipped it open, scanning pages as if looking for a specific detail.

"Lady Honoria," Gideon said, focusing in on the young woman, who still looked shocked at the revelation regarding Ophelia Winters.

She barely lifted her head, only offering him a dazed glance. When she did, he continued.

"James Lockhart told me that he asked you to marry him and you'd agreed, but you said—"

"He never asked her such a thing," Lady Alice snapped, anger tightening her jaw. "He never would."

Lady Honoria lifted her head at that, glancing briefly at her sister. "He never asked me, Inspector."

Gideon nodded. "And yet he said he did."

"That is a lie," Lady Alice insisted.

"Yes, I believe there have been a few lies spoken in the last couple of days," Gideon told Lady Alice honestly.

"Electra." Lady Alice turned toward her. "This is outrageous. Will you let this continue?"

Electra rose from the chair where she sat and moved to perch on the end of the settee next to Alice. She angled her body toward her friend.

"Inspector Pierce is simply trying to find the truth, Alice. Surely, we all want the right man to pay for his crime."

Gideon noted Electra's hands were balanced on her knees. He had a ridiculous wish for her to reach out and touch Lady Alice, for he was convinced the noblewoman would hide whatever truths she knew as long as she could.

Electra looked at Gideon, a question in her gaze.

"Mr. Lockhart did say he was quite smitten with Honoria," Electra confirmed, though she had not been present at that interview.

"That is utter nonsense," Lady Alice said again, shaking her head. "Honoria, tell them."

"I did, Alice, just now. I'm sure the inspector heard me." Honoria's tone had taken on a bit of a chilly edge, and she'd lifted her head fully. Indeed, she seemed more clear-eyed all of a sudden.

"It's an odd discrepancy," Electra said quietly, sympathetically.

"I don't believe him," Alice said to Electra, then shot Gideon an icy glare.

"I take it you would be opposed to the match, judging by your reaction, my lady," Gideon pressed.

Lady Alice smiled, but there was no amusement in it. "I never had to consider my approval or opposition because the very notion is absurd."

Lady Honoria gripped the edge of her gown so tightly that her knuckles had whitened.

"May I ask something completely off topic?" Electra asked him.

Gideon nodded, trusting whatever she intended.

"Did your mother enjoy croquet?"

Both Lady Alice and Lady Honoria turned to look at her, eyes wide.

"What an odd question?" Lady Honoria whispered. "But, yes, she was quite good."

"It's just that there was a little plaque in the earl's chamber. I saw it when I was in the room with you earlier, Alice."

Lady Alice looked at Electra as if she was seeing her for the first time, a bit of shock slackening her features. "You saw what exactly?"

"Oh, a little plaque. A gift, perhaps, from a ladies' croquet club. But the stand seemed empty."

Lady Alice shook her head firmly, but she cast her gaze away from Electra. "I have no notion what you're talking about."

"It was a mallet, I think. Made of crystal, perhaps."

Lady Honoria gasped, then swallowed hard. "It's missing," Lady Honoria said quietly.

"Is it?" Lady Alice turned to her suddenly. "Why didn't you tell me? Good heavens, if the staff are filching things again." She turned back toward Electra. "We had a staff member who stole from us frequently. He was fired, but apparently someone else has now taken up their habits."

"So you acknowledge the crystal mallet now, Lady Alice?" Gideon asked.

"There was a mallet, yes," she said, her tone even and a bit icy. "Perhaps your efforts would be more useful finding my family's missing property, Inspector."

"Someone was seen with the mallet," Electra said in a clear firm voice. "But it wasn't a servant. It was James Lockhart."

Lady Honoria began to shiver as if a chill had taken her, yet she also swiped a hand across her brow, which glistened with a light sheen of perspiration.

"Why would James Lockhart have the mallet?" Gideon asked.

The look that Lady Alice gave him might have cut if it had

been a tangible thing. "You've upset my sister terribly, Inspector. May we please bring this interview to an end?"

Once again, she turned a softer look Electra's way. "Please, Electra. I'm not sure how much more of this I can take."

"I understand," Electra said, then reached out a hand to place it on Lady Alice's where it lay on her lap.

"Don't touch me!" Lady Alice's shout rang against the parlor room windows. She looked terrified, and physically arched away from Electra, who immediately withdrew her hand.

"Alice, if you know why James Lockhart had the mallet, please tell Inspector Pierce."

Lady Alice scoffed and turned her back on Electra, leaning toward her sister as if to comfort her.

"Alice," she tried quietly.

"You brought that man here, and he's been unforgivably rude."

"I'll answer your questions." The voice came from the parlor doorway, and everyone pivoted to see James Lockhart on the threshold, still wearing his overcoat. "Allow Alice and Honoria to go upstairs. I'll take their place," he said, "and you may ask me whatever you like, Inspector."

"James, no," Lady Honoria said, her voice firmer and more confident than Gideon had ever heard it since arriving at Carthorpe.

Lady Alice turned toward her sister, and Gideon could not see her expression, but there was such tension in her body that he saw the tendons in her neck, the tight set of her jaw.

Then she suddenly stood, turning toward James Lockhart. "I won't allow you to speak to the inspector alone," she told him.

"You must. Do you not trust me?" his tone was warm, his gaze full of sadness and what seemed to Gideon like affection.

When Lady Alice gave no reply, he laid a hand gently on

her arm. "Take Honoria upstairs, Alice. I'll come up when we're finished here."

Lady Alice pressed her lips together, tipped her head up, leaning toward him. Gideon had the sudden and shocking thought that they might kiss. And he saw Lady Alice's posture loosen, saw a little smile play at the edges of her mouth.

Finally, she turned away from James Lockhart and looked back at Electra. She moved closer, leaned toward her, and whispered something in her ear that Gideon could not hear. Whatever she said, it was more than a few words. She whispered at length, then withdrew, reached for her sister's hand, and they strode together toward the threshold.

As Lady Alice approached James Lockhart, he shifted his gaze toward her. His eyes were fixed solely on her. She did the same. Gideon noticed that their hands brushed as Lady Alice strode past him, but they exchanged no words.

ELECTRA RESUMED her seat as James Lockhart swept into the room, peeling off his overcoat and throwing it over the back of the settee before sitting down in the center. He leaned forward, elbows braced on his knees and fixed his eyes on Gideon.

"Let's have an end to this, Inspector," he said with calm resignation.

Before Gideon could jump in with his questions, Electra cleared her throat, drawing Lockhart's attention.

"When did you fall in love with her?" she asked him.

"You mean Honoria?" He hadn't looked at her yet and seemed hesitant to turn her way.

"No, Mr. Lockhart, I don't. And I suspect you know that I don't mean Honoria."

He ducked his head a moment, and when he finally did shift toward Electra, there was a sheen in his eyes.

"Did she tell you?" he whispered.

"Yes." She hadn't told Electra that in so many words. Before she'd left the drawing room, she'd whispered that Alex Winters was the killer and that she could prove it incontrovertibly.

But Electra had sensed something from her that she hadn't since the day she'd arrived at Carthorpe. A kind of overwhelming affection, and it reflected exactly what she'd seen in Alice's sketchbook. The loving way she'd captured James Lockhart's face again and again.

"She didn't do this thing," he told Electra. Then to Gideon, he added, "She had nothing to do with it, Inspector."

Gideon frowned, a question in his eyes as he glanced Electra's way.

"How did it come about?" Electra asked him.

James Lockhart let out a weary sigh, scrubbed a hand across his jaw, and said, "Henry was not what he appeared to be. There was nothing respectable about my brother. I don't know why he turned out the way he did, but I watched him hurt others from the time we were children."

"Including Alice," Electra said, needing Lockhart to say what she suspected was true.

"Alice. Honoria. Miss Winters. There are more, but you, Miss Poole, seem to know who matters most to me."

"Lady Alice," Gideon said.

Electra understood that he needed James Lockhart to spell it all out plainly.

"Yes," Lockhart said simply. "She wouldn't...end the engagement. Her father was always the excuse." Lockhart lifted a hand, emphasizing his point. "She does love me. Make no mistake about that, but how could I continue to watch him wreak destruction wherever he pleased?"

Lockhart's eyes had taken on a kind of wildness. "It was a blessing, what I did. All of it is at an end now. No more suffering for any of them."

"Except Mr. Winters." Gideon watched him cooly, offering no reaction as Lockhart's emotions peaked.

Lockhart scoffed and waved a hand in the air. "That was not my doing. Winters made himself the perfect scapegoat, and Alice insisted on ensuring that Ormsbee would find what he needed to hang him."

"The coat. The button," Electra said. "And the séance? Was that planned too—"

"No," Lockhart shouted, his protest too strident. His eyes had widened. He looked panicked, as if realizing he'd already admitted too much. "Alice is not at fault for any of this. I take full responsibility."

"You confess to murdering your brother?" Gideon asked.

Lockhart ran a shaking hand through his hair. "I ridded the world of a menace, Inspector. A reprobate. A defiler of young women. I cannot regret it."

"And Lady Dalrymple?" Electra asked. Her heart ached sharply, fearing his answer.

He stilled then and dipped his head. "I know nothing of Lady Dalrymple's death," he finally said to Gideon, voice stripped of all the emotion that had overtaken him. "I was not at Carthorpe when the poor lady…"

"Dr. Brownlow says a portion of the medication he gave to treat the earl was missing prior to her ladyship's death."

Lockhart smiled. "Brownlow is a man of some years. Perhaps he forgot how much he'd administered."

"You're still protecting her," Electra said. He'd already acknowledged Alice's involvement, and as she thought of the vision, of Honoria encountering him as he retrieved the crystal mallet, she suspected Honoria knew too. It wasn't one man's anger at his brother that had brought about the viscount's murder. It was a conspiracy of those he'd wronged, those he'd harmed.

"I don't know what you're referring to, Miss Poole."

"Alice, Mr. Lockhart. You're protecting Alice because you love her."

"I will always protect her," he snapped, his body all but vibrating with a stew of emotions, so volatile Electra had a hard time sorting them out.

More quietly, Lockhart said, "That is why I am speaking to you now."

"And if it's found that Lady Dalrymple was poisoned?" Gideon asked. "Will you claim responsibility for that too?"

Lockhart said nothing.

"Tell us then. How was it done to Lord Lockhart?"

"I struck him in the hedge maze, from behind, with a mallet."

"The crystal mallet?" Electra asked him.

"Yes." Lockhart's eyes flickered wider as he answered Electra. "How did you know that?"

Electra did not explain her visions to James Lockhart. There was no need. His very answer was confession enough.

"Where is the mallet now?" Gideon asked.

"Gone," Lockhart told him. "Smashed. The pieces tossed into the Thames."

Gideon let out a beleaguered sigh at that.

"You will need to provide a full confession to Sergeant Ormsbee," Gideon finally said.

"May I speak to Alice first? I must be the one to tell her."

"Not alone, no." Gideon seemed to have lost patience for the young man. "Either I or Constable Withers will accompany you when you speak to her."

"I can accompany him," Electra offered.

"No," Gideon's answer brooked no argument. "Not you."

Electra wasn't offended by his tone. She understood the protective impulse, especially now that James Lockhart was a confessed murderer.

"I don't want you embroiled in this any more than you need to be, especially when the papers get a hold of this," he whispered. "I'll speak to Lady Alice."

"I'll make it easy for you, Inspector."

They all turned to find Lady Alice occupying the same spot on the threshold where James Lockhart had stood a few minutes earlier.

Lockhart got to his feet and moved toward her. "Alice, no."

"I heard you shout. I had to come down. I won't let you do this alone. Not when you were the one who saved me." Alice lifted her hand to cup James Lockhart's cheek, much as Gideon had done to her not an hour ago. "I want to tell the truth now, my love."

Electra bit her lip at Alice's tone. There was no pretense, no anger or defensiveness. She sounded raw and utterly sincere.

Gideon stood beside her, his posture tense. She knew he must be eager to have Alice's confession.

"Shall we all have a seat?" Electra asked.

Gideon turned a look her way. He had just told her that he wanted to protect her, but he gave her the slightest of nods, as if to indicate that she should remain.

Alice and James approached the settee he'd just occupied, and Electra was not surprised to see their hands linked as they sat down next to each other.

"Ask me what you will, Inspector." Alice sounded tired and resigned. None of the fire that had blazed in her eyes just minutes ago seemed to flicker there anymore. Just a steely resolve.

"Tell me how this plan unfolded, Lady Alice," Gideon said.

"He was never going to stop," she said matter-of-factly. "I found out about Ophelia Winters and other young ladies. I found a diary he kept. He noted things about ladies he'd violated."

A shudder of revulsion skittered down Electra's spine, and Alice turned a look her way, as if she'd noticed her reaction.

"Alex Winters was blackmailing him. I beseeched him. James tried to reason with him, but none of it made any difference. He'd gotten away with it several times. Who was going stop him?"

Alice licked her lips, and James seemed to notice.

"It was Honoria that tipped the scales for us," he said. "When we learned he had forced himself on her. She'd fought him. Scratched him. I saw the scratches myself, even as he denied her account to my face."

Alice tightened her hold on James's hand, her knuckles whitening.

"So we made a plan," she said. "A house party. A séance and your presence, Electra."

"Me?"

Gideon swung a look Electra's way and when their gazes met, she saw the worry in his eyes.

"What does Miss Poole have to do with this?"

"We had no real proof," Alice said quietly. "Henry destroyed the diary after I found it. He paid off the families of other young ladies, and I don't know any of their names. He'd only used nicknames he'd given them in the diary." She shook her head as if shaking off the memory.

"So all we had were the stories of two young ladies, neither of whom wanted the truth of what had happened to them out." Alice lifted her gaze to fix it on Electra. "But you'd gained notoriety, Electra. Your psychic abilities were renowned and proven. For heaven's sake, you foresaw a lady's death."

Electra felt the immediate urge to point out that she had not helped that lady by telling her of the vision, a guilt that still weighed on her.

"I thought if you saw Henry assault me, if you saw his memories at the séance..."

Gideon leaned forward in his chair. "But Lord Lockhart never attended that séance."

"Originally, he was meant to," James Lockhart admitted. "But then Henry went outside to speak to you, Miss Poole, and Alex Winters trailed after. I had to take the opportunity because I knew suspicion would fall on Winters."

"The weapon was buried?" Electra surmised.

"Yes," James acknowledged. "I didn't know exactly what moment it would happen, only that it had to be done during the house party."

"You always intended to frame Alex Winters?" Gideon asked.

Alice and James looked at each other, and both nodded. "Yes," Alice confirmed.

"Why?" Electra couldn't help but ask.

"It made the most sense," Alice said as if the answer should have been obvious. "He would come when invited. He hated Henry, and if not for the money Henry paid him, he would have wanted him dead."

"He did threaten to kill him years ago," James added. "After what he'd done to Miss Winters."

"But he didn't," Electra said. "You did, and you were willing to let him go to prison."

Gideon drew in a breath and asked, "And Lady Dalrymple?"

"She saw James in the hedge maze," Alice said, her voice eerily calm. "I thought to protect him."

"Alice..." James didn't finish whatever he'd intended to say.

When she turned a look his way, she smiled. "I didn't realize he would come forward to protect me, but I should have known he would."

"There's nothing noble in it," Electra said. She couldn't hold the words back, nor the tears that welled in her eyes. "Your own aunt. Your own brother. Confessing is the least you can do—"

"Electra," Gideon said softly. "They'll face justice for this. When Ormsbee returns, we'll make sure of it."

Electra swiped at the tear that slipped down her cheek and looked into his eyes, seeing only empathy returned. That strengthened her.

"You intended that I would join you for tea," Electra said, struggling to keep the emotion from her tone. A part of her wondered if her childhood friend would have harmed her too.

"Yes," Alice said to her. "I hoped we might talk more about whatever my aunt saw during her session with you, but you didn't come down. And she…" Alice glanced at James, then at Gideon. "She spoke to me of her recollection, and she had spotted James. Though she could not identify the man she saw, I feared she might recall more."

Electra could hardly bear to look at Alice. It was like sitting across from a stranger, and all she'd thought she'd known about her fell away.

"I must ask about Lady Honoria," Gideon said when he'd turned back to Lockhart and Alice.

"She was not part of this," Alice insisted, "though in the aftermath, she did come to suspect what had happened."

"Honoria bears no responsibility for any of this," James agreed. "But I cannot say I regret that she will never have to face my brother again."

Electra could not deny that they'd rid the world of a terrible man, but Lord Lockhart should have faced justice. Still, she knew that Ophelia's and Honoria's claims might not have been believed. And their reputations and lives would have been forever marred by merely telling the truth.

Women's claims against a man, especially a nobleman, were often dismissed. A nobleman's denial would invariably trump a young lady's account.

"Ormsbee will return directly," Gideon told them, "and will no doubt wish to take both of you into custody to stand before a magistrate."

"May I speak to my sister first?" Alice asked.

"With Constable Withers or myself present, yes."

"Could Electra go with me instead?"

"No." Gideon's answer emerged swift and with clear finality.

Electra felt a measure of gratitude. She'd already been a pawn in Alice's scheme and would not allow that to happen again. And, somehow, despite the confession of the pair of them, she felt that the whole truth had not yet been revealed.

Chapter Nineteen

When Ormsbee returned, he decided to bring James Lockhart into custody and allow Lady Alice to remain at Carthorpe. She was to keep to her room with a constable on duty, ensuring that she remained there until both she and Lockhart would appear before the local magistrate the next morning. Ormsbee insisted that it was a more reasonable place of containment for a gently bred young lady than the local lock-up.

Gideon told him that he and Electra wished to speak to Lady Honoria, and Ormsbee had balked at first. He eventually consented, even permitting Electra to be present, though he insisted on leading the interview himself. Gideon made one further request, and Ormsbee agreed, asking a footman to go into town with a message to Mrs. Markland, who Gideon wanted to question again in the light of Lady Alice's confession.

They decided to speak to Lady Honoria in the house's library, since it had been a room she felt comfortable in, and the parlor now carried the distress of her aunt's death.

By the time Lady Honoria entered the room, she looked far different than the rose-cheeked young woman Gideon had questioned so recently. The color had leached from her face, and the spiritedness she'd exuded seemed to have faded too. She'd lost her aunt just hours ago, and she would lose her closeness with her sister too, depending on the length of the sentence Lady Alice received. Her eyes appeared sunken, her expression flat, as if she couldn't even feign the polite smiles and open expression he'd noted the first time he'd spoken to her.

Lady Alice had been given a chance to speak to her sister before being sequestered to her room. According to Constable Withers, the two had consoled each other, embraced, and though they'd whispered, as if they might evade the constable's hearing, he did hear Lady Alice urging her sister to "say nothing" and assuring her that she "need not say a thing."

Gideon recalled Electra's comment and had asked Withers one crucial question: had Lady Alice conveyed to her sister all that she and James Lockhart had confessed. When Withers told him that she hadn't, he suspected Electra was right. Unless Lady Alice had told her sister everything before coming down to the parlor to be questioned, which was a possibility too.

Gideon wondered, as he, Ormsbee, and Electra had taken chairs in the wood-paneled library and Lady Honoria had settled on the settee, whether they would get any truth out of her. Perhaps she would heed her sister's urging to not share anything more of what she knew of the plot to kill Lord Henry Lockhart.

"Lady Honoria, are you aware of the confession your sister and James Lockhart made a few hours ago?" Ormsbee began, clearly drawing on Withers's report of the sisters' conversation.

Lady Honoria lifted her weary gaze to Electra first before sliding it back to the sergeant. "I know that she claims to have conspired with James, who admitted to killing Lord Lockhart."

"Claims to?" Ormsbee interjected. "Do you not believe your sister?"

Lady Honoria licked her lips and then began to tremble. "All of it is dreadful, and I wish Alice wasn't caught up in any of it."

Gideon glanced at Electra. Ormsbee indicated that she could come as an observer and perhaps as a measure of support for Lady Honoria, but Gideon wished Electra could ask the most delicate of questions.

"Miss Poole and I," Gideon began, "spoke to Ophelia Winters earlier today."

Lady Honoria's gaze sharpened suddenly and what seemed to be wariness tightened her jaw.

"She told us that Lord Lockhart committed an improper assault upon her some years ago."

"That's dreadful." Lady Honoria's eyes widened, but too wide. Gideon sensed the false surprise in her response, and it persuaded him of Miss Winters' suspicion that Lady Honoria had suffered similarly at the hands of Lord Lockhart.

"Did he harm you, Honoria?" Electra asked softly.

Gideon half expected Ormsbee to forestall her from asking further questions, but the sergeant kept his gaze fixed on Lady Honoria.

The young woman gave Electra a look of surprise and then scoffed. "I certainly would have said as much if he had."

"But he was in your bedchamber," Electra said, her voice soft and low.

Gideon knew she had not witnessed what she spoke of first-hand, that Electra had not been present in the moment she spoke of, but thankfully Ormsbee did not.

Color suddenly rushed back into Lady Honoria's complexion, two splotches of red on her cheeks. "Alice wouldn't have confided that to you," she whispered, eyes glittering as she looked at Electra.

"So you confirm that he was?" Gideon asked, keeping his

voice as low as Electra had. He understood this would likely be the last thing a young lady would wish to confide, let alone be interrogated about.

Lady Honoria cast her eyes down to the carpet, unblinking, staring as if considering what to reveal and what to protect. "I do not wish to speak of it, but I will only say that he was not *invited* to my room. I fought him. Scratched him. He begged me not to speak of it to Alice, but Alice found us."

Gideon considered the tangle of the relationships, and the pile of motives that might cause two gently bred noble ladies to conspire with the brother of a man who'd tormented them both. He had sympathy for them, and he suspected a jury might too.

"Did Mr. James Lockhart know of this incident?" Ormsbee asked.

Lady Honoria nodded.

Ormsbee glanced at Gideon, then turned back to Lady Honoria. "There seems to be some confusion about whether you are engaged to Mr. Lockhart."

Lady Honoria looked at Ormsbee. "We were never engaged, but the pretense was enough to hide the truth from Lord Lockhart."

"Of your sister's involvement with James Lockhart?"

"Yes," she admitted, then pressed her lips together. "His lordship was quite vain. I sometimes think even if he harbored suspicions, he would never have believed that Alice had once begged our father to allow her to marry James."

"Your father refused, I take it," Gideon said.

"Vehemently. Lord Lockhart held the title and Father always dreamed of us marrying well. He didn't know what sort of a man Henry Lockhart was."

She squeezed her hands together in her lap, then glanced up, gaze locking on Electra first. "Ophelia was very brave to tell the truth."

"She doesn't want to see her brother go to prison for a crime he did not commit," Gideon pointed out.

"But, yes," Electra added quietly. "She is brave."

"And now she has a measure of justice," Honoria said, her voice little more than a whisper as she looked at Electra, almost as if beseeching her to understand or acknowledge the claim.

"Did you know of the plot, Lady Honoria?" Ormsbee asked. "To kill Lord Henry Lockhart."

The young noblewoman looked at Ormsbee with what seemed a fresh sense of resolve, shoulders squared, eyes sharper.

"I know nothing about any plot, Sergeant Ormsbee."

"Forgive me for asking," Gideon says, "but regarding your aunt. Did you know—"

"No." Her eyes immediately welled with tears, and he believed her when she shook her head. "I could not fathom why anyone would want to do her harm."

She dipped her head, dabbing at her eyes with a handkerchief, and Gideon felt her tears were genuine. Yet that did not mean she did not know more than she was willing to admit.

He glanced at Electra as if she might provide some further answer, but her expression was one of pure sympathy. She looked as if she wished to reach out to Lady Honoria and offer her comfort.

They would get no more out of her this day. Of that, Gideon felt certain. He could see that she'd steeled herself now, after her admission about Lord Lockhart.

Ormsbee looked at Gideon, almost exasperated, as Lady Honoria continued to weep quietly. "Thank you for answering our questions, Lady Honoria," he finally said.

As soon as he did, Electra rose from her chair and went to sit next to Lady Honoria on the settee. She laid a bare hand gently on her arm, and Lady Honoria laid her hand over Electra's, as if welcoming the comfort she offered.

Ormsbee eased off his chair to stand, glancing at Gideon to do the same.

"We have some matters to settle, Inspector, if you'd follow me back to the dining room."

Gideon began to follow the sergeant out of the room, but he turned back as they reached the threshold.

Electra looked up at him, sensing his gaze on her. She gave him a slight shake of her head, and he took it to mean she had either seen nothing when she touched Lady Honoria, or what she'd seen provided no other evidence of her involvement in the plot to kill Lord Lockhart.

Chapter Twenty

Electra busied herself with packing the traveling case she'd brought to Oxford while she awaited Gideon's return from court. Though the appearance of Lady Alice and James Lockhart had been scheduled for late morning, it was well into the afternoon now and Gideon had not yet returned. She suspected there were matters to resolve with Ormsbee, but she hoped they wouldn't detain him in Oxfordshire much longer. The desire to leave Carthorpe Hall was almost a physical weight upon her shoulders, though she didn't wish to return to London without Gideon.

A knock sounded at her guest chamber door and she opened it to find Honoria. She looked exhausted and somber. How could she be anything else after all that had occurred?

"I've been sitting with Father, but Dr. Brownlow says he's doing a bit better. Now I feel as if I should have gone to the magistrate's court."

She looked up at Electra, almost beseechingly, tears welling in her eyes. "I'm not sure what to do with myself."

"Would you like to come in and sit with me?"

Honoria nodded and they settled in the chairs arranged near the fireplace.

"Is there anything I could have done if I'd gone?" she asked quietly once they were seated.

"In what regard?" Electra asked.

"If I...admitted what Henry did to me, what he tried to do," she amended. "Could mercy be given to Alice and James?"

"That is likely a question for Sergeant Ormsbee, but Inspector Pierce told me that they will likely be tried in separate circumstances. James, as the new Lord Lockhart will be subject to trial in London by the House of Lords."

Honoria clasped her hands together fiercely. "It is still so hard to believe how terribly everything has unraveled. My dear aunt. That Alice could so such a thing..."

Electra nodded. She struggled to make sense of it too, no matter how she tried to reconcile the quiet, artistic young woman she'd thought she knew.

"I take it Alex will be freed," she said quietly. "It's dreadful what's happened to him too. And to know that Ophelia suffered Henry's attentions."

Honoria bowed her head, then lifted it and traced her gaze around the room. Tears slipped down her face, and she swiped them gently each time one fell. She noted Electra's traveling case and shot her a worried frown. "I take it you will be leaving Carthorpe soon?"

"I should return to London."

"Of course. If not for Father, I would wish to leave too. It's a very bleak place now."

Electra felt sympathy for Honoria and reached out a hand to lay it against the young woman's clasped hands. Electra's hands were bare, but no images came. Only an enormous sense of sadness and grief.

As they sat in the quiet but for the snap of the fire, Electra heard the familiar sound of gravel crunching in the carriage circle. She stood and went to the window, knowing it was likely Gideon and Ormsbee.

Both gentlemen stepped down from the carriage, and Electra noted that they were alone. As anticipated, it seemed that James and Alice had been taken into custody after submitting their confessions and being charged with murder.

"Alice isn't with them," Honoria said as she came up to stand beside Electra.

"Inspector Pierce told me they'd likely be held at Oxford Castle Gaol."

"Will I be able to visit?" Honoria asked quietly.

"Yes, I suspect you will be able to." Electra recalled from the Becknell case that when a noble was taken into custody, they were often afforded privileges that commoners were not. Though she wasn't certain that applied to a man who'd gained a title by killing his predecessor.

"That's some slight consolation."

Despite her own desire to leave Oxfordshire with Gideon as soon as they could, Electra couldn't help but imagine the desolation Honoria might experience at Carthorpe on her own.

"Is there anyone who might come and stay with you? Family or—"

Honoria let out a quiet, bitter scoff. "After all of this, Electra? Our family was never the most fashionable or popular, but no one will wish to visit Carthorpe now. The ignominy and scandal will linger."

Having been swept up into an aristocratic murder case herself, she knew Honoria's fears were well-founded.

Before she could think of anything else to say, someone rapped at her door, and she hoped it was Gideon.

"Electra?" he called through the panel.

"I should go and make sure my father is resting," Honoria said. She crossed the room and opened the door.

"Lady Honoria," Gideon said, then glanced at Electra.

"Do come in, Inspector. I was just on my way out." Yet Honoria made no move to depart. "My sister?" Her voice quavered as she asked. "They will not let her come home again, I take it."

"No, my lady. She will be held on remand until her trial." Gideon glanced at Electra again, as if he understood she would be concerned about the details of her friend's fate too. "Sergeant Ormsbee says they've arranged special accommodations for her."

"And I may visit?" Honoria asked.

"Yes, I'm sure that can be arranged."

"Thank you, Inspector." With that, Honoria departed and Gideon stepped inside, closing the door behind him.

He came so close that Electra had the urge to reach for him. Since the previous night, and the death of Lady Dalrymple, she'd been so uneasy that she'd been unable to sleep more than a couple of hours.

"Alex Winters has been released," he told her.

"That's a relief."

Gideon studied her as if waiting for some greater reaction, but whatever he suspected about her feelings for Alex Winters, he was mistaken.

"Ormsbee gave me to understand that he and his sister will be removing to London until the furor over this case diminishes."

"I suspect that won't be for a long while."

Gideon nodded. "While in the village, I also called on Mrs. Markland."

"Oh?"

"She admits that she lied when I spoke to her previously. Lady Dalrymple wasn't the one who reached out to her about the séance. Lady Alice did so, and that request came prior to the start of the house party. Lady Alice asked her to say that Lady Dalrymple had arranged the event, claiming that Lord Lockhart would be appalled if he learned that Lady Alice had."

"So it was all strategized, a plan concocted before I arrived." Electra turned away, struggling to reconcile that someone she believed she knew was so cold and methodical about another's demise.

"You've begun preparing to depart," Gideon said as he came to stand beside her.

He was close enough that his nearness itself brought her a measure of comfort that eased her jangled nerves.

"I suspect Honoria would be grateful if I remained longer, but I want to go home." Electra looked up at him. "And you? When will you return?"

"Ormsbee no longer requires my assistance, so I'd considered returning on the evening train." He hesitated and then asked, "Shall we go together?"

"Of course. I want to leave here when you do." Electra offered him a smile. Gideon had come to Oxfordshire for her sake, after all.

A few hours later, they'd said their goodbyes to Lady Honoria and were afforded one final use of the family carriage to deliver them to the train station.

Electra stood in the carriage circle with Gideon as the footman secured their travel cases, thinking of her arrival not so many nights ago. The house's windows had been alight and shadowy figures had moved beyond the glass. Now the windows at the front of the house were mostly dark.

James Lockhart had come out to fetch her and draw her into the tangle of a plot she'd had no inkling about. It reminded her suddenly how much she was at the whim of her abilities. Why hadn't some future vision come the moment he'd touched her, warning her of what would unfold?

As she stood in contemplation, movement near the hedgerow caught her eye. In the distance, a young man, his figure shadowy and faded, strode out of the hedge. Then the image of the young man dissipated like fog scattering as he proceeded toward the front of the hall.

Coldness seeped into her bones, and a chill skittered down Electra's back. She blinked, wondering if it had been some fragment of a vision. Yet she'd not felt the jolt that usually preceded one. Nor was she touching anyone or any object which might give her access to memories.

"Electra?" Gideon asked. "What is it?"

"Nothing. Can we depart now?"

He handed her up into the carriage, and they arrived at the station just in time to board the London train. Only when they were in a car, sitting side by side, did Gideon turn to her again. She'd felt his gaze on her in the carriage, but he'd let a companionable silence settle between them. But he, like her, was too curious by nature to not inquire about why she'd become quiet and pensive.

"Are you all right? The last few days have been..."

"Yes, they have been," she said, not needing him to find the right word for all the tragedy that had unfolded at Carthorpe Hall. "But, yes, I'm all right. Or at least I soon will be."

That seemed to satisfy him, but only for a short while.

"And when we return to London?" he asked. "What will you do? Before you departed, you were uncertain."

She stroked her gloved fingers down the row of buttons along her coat, then folded her gloved hands in her lap. In all her waiting that morning, it was a question she'd been pondering too.

"I don't want to stop," she finally confessed. "Using my abilities, I mean. But I fear I still have so little control, so little certainty, about them."

Gideon tipped his head, brows arched as if surprised by that declaration. "Your abilities have proven to be reliable on multiple occasions."

Electra didn't even attempt to hide her smile at that admission from a man who'd been so dubious the previous fall when he'd walked into one of her sittings at the Redmayne townhouse. But then her smile fell and a wave of grief pinched at her chest.

"Yet I failed Lady Dalrymple. I saw a vision when I conducted a sitting with her. And it felt very like when I saw the vision last fall, as if I was foreseeing a future event."

"And did you not tell her about the vision?" Gideon asked.

"No, I did," Electra insisted. It was what she'd failed to do last year. "But the vision was different than...what ultimately happened to her. I saw her taking tea in the conservatory, but she died in the parlor."

"Perhaps she avoided the conservatory because of what told her."

Electra looked up into his warm brown eyes. "Yes, she said she would avoid it, but—"

"You bear no fault in what happened to Lady Dalrymple."

Electra nodded. "But even warning her changed nothing."

Gideon drew in a long breath and let it out slowly. "So you foresaw danger, but her choice altered the course of how it occurred."

"If only I'd seen Alice. If only I'd sensed the truth about her. Or James Lockhart."

Gideon reached out and placed one of his large hands over her folded ones.

"Your observations helped uncover the truth."

When she looked up at him and nodded, accepting his reassurance, he lifted his hand from hers, leaving her feeling oddly bereft.

"I want to gain more control over what I sense, over when visions come, if I can."

A smile curved his lips. "Then I am certain you will. I don't know if I've mentioned this, but you are one of the most determined young ladies of my acquaintance."

Electra chuckled. "I believe *stubborn* is the word you use most often."

"Tenacious then."

"Tenacious sounds enough like a compliment that I shall accept it."

Gideon smiled.

For the rest of the journey, they made light conversation, avoiding further discussion about the previous days. After arriving in London and securing a cab, Electra savored the familiar sights and scents of London. Not anything like the bracing freshness of the countryside, but it was home.

Gideon insisted on depositing her in Russell Square first, and he helped her exit the carriage.

"I will see you soon?" he asked when he'd settled her travel case at her feet.

The question surprised her, but it didn't displease her.

"I take that to mean the offer to come to Sunday dinner with you and Mrs. Perkins still stands."

"Of course," he said earnestly.

Electra smiled. "Or perhaps we'll see one another the next time you have a case and require my assistance."

His dark brows winged up at that, and he looked decidedly

less eager than he did about the prospect of them sharing a homecooked meal. But something had softened. She didn't sense the hesitance in him that she had last year.

"We shall see," he finally said.

After his cab had rolled away and she turned to approach Cordelia's front door, Electra felt hopeful in a way she hadn't for many months.

Also by Christy Carlyle

Electra Poole Mysteries

A Grave Gift

A Deadly Invitation

About the Author

Fueled by Pacific Northwest coffee and inspired by multiple viewings of every British costume drama she can get her hands on, USA Today bestselling author Christy Carlyle writes sensual historical romance set in the Victorian era. She loves heroes who struggle against all odds and heroines who are ahead of their time. A former teacher with a degree in history, she finds there's nothing better than being able to combine her love of the past with a die-hard belief in happy endings.

Contact Christy at christy@christycarlyle.com or find out more at www.christycarlyle.com

OLIVERHEBERBOOKS

A small press bound by the belief that every voice matters.

Sign up for our newsletter to learn about new releases and more.
https://oliver-heberbooks.com/subscribe/

Follow us on social media:

facebook.com/oliverheberbooks

instagram.com/oliverheberbooks

amazon.com/oliverheberbooks

youtube.com/@OliverHeberBooksPublisher